TANGLED SECRETS: A SUSPENSE THRILLER
Copyright © 2024 by S.F. Baumgartner



ISBN 979-8-9894474-4-2
Library of Congress Control Number: 2024905964

Edited Brilliant Cut Editing and Represent Publishing

Formatted and Published by Represent Publishing

Cover Design by 100bookcovers.com

# TANGLED SECRETS

# TANGLED SECRETS

A Suspense Thriller

## S.F. BAUMGARTNER

# AUTHOR'S NOTE

To all readers, especially residents and those familiar with the state of Florida, I wish to clarify that the town of Marian and the Mirror Estate are purely fictional creations for this series.

All characters and events depicted in this novel are born from my imagination. Any resemblance to actual people, living or dead, or to real-life events is entirely coincidental.

# RECAPS



*BURIED SECRETS - WHERE IT ALL BEGINS, BOOK 1*

Twenty-five-year-old Dylan Roche barely has time to mourn his mom before an attorney appears with an invitation to his long-lost maternal grandmother's opulent estate. Eager to learn about the family he believed dead, and armed with a mysterious key his mom gave him before her death, he's ready to uncover what he believes are buried family secrets.

After a lifetime of scraping by with his mom, he's shocked she grew up wealthy. But, while the estate is lavish, something's off, and he can't shake the haunting feeling that he's being watched. As he delves deeper, he unearths his family's dark history tied to organized crime. His focus, however, remains unshaken, latched onto what the mysterious key unlocks.

At last, he locates the buried box the key opens. Then, along with those buried secrets, he discovers that the ever-present, sinister aura he's been sensing is his mother's twin sister, believed to have died shortly after birth. Very much alive, this ghost is now a criminal mastermind out to kill him. Although he dodges her murder attempt, he's left questioning everything he thought he knew about family, trust, and his past.

## *LIVING SECRETS, BOOK 2*

Twenty-two-year-old hotel worker Lily Tso has grown up in Hong Kong believing she's an orphan. Then her mother, Olivia, who's alive and working for the US government—possibly as a spy—entrusts Lily with a mission. Lily is to deliver an antidote for an experimental biological weapon to her father, US Senator Simon Roth.

FBI Special Agent Kyle Peters is assigned to get Lily safely to the US and to her father. Posing as her boyfriend, he works with Dylan Roche, a young tycoon asked to assist them. But the trio soon finds themselves pursued by mysterious assailants in a harrowing life-or-death chase.

Undercover Agent Olivia Tso, code-named Phoenix, has infiltrated the organization run by the Ghost (Dylan's aunt) and thinks she can stay in the background during this operation. But when Kyle's shot, Dylan injured, and Lily kidnapped, Olivia must join forces with Simon, her former lover and Lily's father, and an FBI task force led by Ron Peters, Kyle's father.

Symptoms of the bioweapon soon start to appear among the population. After multiple setbacks, the team locates Lily. They deliver the antidote and other critical information to Simon. While a few casualties occur due to the virus, global catastrophe is ultimately contained.

Now, Lily's reunited with her long-lost parents, but a new world of familial connections and covert operations awaits this fast-becoming tight-knit group.

## *FORGOTTEN SECRET, BOOK 3*

In Forgotten Secret, Clara Khoury, a magazine writer who lost her memories two decades ago, faces a turning point when a TV news report about a grisly discovery triggers a fragment of her past. Married to Dr. Michael Khoury and mother to Faith and Jason, Clara's led a stable life until this moment.

Driven to investigate the murder for a magazine article, Clara embarks on a journey, but each step leads her closer to her forgotten history. As her investigation unearths troubling hints about her past, her persistence attracts attention, including attempts on her life.

Despite mounting evidence and suspicion, Clara refuses to believe her husband, who once saved her, could be involved. Then their daughter, Faith, is abducted. Concurrently, a criminal mastermind known as the Ghost seeks to live on Mirror Estate and, in exchange for the privilege, provides a lead to a man named Ray Ho.

Eva, operating undercover to uncover the truth about her aunt Clara, whom she believed was tracked, stumbles upon Faith instead. Unaware that Faith is her cousin, Eva rescues her with the help of a task force.

The climax reveals a harrowing past event: At a party, Clara witnessed her friend's ex-boyfriend assault and kill her. Then Ray Ho's men, called in to clean up, took both women. While Clara's friend's body was left in the building where her remains were eventually found, Clara was intended to be sold. However, Clara recognized Ray Ho from her part-time job at the foundation and became a liability. Unable to risk being exposed, Ray Ho shot Clara, leading to the traumatic amnesia that defined her life for the next two decades. This revelation ties Clara's fragmented past with the present, culminating in a dramatic and poignant conclusion.

# Relationship Chart

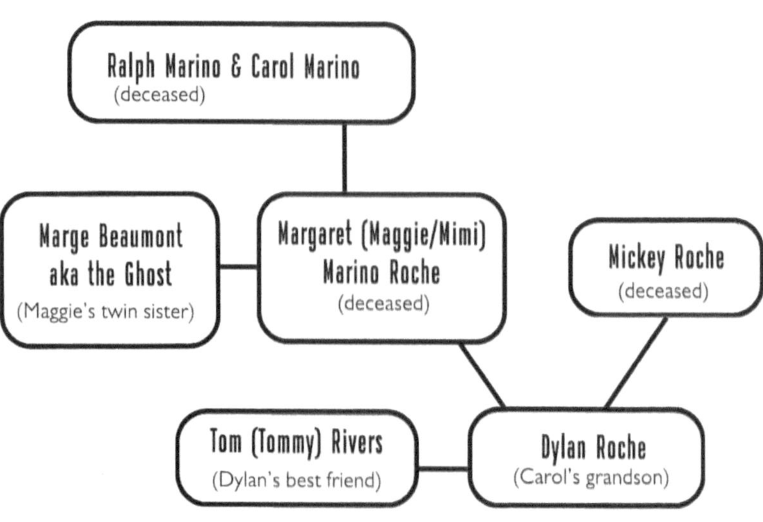


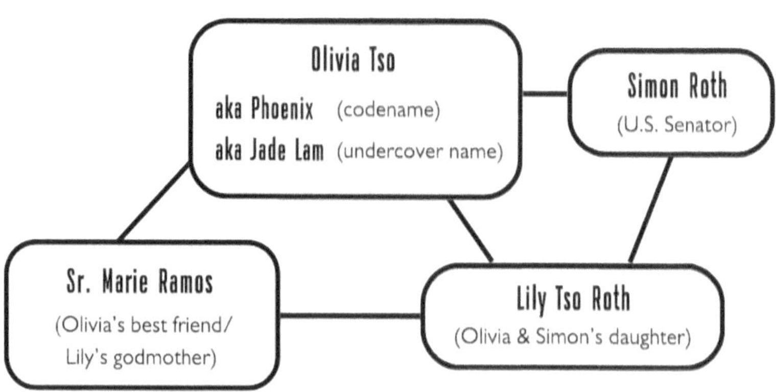

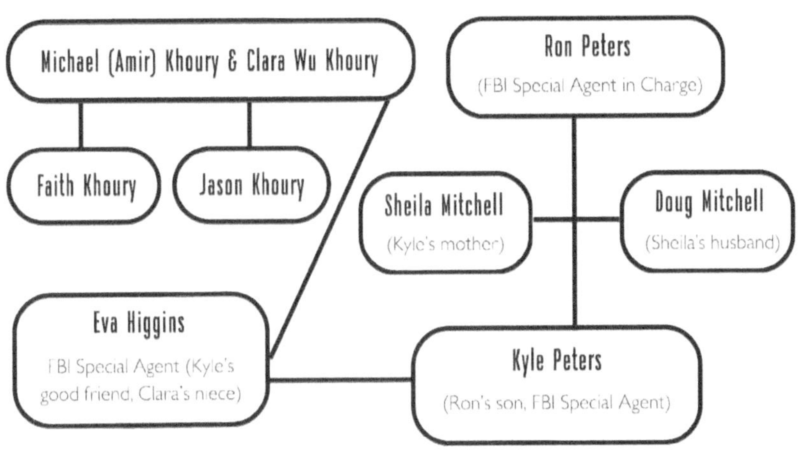

Michael (Amir) Khoury & Clara Wu Khoury
Ron Peters
(FBI Special Agent in Charge)
Faith Khoury
Jason Khoury
Sheila Mitchell
(Kyle's mother)
Doug Mitchell
(Sheila's husband)
Eva Higgins
FBI Special Agent (Kyle's good friend, Clara's niece)
Kyle Peters
(Ron's son, FBI Special Agent)


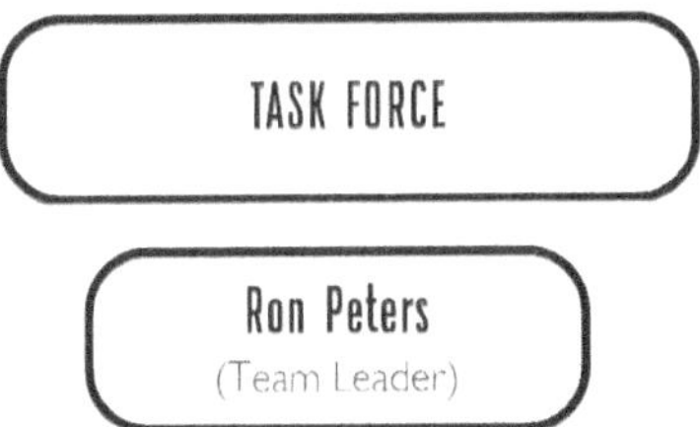

TASK FORCE
Ron Peters
(Team Leader)


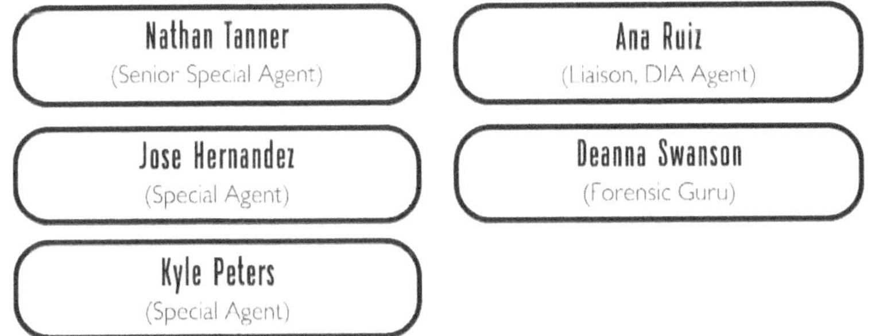

Nathan Tanner
(Senior Special Agent)
Ana Ruiz
(Liaison, DIA Agent)
Jose Hernandez
(Special Agent)
Deanna Swanson
(Forensic Guru)
Kyle Peters
(Special Agent)

# PRAISE FOR BURIED SECRETS - WHERE IT ALL BEGINS: BOOK 1

I felt that the author wove a story that had twists and turns with unexpected moments sprinkled here and there.

— DELPHIA, GOODREADS

They say that dynamite comes in small packages. This one was definitely loaded with plenty of information that will blow your mind.

— TAMMY, GOODREADS

What a great story! This had enough thrill and mystery to draw me in even though it was a short novella.

— MEGAN, GOODREADS

# PRAISE FOR LIVING SECRETS: BOOK 2

A great crime novel! Loved that it picked up right where the prequel left off. Loved all the chasing of Lily and who was after her. Loved the cliffhanger and can't wait to read the next one!!

— KRYSTA, GOODREADS

The book is one you will not want to put down, and if you read it at night, you will jump at every noise and check the locks on your doors and windows. Highly recommend.

— BARBARA, GOODREADS

Edge of your seat reading that keeps you guessing until the end. Plenty of drama with twists and turns that keeps you going until the end. Great characters to follow along on this adventure. Good read.

— RHONDA, GOODREADS

# PRAISE FOR FORGOTTEN SECRET: BOOK 3

I am exhausted!!! This is an absolute whirlwind and it kept me guessing from the very beginning. I loved Living Secrets and I can safely say, this is even better! I'm not even going to say it's a "one more chapter" book, it's an "I read it in a day book." An amazing plot, great characters, and so many twists and turns your head will spin. I'm loving this series, if you like your fast paced psychological suspense books, give this a go!

— VICKIE, GOODREADS

WOW, TALK ABOUT NEEDING A SCORE CARD TO KEEP TRACK!! I enjoyed Clara's story, and I thought I knew who the culprit was, but I was wrong given all of the players involved! I SURE HOPE THERE'S ANOTHER BOOK IN THE WORKS!!!

— BECKY, GOODREADS

AWESOME BOOK !!! This is a great psychological suspense thriller that I would recommend to anyone. This is a fairly new author to me and I love everything I have read so far.

— MICHELLE, GOODREADS

# PRAISE FOR TANGLED SECRETS: BOOK 4

These books are so addicting—I don't want to do anything else except for finishing the book! The suspense and anticipation was awesome. Getting reacquainted with all of the characters—Olivia, Dylan, Lilly, Ron, Grace, etc. were all great.

— LAURA, GOODREADS

The book has infinite layers, the plot is intriguing and secrets are way too deep. The world is dangerous. The book is filled with twists and turns. The ending shook me.

— RUDRASHREE, GOODREADS

This book had amazing characters, many with secrets that seem to connect them all together. The storyline is intriguing & mysterious. I was always wondering who the person was that had their hands in both sides of the game. The ending left me shocked and ready for the story to continue.

— LUNAWOLFWY, GOODREADS

"Drug trafficking is a global illicit trade involving the
cultivation, manufacture, distribution, and sale of
substances which are subject to a drug prohibition
laws."

— UNODC (United Nations Office on Drugs and Crime)

# PROLOGUE

## PARK HILLS PRIVATE SCHOOL

*GRACE*

In the bustling school auditorium, whispered chatter further tinted the air already thick with the scent of pine from the festive decorations. Grace Benson, her heart aflutter, perched at the grand piano, her fingers ready to dance over the keys. This was her moment, her first time directing the school's Christmas program, and she'd embraced it with both hands.

As the lights dimmed, she took a deep breath, steadying herself. No time for fretting now. The first class, a group of third graders, shuffled onto the stage, their faces alight. From there, the night progressed in a whirl of color and sound. Each class brought their unique flair to the stage, performing dances and songs they'd practiced for weeks.

Then the finale arrived—the nativity scene. She'd taken great care in selecting children from each grade, from kindergarten to fourth grade, to participate.

The stage transformed into a serene Bethlehem scene, complete with a manger and makeshift stable. The children, dressed in their costumes, took their positions with a seriousness that belied their years. Mary and Joseph, played by a pair of fourth graders, stood by the manger.

As she began the gentle, familiar strains of "Silent Night," the children started their performance. The shepherds, a group of second graders, entered from stage left, followed by the wise men adorned in sparkling costumes. The angels, a chorus of kindergarteners and first graders, flanked the stage, their voices joining in the song to create a heavenly sweetness that seemed to lift the entire auditorium.

Smiling, she watched from her piano. The children were more than rising to the occasion—they were shining. Of course, the audience was mostly family members, guardians, and relatives. A lot of them slid their phones up to record when their kids took the stage.

As the evening's last notes faded and the auditorium began to empty, parents approached her, each of them beaming. Their words washed over her, filling her with a warm sense of accomplishment. She greeted every compliment with a humble smile, her heart still racing from the night's success.

Amid the departing crowd, Mrs. Montez, the mother of one of the kindergarten angels, made her way toward her. Her face was alight as she began in Spanish, her words tumbling out in a fluid, lyrical stream.

Caught off guard, Grace managed a smile. "Solo hablo un poco de español," she inserted, her accent betraying her lack of fluency. The woman's eyebrows shot up, a reaction she had seen before. She could almost read the thoughts behind that astonished look—her being Latina often led people to assume she could speak Spanish. After the last of the parents had left and the children were safely in their care, she began to pack her things up.

"Are you ready to go?" Jenny, one of the school secretaries, hollered from the back. "It's dark out. Ned wants to know if you need help carrying things."

"No, I'm good. But tell your husband thank you from me. We're coming back to clean up this mess tomorrow anyway." School closed for the Christmas break until the first week of the new year. But Grace and those who helped with the program had to clean up.

"Okay, I'll see you tomorrow."

With the school quiet now, she stood alone in the empty auditorium. As she locked the piano and gathered her music sheets, a shadow caught the corner of her eye. She turned toward the door. Did Jenny come back?

"Jenny, is that you? Ned?"

Silence.

She was imagining it. That was it. She gathered her things and headed out to the parking lot. After dumping her stuff in the back seat, she got in front and started the car. The drive home was less than ten minutes, but a pair of headlights had stayed behind her since she left the parking lot. She turned into her apartment complex. The headlights stuck with her. Heart pounding, she remembered reading a post on social media about situations like this. Instead of parking, she turned back around, headed to the closest police station, entered the lot, and honked.

An officer came out. "Ma'am, is there a problem?"

"Yeah, a car is following me." She twisted in her seat to point it out, but it was, of course, gone.

He looked to where she pointed. "Stay here, ma'am."

He walked to the curb, checked up and down the street, and came back. "Sorry, ma'am. I don't see any car out there stopping or acting suspicious."

The officer offered to escort her back to her apartment building. She accepted the offer. She knew the car was there. Or perhaps it was simply traveling in the same direction? But why follow her to her apartment complex? Then again, why would anyone follow her?

# CHAPTER 1

## MIRROR ESTATE

*SHEILA*

"I need help. I think my husband is a spy," Sheila Mitchell declared as soon as she walked in the door, her urgency seeming to drop the room's temperature a few degrees.

Ron Peters, her ex-husband, and Kyle, their adult son, exchanged puzzled glances. They were both square-jawed men, Kyle about an inch taller than his dad, their careers in the FBI evident in their no-nonsense demeanor.

"What kind of spy? Industrial spy? Corporate espionage?" Kyle asked as he led her to a room off the foyer, gestured for her to sit on the beige velvet couch, and took a seat in a matching chair.

Ron followed and sat in an accent chair across from her. "Has something happened?"

She shook her head, took a deep breath, and clenched her hands in her lap. If anyone could make sense of her fears, it would be these two. "No, I mean like James Bond."

Ron arched his brow. "And what made you think that?"

"It's just—things have been weird lately. Doug has been

taking secret phone calls, disappearing for hours. I found a second cell phone in his drawer."

"I'm sorry, Mom, but, um"—Kyle shifted in his seat—"could he just be, um, having an affair?"

She twisted her fingers together, her knuckles turning white beneath the pressure. "But how do you explain his abandoning credit cards and going cash based altogether? We're not on any credit counseling. And I overheard him speaking in Spanish and some other strange languages. I didn't even know he spoke so many languages. I don't know what to think anymore."

"Okay." Ron held up a hand. "Have you confronted him about this?"

"I'm scared to. What if he's involved in something dangerous?" Her voice trembled. She flexed her shaky hands in her lap and surveyed the luxurious décor. Vaulted ceilings crowned an elegantly furnished front room. A chandelier, worthy of a small palace, sparkled overhead. Voices and the rustle of people milling around drifted from the deeper interior. When had Ron become friends with people who lived in places like this?

Her gaze drifted to the bay windows overlooking an expansive lawn framed by towering trees on acres of land. Clearly, her ex-husband had contacts that existed in a different tax bracket altogether. She frowned. "You're not here on a case?"

"No." Head tipped to one side, Kyle gave her an are-you-serious look. "Back when you asked me, I wouldn't have known we'd be called out on a case. We're here for a Christmas party."

"Oh, I just thought—never mind." It was the day after Christmas, but... During their marriage, Ron was always working. Holidays meant nothing to him. One of the reasons they split.

Her ex-husband braced his hands on his knees, leaning forward, his gaze meeting hers. "Listen, what you told us doesn't seem like much. But, for your peace of mind, we'll look into it discreetly. In the meantime, I suggest you go about your business. Unless he starts threatening you, don't fret too much."

She exhaled, her stomach tightening into knots. How ironic to be here, seeking help from her FBI ex-husband about her current husband, whom she suspected of espionage.

A young man rounded the corner and approached. His smile radiated a disarmingly casual charm. "Grandma sent me," he announced, grinning at Kyle. "She'd like to invite your guest to join in the fun."

Kyle nodded. "Mom, this is Dylan Roche. His grandmother is Carol Marino. Dylan, my mom, Sheila Mitchell."

Marino. The name clicked like a missing puzzle piece snapping into place. She'd heard about M&M Enterprises. Other than real estate development, they were also the parent company of Marino Hotels Worldwide. Their headquarters was in Orlando. So… Mirror Estate, with its sprawling acres and gated luxury, belonged to the Marino family. That's the league Ron and Kyle were in these days.

Dylan's smile never wavered as he led them down a grand hallway. The murmuring voices grew louder when they approached an opulent set of double doors. With a flourish, Dylan swung them open and ushered her into a room pulsing with holiday energy and sweet with sumptuous treats.

As soft strings of a quartet in the corner underplayed the conversations, an elegant older woman sat amid her joyous guests, a commanding presence even as she chatted with a priest with thinning hair. After Dylan introduced Sheila to his grandmother and Fr. Phil and the others, she scanned the room and paused at a familiar face. Simon Roth, the senator who resigned recently. By his side stood a striking Asian American woman—Olivia, his new fiancée, if she caught the name right—and Lily Roth, their daughter, who looked too young to be holding a cocktail. From the way Kyle introduced her, Lily meant something to him. But then, Lily and Dylan looked pretty cozy together. Hmm…

Nearby, another woman caught her attention. Asian as well.

Introduced as Clara, she was deep in conversation with her husband, Dr. Michael Khoury. Their daughter, Faith, chatted with Lily, and their teenage son, Jason, ignored it all, engrossed in his phone. Next to him stood another young man about Kyle's age. Someone said he was Tommy, Dylan's best friend. He and Jason appeared to be playing some games on their phones.

And there was Eva Higgins, Kyle's childhood friend. What was she doing here? Ah, so Clara was Eva's aunt. Small world.

Ms. Marino stood up and stepped forward with a smile. "It's a pleasure to finally meet you."

"The pleasure is mine," Sheila replied, still somewhat over-whelmed by the glittering social tapestry she'd walked into.

After a decent amount of time mingling and engaging in small talk, she felt it was time to go. She caught Ron's and Kyle's attention from across the room and subtly gestured toward the exit. They made their way over to her.

"I should head out."

"Okay. We'll look into your concerns about Doug. You'll hear from us soon." Ron clamped a hand on her shoulder. "In the meantime, try to relax. Have a good rest of the holidays."

"Thanks. You too." Though how would she manage that while anxious about what they might uncover?

Her shoulders already somewhat lighter since she'd given away part of her burden, she made her way to Ms. Marino, who was finishing a conversation with the former senator. "Ms. Marino, just want to say goodbye. The estate is very beautiful."

Ms. Marino stood up again. "Thank you. I hope to see you again soon."

"Likewise." Sheila returned the smile, then gave a polite nod to the senator and the others in their circle.

After saying her farewells, she walked out of the Mirror Estate, her heels clicking against the marbled floors. The grand double doors closed behind her, sealing off a world she was only beginning to understand. As she drove, she rehashed the reason she'd been there in the first place. Was she overreacting? Maybe Doug was having an affair. How oddly relieving that would be. Or would it be? What was worse?

She shivered. Hopefully, Ron and Kyle would discover the answers.

# CHAPTER 2

## M&M ENTERPRISES

*LILY*

A tingle with anticipation, Lily Roth walked into the office building. After completing the accelerated management trainee program, she was stepping into her new role, and it was no small task. No longer a glorified secretary—a role she filled back in Hong Kong—she was now in charge of the Marino Private Select Accounts, an elite VIP program catering to the wealthy and frequent guests. A trial by fire of sorts, given that she was new, but she'd shadowed the outgoing manager before the holidays. She crossed her fingers and quickened her pace. She couldn't afford to mess this up.

Her neat and organized workspace beckoned, and her humming laptop awaited her commands. She settled into her chair and took a deep breath, ready to delve into her responsibilities. Just as she was about to log in, Tommy poked his head into her office. Yes, she had an office—small, but an office, nonetheless.

"Morning." He slapped the doorjamb, his grin too chipper for so early. "Let's grab coffee."

Lily hesitated, eyeing the computer screen, then Tommy. He hiked his eyebrows, waiting. While he seemed like he already had too much caffeine, she really could use a cup. But she couldn't give the impression she was too relaxed on her first day.

Then Dylan stopped beside Tommy. "Cute haircut!"

She glanced at her reflection on the darkened computer screen. Her long hair lost about four inches. The stylist had layered it and told her she looked more professional in this new stylish do. "Thanks. A new hairstyle for the new year and a new job."

"I approve. So, it's not eight yet. You've got a few minutes. Let's go." He jerked a thumb toward the hall, his eyes twinkling with the sort of mischief that made it hard to say no.

"All right." She stood and followed them to the elevator. "Where are we going? I thought we were going to the lounge."

"Nah, we're going down to the café. Your first day. A little celebration is in order." Dylan held the elevator door open for her.

"But—"

"No but." Tommy entered after her, blocking her in. "Remember who you're talking to. The heir to the empire."

Dylan gave an eye roll at the dig. Then after the elevator released them, he led the way into the café where well-spaced glass-topped tables interspersed with thriving money trees, all lit by a bank of windows, offered a relaxing vibe amid the downtown hustle. The morning hostess greeted them and showed them to a table. They frequented the shops down on the retail floors enough to recognize the faces.

"Are you getting used to being Lily Roth?" Tommy asked as a server poured coffee for them.

"Yeah." Lily grinned and brought the cup up for a sip. "People won't keep asking, 'Where are you from?'"

Tommy quirked a brow. "I didn't."

"That's because you knew, and we went to Hong Kong to

pick her up." Dylan turned his cup in his hand, frowning at the steam. "Do people really ask that?"

"Not all the time, but enough to be annoying." She pressed her palm to the warm cup. "Just because my name is—well, was—Tso, doesn't mean I'm not American."

"That's right!"

"So…" Tommy drummed his hands on the table, drawing the word out like an emcee at an event. "Ready for your first day?"

"I think so." She frowned at the smudges his handprint left. She'd better not mess up whatever had her fingerprints on it today. "It's a big responsibility, and I don't want to screw it up, you know?"

"We've all been there." Dylan reached across to pat her hand. "The first week is always a whirlwind, but you'll get the hang of it."

"And if you ever have questions or get stuck, don't hesitate to ask," Tommy added. "Rhonda filled in for a few days once. Ask her if you need help."

"Thanks, guys. I appreciate it." She settled back in her padded chair, more relaxed than when she walked into the office.

The guys ordered pastries, but she declined. She had breakfast already and didn't need the extra calories. The clock ticked closer to eight. "I should get going." She pushed back her chair, the metal legs grating on the tiled floor. "Big day ahead. Speaking of… you have a big day too. Mom said you guys were going to see your aunt today, Dylan."

He nodded. "Might as well get it over with. See what she wants."

"Well, be careful." After all, his aunt, a notorious criminal mastermind, tried to kill him last year. Now, she was in federal custody pending litigation and "deals."

"I will. And you have a great first day."

As she was leaving, Tommy murmured, "Aren't you gonna tell her?"

Huh. She slowed her steps, but she was too far away to hear Dylan's response. Her heart fluttered. Was he going to profess his feelings for her? No, she shook her head. They hadn't even gone on an official date yet. On the other hand, she'd gone out with Kyle a couple of times. When she met Kyle, she felt a connection. Now, she wondered if that had been nothing more than infatuation.

*Stop thinking about them. Time to work!*

# CHAPTER 3

## FEDERAL DETENTION CENTER

*DYLAN*

Dylan's shoes clicked against the linoleum floor as he followed Olivia Tso through the Federal Detention Center's mazelike interior, passing one security checkpoint after another. The tense atmosphere carried the weight of subdued emotions and unspoken stories. Despite the environment's sterility, it felt anything but clean. He'd never been to a prison before, and everything from the guard's cold gazes to the stark, imposing walls felt foreign.

Finally, they entered a nondescript room furnished with nothing more than a table and chairs. Earlier, Olivia had explained this was an attorney visiting room, so they wouldn't be directly supervised.

"She'll be cuffed to the table. You don't need to worry about her." She walked in after him.

He nodded, still grappling with the surreal situation. He stood, gripping the back of a chair. Then the door across the room creaked open, and guards escorted the Ghost in. Shackles clanged against each other as they secured her to the table. The guards left, locking the door behind them, leaving just him, Olivia, and his aunt.

Staring at the Ghost was like staring into an abyss. She was the mirror image of his late mother, an identical twin. Yet where his mother's eyes had been warm and nurturing, the Ghost's were ice-cold, void of any emotion that could be termed as human. It wasn't just that she had tried to kill him a few months back. It was also the unsettling sensation of seeing a distorted reflection of someone he had loved and lost.

"So, you've come." The Ghost finally broke the silence, her voice unnaturally calm.

He tightened his grip on the chair, the elevated position somewhat assuring. "I have. You asked to see me. What do you want?"

The Ghost turned to Olivia. "I'd like to speak to my nephew privately."

"That's not gonna happen."

The Ghost shrugged. "Well then, I guess that's it."

"You need to give us another name. Remember your deal?"

"I will after I speak with Dylan alone."

Chills shivered over him. What did she want from him? Needing to find out, he took a deep breath. "That's okay, Olivia." He pushed the words out with his exhalation. "I'll be fine. Like you said, she can't hurt me."

Olivia eyed him before giving a tight nod. "All right." She stood up. "Five minutes. I'll be right outside."

Her boot heels thudded on the floor. The door clicked behind her.

The Ghost's lips quirked. She eyed the chair he gripped. "You look ready to hold that thing up like a lion tamer." She rattled the chains holding her back. "I assure you this lioness is harmless at the moment, docile as a kitten."

He doubted that. But, called out, he slid into his seat and flattened his palms on the chill metal table between him and his aunt. "Now, what do you want?"

"What do you know about our family business?"

"You're not involved in 'our' family business. The Marino family only operates legitimate businesses now."

She smirked, twisting up his mother's lips on the impostor's face. "I'm afraid you're the one out of touch of the family business. Don't you want to know how our ancestors made their fortune?"

"I already know their criminal past." Two could play this game. "Why do you want to live on the Mirror Estate grounds?"

"It's our ancestral home. Why shouldn't I live there?"

"You forfeited that right when you wanted to kill me."

"I wasn't going to kill you. I only wanted you to give me what your parents found. After all, it belongs to us."

His brows furrowed. Was she talking about what he thought she was talking about? No way would he hint that he'd found anything besides what she had seen that fateful night. "As I recall, you said any treasures were just legends. And you saw the box. I gave everything to the authorities."

"Come now, you're a Marino—you're smarter than that. And you'd better believe *I'm* smarter than to believe that." She leaned forward. The shackles clanked. "We can work together."

He chuckled. "You and me? Not in a million years."

The door opened, and Olivia stepped in and sat down. "Time's up."

The Ghost's eyes flared at the corners, the rage fleeting, but he saw it. Maybe she wasn't an abyss after all. Now, she sat back.

"We need a name," Olivia reminded her.

"Hector Martinez."

The name meant nothing to Dylan, and Olivia's poker face revealed a further nothing.

The Ghost continued. "In case you didn't already know, he's

a kingpin of the cartel known for elusive maneuvers and brutal tactics."

Olivia held up a hand, her dark eyes piercing. "Details, we need actionable details. Addresses, contacts, operations —anything."

The Ghost's gaze flickered between them before settling on the table, almost as if she were contemplating how much to reveal. "Martinez has been spreading his wings, so to speak. The Orlando area has seen an uptick in his operations."

"That's it?" Olivia interjected. "That's like saying it rains in Seattle. We need something concrete."

The Ghost snorted. "If I gave you everything on a silver platter, what would your task force buddies need their badges for? Check with your DEA. They'll have some information to share."

Olivia clenched her jaw, visibly suppressing her frustration.

"By the way, how is the construction going for my new accommodation?" The Ghost shifted. The shackles rattled, the echo resounding in the small room.

"It's going," he said. This would be the first day the contractor started retrofitting the old orphanage. He'd seen the construction drawings. They planned to preserve as much of the building as possible and only use parts of it. An electric fence separated that from the rest of the estate.

Olivia stood, signaling the end of the visit. He followed. The task force would now be working on nailing Hector Martinez. Thank goodness, that wasn't his job.

Out of the room, Olivia stopped him with a hand on his arm. "What did she want?"

"She was trying to recruit me, so to speak."

Her grip tightened, and her high forehead crinkled with her frown, her beauty a reflection of Lily's. "What do you mean? Recruit you?"

"She wants something on the estate grounds. And she thinks I can get it for her or help her find it."

"What is it?"

Just how much did he want to tell Olivia about the buried treasures and the map he and Tommy had found? "Rumor has it my ancestors buried some treasures on the estate grounds."

"And she wants it?"

He shrugged. "I guess. Remember it's only rumor."

Her hand slid away. Still, she stared at him before resuming walking. "I wouldn't worry too much about it. It would've been found by now if it existed."

He made a noncommittal sound.

"I'm heading back to the task force office." She strode to her car once they were outside. "Oh, Dylan?"

"Yes?"

"You'd better make your move."

His brows went up. "Huh?"

As she got in her car, she smiled. "You know what I'm talking about. You have the advantage. She works with you."

# CHAPTER 4

## M&M ENTERPRISES

*LILY*

Lily slid into her desk chair with a sigh after lunch. The morning had been uneventful—organizing pens and papers, syncing her email, answering calls. It was the calm before the storm, but for now, she was okay with the quiet.

As she was considering whether to dive into the training manuals or continue customizing her workspace, her office phone buzzed, and Janet Reardon's name flashed on the display. The director of sales and marketing, Lily's boss. Her heart skipped a beat.

"Could you come to my office, please?" Reardon requested, polite but firm. "I'd like to speak with you."

"Of course," Lily answered, keeping her voice steady. She glanced at her reflection on the computer screen, smoothed her blouse, and took a deep breath before hurrying from the room. What could Reardon want?

A mahogany desk dominated Reardon's spacious office, and floor-to-ceiling windows offered a panoramic view of the city skyline. The stocky fortyish woman looked up from her computer and tucked wavy brown shoulder-length hair behind her ears as Lily entered. "Ah, Lily, come in. Have a seat."

"Thank you, Ms. Reardon." Lily smoothed her skirt beneath her as she took the proffered seat across the desk.

"Janet, please. We're casual here. First off, welcome to the team." Janet eyed her, looking for what? Signs of discomfort, maybe? "I'm sure you'll find your work here rewarding. If you ever have questions or need help, don't hesitate to reach out to me or anyone else. We're a team here."

"Thank you. I appreciate the warm welcome." Lily exhaled in quiet relief. So, it was a meet and greet, not some urgent problem.

"Good." Janet narrowed her eyes behind her red-framed glasses, her tone growing more serious. "Now, you're taking charge of our Private Select Accounts."

"Yes."

"Excellent. As you might already know, this is one of our most prestigious programs. It's not just another loyalty program —it's a VIP service catering to our most affluent and frequently returning guests."

Lily nodded at the gravity of Janet's words.

"Retention rates, exclusive offers, personalized services— these are the elements that make or break the program. I expect detailed monthly reports, as well as your input on how we can improve or expand the program." Janet slid off her glasses and rubbed the bridge of her nose. "Do you follow?"

Lily nodded again, more vigorously this time. "Absolutely. I am ready to give it my full attention."

"Great. That's what I like to hear." Replacing her glasses, Janet offered a smile. "We've had a good run, but we want to make it great. I'm counting on you to bring fresh ideas and energy to the table."

"I'll do my best."

"Perfect. If there's nothing else, you may return to your desk."

Moments later, Lily settled into her desk chair. Her fingers hovering over the keyboard, she logged into the Private Select Program's interface. As she scrolled through the list of VIPs, a name caught her eye: Toby Filmore.

Her heart lurched. Toby Filmore. The guy she had suspected of stalking her before the holidays. And here he was, listed as a VIP.

"Okay, Lily. Let's see what's going on here." She clicked on his profile and examined the information available: the date he joined the program, his room preferences, his stay frequency, the locations he visited. Huh. He'd joined the program a few months ago—around the time she moved to the US. A shiver went down her spine.

Toby stayed at the hotel for three to four days each time, and his visits were remarkably consistent, occurring every three weeks like clockwork. What business would make him frequent Orlando so often? His occupation was listed as business consultant. She stared at the screen. If he had been visiting so regularly, how had she only noticed him last month? Was it mere coincidence, or was there more to it?

She shivered, feeling exposed sitting at her desk. She minimized the program and grabbed a notepad, jotting down quick facts about Toby's stay patterns.

Something didn't add up. The timing of his program membership, his regular but short visits, and the uncanny alignment with her own life events—it was as if he had engineered things to put himself in her orbit. Should she discuss it with her boss? No. This was her first day. She couldn't go in with accusations based on hunches.

Still, the feeling nagged her. Something was off. Maybe she'd ask Kyle's opinion. And Dylan's. She checked the reservation. Toby was due back in about a week.

And while checking Toby's information, she noticed a series of cancellations on another account, often just days after making the reservations. Interesting. One or even two times, she could understand, but upward of a dozen times? Something wasn't right. She checked the registration. The account was registered to Rain Tree LLC. The company's website offered minimal information. Hmm, what to do? It wasn't her job to investigate such a peculiar pattern, or was it? She oversaw the Private Select Accounts, so maybe performing an audit was within the purview of her job description.

# CHAPTER 5

## TASK FORCE OFFICE

*OLIVIA*

Amid an atmosphere of focused intensity, paperwork littered the desks, and data flashed across the screens. Olivia sat on the edge of a desk and surveyed Ron and his team —Tanner, Ana, Hernandez, and Kyle—around the big screen in the squad room.

Having retired from her active intelligence operative role, Olivia now acted as the go-between for the task force and the Ghost. That was the result of a perplexing deal the Ghost struck with the US government—stating that she would live on the Mirror Estate grounds and would only talk to Olivia. She now strode in front of the group, ready to brief them.

"Where's Simon?" Ron asked.

"He's talking with a law firm specializing in nonprofits," she replied. Since Simon's resignation from the senate, he'd been consulting with the task force. But his dream had always been to serve the underprivileged.

"I guess he kept his Bar card up-to-date. Is that what he wants to do?"

"He renews every year. He's only talking to them." Olivia turned to the crowd. "We have a new name: Hector Martinez."

Nathan Tanner, the senior agent, cocked a bushy eyebrow. "Martinez, as in cartel kingpin Hector Martinez?"

"Exactly," she confirmed. "We might be dealing with an operation much bigger than we originally thought. I suggest we get in touch with the DEA on this one." She deferred to Ron, the head of the task force.

He nodded.

"I've got a contact at the DEA." Tanner crossed his arms, sinking into his chair. His rugged look and wary eyes always reminded her he'd seen a lot. Maybe not as much as she had, but still. "I'll set up a meeting as soon as possible."

José Hernandez opened a secure browser on his computer even as Ron smiled his approval. "Hernandez, dive into the dark web. If this guy is as connected as we think, there'll be chatter—find it."

"On it, boss." Hernandez's fingers already tapped away on the keyboard. The tech whiz's always-restless fingers and the circles under his eyes betrayed how much time he spent time lost in his glowing screens and data.

"Kyle." Ron twitched a finger at his son, who was leaning against a filing cabinet. "Reach out to local law enforcement. See if they've picked up anything on Martinez or his operations."

"Yes, sir." Kyle straightened his stance and stepped away from the cabinet. "I'll make the calls right after this meeting."

"What can I do?" Ana Ruiz, the DIA liaison, asked. A strong woman with poised shoulders and an alert posture that gave evidence of her high intelligence, she was the kind of woman Olivia could relate to, connect with if she had time, and trust to make a genuine friend someday.

"Let's see what they dig up first," Ron said. "I need you to give an update on the fake Adam O'Shea. Where are we on the trackers?"

"Ah, yes." Ana glanced at Hernandez. "Olivia must've been right. The guy changed clothes and walked somewhere, maybe even wore a disguise to throw off facial rec."

About a month ago, when the Ghost asked to speak with Olivia, Olivia knew there had to be a leak somewhere. Olivia Tso had been "dead" for more than two decades. For the Ghost to request to speak with Olivia meant someone had talked. Only a handful of people knew Olivia was the operative code-named Phoenix who infiltrated the Ghost's organization during those same two decades. Thanks to lifelike masks and wigs, Olivia had lived as Jade Lam for the better part of her life. As Jade, she'd made her way to be the Ghost's confidante. To get out and not have to look over her shoulder for the rest of her life, she orchestrated the act to have Jade "killed" a few months ago.

Ron and the team had been looking for the leak. Everything pointed to a fake Adam O'Shea who regularly visited the Ghost as one of her lawyers. Olivia managed to place a tracker on his car and on his person. But the guy was good.

"A few good candidates match the guy's height and gait." Ana shrugged, her curly brown bob bouncing with the movement. "But we lost them after a block or two."

Olivia needed to tell him something without the team listening. She pushed off the desk, caught his eye, and looked toward the hallway. Ron gave a subtle nod and rubbed his hands together. Then his rich baritone filled the room. "Let's get to work, folks."

He then followed her to the hallway alcove away from prying eyes.

"I talked to my former handler," she said. "This stays between us."

"Absolutely."

"The real Adam O'Shea is a Company asset. Whoever's impersonating him knows O'Shea's credentials would get him into the detention center. They're now considering it an internal security matter and conducting their own investigation. You'll be hearing from your superior soon."

"Shouldn't we join forces to identify this mole, for lack of a better word?"

She suggested that to Jay Burns, her "boss" and former handler, but he told her it stayed "in-house" for now. "I can't tell you how to do your job. Officially, I'm to tell you to stand down."

"I see. I'll just keep doing my job." Head cocked sideways, he fixed his deep-set eyes on her. "What about Eva's so-called Uncle Bill? Have you found out anything?"

"Uncle Bill" was actually someone Eva had met at a family gathering years ago. And all the evidence suggested he was with the Company. And then her aunt Clara had met an Officer Bill years ago. They now believed this Officer Bill and Uncle Bill were one and the same. However, he remained an elusive figure. According to Eva, she had no way to reach him. Instead, he always initiated contact.

"I asked. An intelligence officer fit the description. My handler only knows of him. Something tragic happened some years ago—he thinks it has something to do with his family." She shivered, thinking of the family she only recently reconnected with. If something happened to Simon or Lily… Her arms crept around herself. "Anyway, he hasn't been the same."

"What's his name?"

"Sorry, he didn't say. You know how it is. You'll have to wait for him to contact Eva again."

His gaze intense, he didn't say anything for a moment. "Could this Uncle Bill be the fake Adam O'Shea?"

"It crossed my mind. But without any proof, it's only conjecture." She lowered her arms, the vulnerable gesture unsuited to a woman strong enough to be Phoenix. And one thing Olivia would never be—vulnerable. "If there's nothing else, I'm heading out."

"Yeah, sure. See ya—Wait!"

"Yes?"

"Thanks for looking into Doug Mitchell. I didn't think it was anything. But just so I can tell Sheila I checked with a spook." He chuckled. "It's for her peace of mind."

The woman—light-brown hair sprinkled with gray, stylish hairstyle, early fifties—showed up at the Christmas gathering. Ron had relayed what Sheila said and asked Olivia to look into it. "No problem." Olivia smoothed a hand down the wrinkles on her slacks. Focusing on Ron's ex was much easier than thinking of something happening to an agent's family. "What made her think of it anyway? People don't jump to *that* conclusion."

"Oh, she found a second cell phone, and, uh, I guess you can call it women's intuition."

"Mm." She'd let that slur go. Knowing Ron, he hadn't meant it as sexist as it sounded. A second cell phone typically pointed to infidelity, not espionage. However, it wasn't her problem. She had other things to worry about, like the fake O'Shea. She'd finagle a way to investigate him.

# CHAPTER 6

## THE MITCHELL RESIDENCE

*SHEILA*

The silk of her cocktail dress slid against Sheila's skin as Doug parked in their garage. The night's business function had been a whirlwind—champagne flutes, small talk with potential clients, polite laughter at recycled jokes. But something had been off. Usually the charming businessman, her husband had been distant, his eyes glazed over as if his thoughts were miles away.

She studied him as he sat in the driver's seat for a moment longer than necessary. "You've been quiet. Everything okay?"

"Just tired, luv." The smile he foisted off didn't reach his eyes.

They moved inside the house, and she kicked off her heels, letting out a sigh of relief. He made his way to the kitchen, opened the wine cooler, and selected a bottle of white wine before filling two glasses. He handed her one before collapsing onto the suede living room couch and loosening his tie.

She sat on the cushion beside him, dug her bare toes into the plush teal area rug, and tested a sip, the wine warming her from the inside out. Doug once teased that the room—with its creamy ivory couch and teal accent chairs and matching rug and throw cushions—looked like one of Sheila's brides attended by gaudily dressed bridesmaids. She almost smiled at the imagery. But as she looked at him, seeming lost in thought, the chilling unease shivered over her.

Almost as if talking to himself, he muttered, "It's not easy to live a double life."

She nearly choked on her wine. "What did you say?"

He shook his head, his eyes snapping back to focus. "Nothing. It's not important."

The air grew thick, heavy with unspoken words and concealed emotions. Her mind raced back to the second cell phone she'd discovered in a drawer some time ago. It wasn't his usual phone, and he'd never mentioned having a second one. Ron had called to report he'd checked with a colleague in the intelligence world and nobody had heard of Doug. He'd assured her that her husband wasn't involved in espionage. So, perhaps Kyle was right?

"Doug?" She twisted the wineglass in her hand, the pale liquid sloshing to the rim. "I found another cell phone the other day. One I've never seen before. Whose is it?"

He blinked and sucked in a sharp breath, color tinging his ears. "Ah, that's just an old spare. Keep it around in case of emergencies, you know?"

"In case of what emergencies?" she pressed, not willing to let him off the hook, not when he sounded squirrelly, evasive.

"If my main phone dies or something." But his eyes avoided hers, and chilly tendrils of suspicion crept further into her mind.

Kyle's words resurfaced. "Are you having an affair?"

Eyebrows raised, eyes wide, Doug half rose from his seat. "No! Why would you even think that?"

She didn't think so.

He reached for her hand and squeezed it. "I promise, no

affairs." His thumb caressed the back of her hand. His voice caressed her ear. "No secrets."

But the words seemed to hang in the air, heavy and uncertain.

As they sat there in the dim light, their wineglasses leaving rings of condensation on the wooden coffee table, she feared something had changed. What did he mean by "living a double life"?

# CHAPTER 7

## TASK FORCE OFFICE

*RON*

R on shuffled through a stack of documents. With the room bathed in the fluorescent lights' sterile glow, his desk at the task force office presented a landscape of organized chaos—papers neatly stacked, computer screens flashing data, and sticky notes displaying incomprehensible scribbles decipherable only to him.

After organizing, he stood, exited the office, and entered the squad room, then paused to nod at the newcomer beside Tanner. Ana and Hernandez got up from their desks to prep. As always, the team gathered around the big screen while Ron stood off to the side.

Tanner gestured to the lanky Black man beside him. "Everyone, this is Agent Jake Cooper from the DEA. He's here to liaise for this operation."

Quick introductions followed. Then Cooper began. "Pleasure to be here." A slight drawl brought his words out low and deep. If not for the intensity of his brown eyes, he'd present almost too laid-back to be an officer. "We've got an inside man deep within

Martinez's cartel. The situation there is volatile—lots of mistrust, confusion. We've been successful in intercepting some of their shipments. It's primed for you guys to move in."

Ron rubbed his jaw, appreciation filling his chest. "I understand this is a joint operation with the DEA."

"Yes, sir," Cooper confirmed.

Hernandez jabbed the remote, and his computer display showed up on the big screen. "On the dark web, chatter indicates there's a buy scheduled in two days. If we act, it has to be then."

"All right." Ron drummed his fingers on a nearby workstation. "So we've got a time-sensitive window. We need to coordinate this sting down to the last detail. Kyle, what did local law enforcement have to say?"

Kyle looked up from his notepad. "Local PD is willing to provide any assistance we need. They've been wanting to crack down on this for months."

"Good." Ron stilled his fingers, the calm of planning an operation taking over his every muscle. "Ana, I'd like you to help with the sting operation. You did some undercover work before. And you can put the other investigation aside for now."

As Olivia predicted, word had come from the director to let the CIA take over. However, Ron would still pursue Eva's Uncle Bill angle.

Ana raised her brows, met his eye. She'd understand she couldn't talk about the fake Adam O'Shea in front of Cooper.

Ron swept his gaze across the room. "Listen up, everyone. We have one shot at this. I want every detail covered, every contingency planned for. We're moving in conjunction with the DEA on this, so communication is key. Tanner, you'll be the point of contact with Agent Cooper here."

"Yeah, boss." Tanner nodded.

"Let's regroup in twenty-four hours with final plans and contingencies. All right, get to work."

The room sprang to action, each agent diving into their

respective tasks, the atmosphere now charged with a focused energy. As the task force dispersed, Ron caught Cooper's eye. "This is a big operation. Glad we're on the same team."

"Likewise." Cooper clapped him on the back. "Let's catch this guy."

As Cooper was escorted out, Ana caught up with Ron. "What was that about putting the fake O'Shea investigation aside? Don't we need to find the mole?"

He led her to his office. "The Agency is treating it as an internal security matter. For now, anyway. We'll continue to monitor the situation. But our priority right now is Martinez."

Her expressive brows furrowed. "Why is it an internal security matter?" She pushed her curly hair back from her cheeks and leaned against the door she'd closed behind her. "Did Olivia confirm the guy is an intelligence officer?"

"Sorry." He held up both hands. "There's only so much I'm allowed to say. Speaking of… Where is she anyway?"

"Don't know." She shrugged. "Didn't she tell you?"

He shook his head. Was Olivia getting into her old spy tricks?

# CHAPTER 8

## THE ROTH RESIDENCE

*OLIVIA*

Olivia's fingers danced across the keyboard, the rhythmic tapping a hypnotic counterpoint to her laser-focused gaze. Three computer screens flickered in front of her, each displaying different pieces of an intricate digital puzzle. In her workspace—a dedicated room in Simon's house, far from prying eyes and interruption—laptops, gadgets, and cables littered her expansive wooden desk. The soft glow from the computer screens illuminated her as she dove deeper into the virtual rabbit hole, one encrypted file at a time.

Her mission was clear, albeit unsanctioned. Ever since her last talk with Jay Burns, she'd intended to go rogue to get answers. Jay had said it was an internal matter now, but she was less than keen to trust anyone. Someone was targeting her. Someone knew enough about her to let the Ghost know. Jay had given her just enough to go on—hints about an incident that happened "ten, fifteen years ago."

After bypassing firewalls and intrusion detection systems—a task she could do almost as naturally as breathing—she "borrowed" access to a classified database. One she shouldn't, technically, have access to anymore. According to Jay, something had changed this asset years ago, and so she sifted through personnel files dating back more than a decade.

She had narrowed it down to eight possible people. Eight individuals whose profiles fit the shadowy outline of the man known as Bill. She then cross-referenced the list to the few who had known about her. *Dang!* There was no intersecting point. All right, she would have to work with the eight digital avatars of individuals. She paused to make some notes, jotting down timelines, code names, and potential motivations.

Then Simon walked by, his steps soft on the thick carpet. He was coming up the stairs to the alcove, his eyebrows lifting at the sight of her high-security setup.

"Ah, playing cyber sleuth again, I see." A half smile quirked his lips. Now that he wasn't a senator anymore, he ditched the daily suit habit. Today's blue-striped shirt was paired with dark pants.

She minimized the classified windows and swiveled her chair to face him. "I've got to get to the bottom of this. I can't wait for the Company to clean up its own mess."

He entered the room and scanned her notepads and the cryptic codes on the computer screens. "I understand. Just be careful. Very careful."

"I always am." At the contemplative look in his eyes, she tipped her head to one side. "What's on your agenda today?"

"I, uh, well, I was going to make some coffee. Want a cup?"

She shook her head, her thoughts still racing. "No thank you. What's on your mind? You look like you're contemplating life's mysteries."

He chuckled and eased into the leather armchair pushed off in the corner, the comforting furnishing an afterthought to the intensity of her dedicated space. "I had a conversation with Ms.

Carol during her New Year's Eve function. She's asked me to run the Marino Foundation."

"Oh?" Her hand went to her chest. He'd always wanted to do something that would make a difference. "And how do you feel about that?"

"It's tempting. A different pace entirely, but meaningful. It could be an opportunity for positive change."

"I think it's great. This sounds just like something you said you'd want to do way back when."

Nodding, he pushed to his feet. "Yes, but nothing is set in stone yet."

"Well, whatever you decide, I know you'll be brilliant."

He crossed the room and leaned in, planting a soft kiss on her forehead. "And whatever you're digging into, I know you'll find what you're looking for."

As he walked out, her gaze returned to her computer screen. Eight names, eight potential threats. Resolved and more determined than ever, she reopened the minimized windows and got back to work.

*Which one are you?*

# CHAPTER 9

## GRACE'S APARTMENT COMPLEX

*GRACE*

Grace turned the key in her apartment door, still thinking about the first day after Christmas break. She pushed the door open and stepped into the familiar comfort of her home, but something felt amiss. The air seemed to hang differently, almost as if the apartment's very atmosphere had shifted.

She paused, her hand still on the doorknob, and scanned the entryway. The accent table, usually nestled against the wall, was now conspicuously farther away than usual. She furrowed her brow and murmured, "That's odd."

Of course, the complex's maintenance guy might have come in for some work, but she hadn't requested any repairs recently.

Shrugging off the uneasy feeling, she tried to go about her evening routine. She hung up her coat, slipped off her shoes, and made her way to the kitchen. As she prepared a light dinner, her mind drifted back to the displaced table. The small change was more than enough to unsettle the delicate balance of her well-ordered world.

After eating, she'd practice piano. Even though it had been

years since her last piano lesson, she liked to keep her skills up. A couple of school parents already asked if she'd give their children piano lessons. Soon, she hoped. She needed a way to make some extra income.

She sat at her electronic piano, flicked on the switch to turn it on—but wait. Wasn't that peculiar? The piano settings were different—not drastically, but noticeably. Her favorite presets, tailored to her playing style, were altered. A chill ran down her spine. Her fingers hovered over the keys. But... "This can't be right."

She scrolled through the settings to find her usual configurations. "Did I change this and forget?"

No. Her memory was impeccable when it came to her music. And she was only twenty-five. She couldn't be that forgetful.

Unease began to coil in her stomach. First the table, now this. Something was off. She stood and paced the room. "Am I going crazy?" she asked the empty room, half-expecting an answer. Was someone in the apartment? *Be with me, Lord!*

Her gaze wandered around the apartment, searching for anything else amiss. Everything else seemed in place, yet the nagging feeling of something being wrong persisted. Should she call a friend or the building management? Or would she sound paranoid? Indecisive, she bit her lip and hugged her arms around herself, rooting in the middle of the floor while scowling at her phone on the accent table.

Best to double-check her apartment, room by room. She started with the living room, scrutinizing every detail, every item. Everything was as she had left it in the morning. The same went for the bathroom and bedroom—nothing out of place, no sign of an intruder.

Returning to the living room, she sat on the couch and rubbed the shivers from her arms. The logical part of her brain suggested there must be a simple explanation, but her unsettled gut disagreed. She took a deep breath to calm her racing heart.

"Okay, think. Maybe I moved the table and forgot. And the piano… Maybe a power surge reset the settings?" Though her explanations didn't convince her, they were all she had.

Shaking off the paranoia, she slid onto the piano bench and began playing. Music had a way of relaxing her and transporting her to a happy place. Her mom called, and they chatted. But she didn't tell her about the table or the piano settings. Mom would say "come home" or "call 911." Afterward, Grace prepared lessons for the next day.

As she brushed her long hair to prepare for the night, she tried to reassure herself. "It's probably nothing," she whispered in the darkness.

But in the responding silence, her questions lingered.

# CHAPTER 10

## M&M ENTERPRISES

*DYLAN*

The morning light filtered through the blinds, casting linear shadows across Dylan's office. It was early, the office complex still a sanctuary of silence before the day's hustle, and his space still neat but lived-in, an office phone, a collection of reports, and a computer.

He settled into his leather chair, the door creaked open, and Tommy strode in, as punctual as ever, carrying two steaming coffee cups from the lounge.

"Morning," his best bud greeted, his voice tinged with the kind of cheer only morning people possess. He set one cup on Dylan's desk.

Dylan savored a sip, the caffeine beginning its magic. "Thank you."

Cradling his own cup, Tommy settled into the chair opposite Dylan's desk. "So, how was your visit with your aunt?"

"I was right." Dylan leaned forward and pitched his voice low. "She wants the treasures. She tried to recruit me."

Tommy's eyes went wide. "What? Is she nuts? She tried to kill you not that long ago. Now, she wants to partner with you?"

"I know. Crazy." Dylan swallowed another sip. "Anyway, guess what Olivia said? She told me to make a move."

"Make a…" Tommy's mouth formed an *O* shape. "Lily. Of course! I guess you'd better heed the advice."

"I don't know. There's Kyle."

"Ask her. Or him. See if they're an item. If you ask me, I'd say her mom's right and she's waiting for you to make a move."

Dylan drank his coffee, contemplating the best approach.

"Speaking of Lily…" Tommy sank back in his chair and hooked an ankle over his knee, his loafer bobbing. "Tell me again why you don't want to tell her about the map and those old papers we found in the estate."

After setting his coffee down, Dylan rubbed his palm over his face. "I'd like to keep it private for now. Besides, the map we found is useless without the other half. I've gone over it a dozen times. It's a dead end as it stands."

Tommy gripped his upraised knee, his eyebrows knitting together. "And the old papers, the news clippings?"

"I'm still sifting through them." Dylan drummed his fingers on his armrests. "Some of it could be related, but I don't want to involve Lily unless I find something."

## *LILY*

Lily stared at the spreadsheets fanned across her desk, the glare of her office computer casting a sterile glow over the papers. She felt like she was on the precipice of something—perhaps a revelation—but the edges were too foggy for her to make it out. With a furrowed brow, she cross-referenced the program's data with the hotel reservation's data for the third time that afternoon. The numbers were supposed to dance in harmony, but something was off. And that made her stomach twist into anxious knots.

A knock at the door jarred her from her numerical reverie. She rolled back her chair, grateful for the interruption. "Come in."

Tommy stepped in and widened his eyes. He nodded at the sea of financial chaos. "Whoa, looks like Wall Street crashed here."

She chuckled, her tension easing a fraction. "Something like that. I'm trying to perform an internal audit of the Private Select Program."

He pulled up a chair and scanned the sheets. "Impressive. But why are you doing this on your second day? Did Janet ask you to?"

"No." Lily bit her lower lip, hesitant to explain more. "I noticed something strange, and I don't want to raise alarm bells without cause. If I'm wrong—and I might well be—I'm not going to create unnecessary drama."

"What did you notice?"

She told him about the two accounts, their bookings and cancellations.

His blue eyes glazed over, but that was his focused expression. "Okay, if I understand you correctly, it sounds like money laundering. But you do need to analyze the patterns. If it's suspicious enough, we'd have to report it as part of the anti-money-laundering regulations."

Her mouth opened to an *O*. "Oh my! I didn't know anything about it."

"You noticed the strangeness." He tapped his temple. "That means you're smart. You caught something suspicious on your first day. Way to go! Remember, sometimes businesses have to cancel at the last minute or make a mistake in the dates, but if it's on a regular basis, it's suspicious."

"Okay, I'll look more closely. I suppose I need to go back a few years and maybe compare notes with the program coordinators in the chain."

"Sounds like a good idea." He stood up. "Better get back to work. See you."

After he left, she went back to the computer. This time, she widened the time frame and geographic location. Maybe everything was all legit, and she was imagining problems.

Huh. These two companies only made bookings and cancellations at the Orlando location. She frowned. Would it be normal for a business to need hotel accommodation only in one location? Perhaps just for customers coming to Orlando? But would they need ten, fifteen, twenty rooms at any one time? The hotel often rented banquet rooms out for big conferences and other events. Companies booked blocks of rooms for their employees or attendees. But those were big companies, whereas these companies offered little information on their websites. She should make a sales call to them.

January 4

# CHAPTER 11

## THE MITCHELL RESIDENCE

*SHEILA*

Sheila sat at her desk where a flurry of papers and to-do lists stretched out before her like a paper maze. Her home office was adorned with wedding paraphernalia—swatches of fabric, color palettes, and a wallboard covered in inspirational snippets and client schedules. The phone balanced precariously between her ear and shoulder as she scribbled down available dates from an overly chatty restaurant manager.

"No, Mr. O'Connell, it needs to be in May. I know that's wedding season, but…" Her patience began to wane, cut by each excitable interjection from the other end of the line. "Great, May 15 for the tasting it is. Thank you. I'll confirm with my clients."

As soon as she placed the phone down, it erupted into life again. She sighed before answering, her gaze drifting to the cup of tea she'd made an hour ago—now cold.

"Sheila speaking, how may I assist you?" she answered, all weariness masked behind her professional tone.

"It's Cindy. I've been struggling with finding a bridal dress shop. Any recommendations?"

She shifted gears. "Of course. Elegant Moments downtown is superb and specializes in custom designs. Another option is White Petals near the Riverside Mall, particularly if you're into vintage styles."

Her client squealed on the other end. "Oh, thank you. You're a lifesaver!"

Sheila smiled. "That's why you hired me. Anything else you need, just call."

Setting down her phone, she leaned back in her chair and allowed herself a deep, restorative breath. That's when she heard it—a thud from the study, followed by a cacophony of rattling noises. She frowned and pushed her chair back. Doug wasn't home, so it couldn't be him. Intrigued more than alarmed, she made her way to the study.

As she entered the room, her gaze skimmed the towering mahogany bookcase dominating one wall. There, perched like a gargoyle, was Skippy—Doug's mischievous tabby cat—looking as pleased as a cat can look.

"Skippy! What have you done now?" she chided.

Below the bookcase lay a fallen book, its pages splayed open. She raised an eyebrow at the bulky volume on cryptography. Since when was Doug interested in that? She glanced at the top of the bookcase. And why would he place a book up there?

Curiosity getting the better of her, she grabbed a chair and climbed up to investigate. Behind where the book had been, she found a small, nondescript box tucked into a shadowy nook. Her heart pounding, she took it down and opened it.

Nothing could have prepared her for what she found.

First, there was a gun. She didn't know Doug had a gun.

Then, there were several bundles of cash in different currencies and a stack of bearer bonds. She couldn't say how much, but the US stack was all hundred-dollar bills, probably ten or fifteen of those in the stack. And the top bearer bond was for ten thousand dollars.

The room seemed to shrink around her, each wall inching closer as if to suffocate her. She stumbled back, her eyes locked on the cash concealed within the box.

She sat and gripped the edge of the desk, her mind racing through every moment she'd spent with Doug, everything he'd told her. Where did all the cash come from? Why the different currencies? Was he preparing to flee the country and go somewhere? And most curious of all, why did he hide it? From her?

Her phone rang, shattering the fragile silence. She glanced at the screen—the client who'd been calling about floral arrangements. She took a deep breath and composed herself, silencing the ringtone. There were urgent matters to attend to, but she couldn't ignore this discovery.

Skippy jumped from the bookcase, landing on the carpet, oblivious to the crisis he'd triggered. Focused on the innocent feline, she sighed. If only life were as simple as knocking down books and climbing furniture.

Sheila closed the box and tucked it back where she'd found it. There had to be a legitimate reason. She'd confront Doug when he returned, and he'd explain. But for now, she had weddings to plan, brides to consult, and—most jarringly—reality to question.

Back at her desk, she took a few deep breaths. Her phone buzzed with a new email, a reminder that the world continued to spin outside of her imploding personal life. With a heavy sigh, she opened her laptop and reinserted herself in the realm of seating charts and flower arrangements.

The work could continue, yes, but the trust, the bedrock of her relationship, was now a field of quicksand. Would she ever find solid ground again?

And so, she worked—each keystroke a distraction, each call a diversion—as she grappled with the sand disappearing underneath her, uncertain where it would lead but knowing she had no choice but to follow it to its unnerving end. And the nagging thought remained, lurking in the recesses of her mind like an unwelcome ghost.

Who was Doug, really? Why all the cash? And different currencies?

# CHAPTER 12

## M&M ENTERPRISES

*LILY*

Lily adjusted her blazer as she walked down the corridor. She'd been enjoying her new role, making sales calls and familiarizing herself with the program. However, those two accounts—Rain Tree LLC and New Life LLC—lingered in her mind like a pair of riddles begging to be solved.

Taking a deep breath, she rounded the corner toward Janet's office. The assistant, Kim, looked up as she approached.

"Morning. Is Janet in?" Lily asked, the casual query at odds with the urgency quickening her heartbeat.

"Yeah, she's in. Want me to announce you?" Kim smiled, her perfectly manicured red-painted fingernails hovering over the intercom.

"That'd be great, thanks."

Kim buzzed through to Janet, who gave the go-ahead. Lily took another steadying breath as she pushed open the door to her boss's office.

Janet scooted her chair back from her computer, put her

reading glasses down, and broke into a welcoming smile. "Come in. How's your day going?"

"Hi, Janet. It's going well. Thanks for asking." Lily slid into a seat across from her boss. "I'm enjoying the work, honestly. It's been a great experience so far."

"That's wonderful to hear." Her boss stacked aside her papers to focus. She sported a new hairdo—a pixie cut. "So, what brings you here today?"

It was time to dive into the matter, so Lily took a moment to collect her thoughts. Her hand played with her own recently restyled long hair. "Well, I wanted to talk to you about something. I've been going through the accounts, and a couple have caught my attention—Rain Tree LLC and New Life LLC."

Janet leaned forward, her eyes narrowing. "Oh? What's going on with them?"

"First off, they don't have any real activity, just a lot of back-and-forth billing but nothing concrete. When I called them, I just reached an answering service. For Rain Tree LLC, the only person I found was a young girl who seemed to know nothing. She said she was just there to 'hold down the fort,' whatever that means. For New Life LLC, I had a similar experience."

The woman's face was impassive. "Hmm… It may sound a little odd to you. But remember some of these companies whose headquarters may not be here can operate with minimal staff locally. Are you concerned about something in particular?"

Not the reaction Lily was hoping for. "Not really. Everything looks… normal, just inactive. Most peculiar is their booking and cancellation pattern." She didn't mention Tommy at this point. After all, she was supposed to report to Janet.

"Oh, what is the pattern?"

Lily showed her boss the charts she printed. Then she explained the reservations and cancellations within days—always for a large block of rooms they reserved and then canceled days later.

"I see. Sometimes, that happens. Let me know if they skipped a bill or something. Otherwise, I suggest you focus on the guests that are here. They need to feel welcomed and taken care of."

"Yes, ma'am." Lily nodded. Maybe she wouldn't mention the anti-money-laundering regulation.

"If there's nothing else—"

She stood up, having been dismissed. "No thank you." She returned to her office. But how puzzling her boss's indifferent reaction had been.

Later that afternoon, a soft knock on her door pulled her attention away from her computer screen, and an ordinary-looking gentleman stood in the doorway, wearing a charcoal suit and a polite smile. "May I come in?"

"Of course." Lily stood and motioned for him to enter. "How can I help you?"

"I'm Trent Lockwood with Rain Tree LLC." He extended a hand for a shake.

Her internal radar blipped as she worked to keep her surprise in check and shook his hand. "Nice to meet you, Mr. Lockwood. What brings you here?"

"I received the email announcing your new role to manage the Private Select Program, and I thought I'd drop by to introduce myself." He took a seat across from her.

"That's very thoughtful of you." Her voice calm, she locked her gaze onto his. How was it possible for him just to "drop by," when her previous attempts to contact the company had led nowhere?

"If you don't mind"—she retrieved a notepad and pen from her drawer—"I'd like to update my contact information for Rain Tree LLC. I'm not sure if what I have is current."

"Absolutely, go ahead," he said.

She read out the on-file phone number and the address, watching his reaction.

"That's correct," he confirmed. "I'm often out of town on business, so we use an answering service to handle incoming calls."

"I see." She jotted down a note. Something felt off, but what? An answering service made sense for a company whose principal was always on the move, but her gut insisted there was more to the story.

"Being out of town so much must keep you quite busy," she ventured, looking for any hint of evasion.

"It does, but it's the nature of our business." Lockwood laced his hands in his lap, index fingers tapping. "However, I'm hoping your program can provide some added value to our company's travels."

"I'm sure it can." Smiling, she sank back in her chair. "We have some excellent benefits. What is it that Rain Tree does?"

"We're an import and export company. Lots of customers coming to check out our stuff."

"I see." She nodded. So where were these customers who never showed up?

Lockwood stood. "It was a pleasure meeting you, Ms. Roth. I look forward to doing business with you."

"The pleasure's all mine," she responded, also rising to her feet. "Take care, Mr. Lockwood."

As the door closed behind him, she sat back down and stared at the notepad where she had written the name Trent Lockwood alongside the Rain Tree LLC information. His visit did little to alleviate her concerns. If anything, it deepened them. It wasn't just the answering service or the vague details about his business trips. It was an unshakable feeling that Trent Lockwood had told her just enough to keep her interested but not enough to ease her suspicions.

"All right, Rain Tree LLC," she murmured. "What are you really up to?"

# CHAPTER 13

## TASK FORCE OFFICE

*RON*

The sight that greeted Ron when he walked into the task force office was not something he had expected. The deputy director, Vera Haskin, a woman with whom he had romantic history a long time ago stood in front of him. She still sported a no-nonsense haircut and a professional suit and pumps. But why had she traveled from DC to the task force when she could easily ask for a video conference?

"Ms. Haskin, what a surprise!" Having opted to be formal, he gestured for her to head to his office.

She followed him and sat on a chair facing him, balancing her laptop bag on her knees. "You haven't changed much. Maybe a little more silver in your hair."

"Thank you. You look great yourself." He couldn't help thinking back to their joint ops a lifetime ago. A beat later, he pulled his mind back to the present. "I hear congratulations are in order."

"Would you mind closing the door, please? And thank you.

You'd have gotten this job if you'd thrown your name in the hat."

He shook off the comment and closed the door. "You know I don't do politics."

She smiled. "Sorry we didn't get a chance to chat at Stan's retirement party."

He shrugged. "You were busy shaking the right people's hands." If the rumor was to be believed, Stan was pushed to retire early. And now, this woman got the job and a new title. Not an assistant director, but deputy director. He sat at his desk. "So, to what do I owe this honor?"

She waved as if swatting a fly. "I'll be stationed here on a temporary basis. Not this task force, obviously. You're in charge here." Her head tilted toward the direction of the satellite office. "I'll be over at the public building."

His eyebrows furrowed. "I'm not aware of any big case that would require your presence."

She drew back, and her amber eyes slanted him a "really?" look. "You don't consider the Ghost a big enough case?"

"Oh!" He glanced at the desk calendar, ensuring he didn't have anything urgent to attend to.

"I'll cut to the chase." She set her laptop bag on the next chair. "I heard you're investigating an Adam O'Shea. True?"

"Yes." He cocked his head to one side, his curiosity piqued. "In fact, he's linked to the Ghost. Well, the fake one. Evidently, the real one is an Agency asset. And we're told to stand down."

Vera sighed, looking past Ron as if contemplating how to proceed. "Great. I don't need to repeat the order, then."

"May I ask why?"

Vera leaned back, pressing her lips tight in visible displeasure. "I was informed that this particular Adam O'Shea may be leaking classified information. Information sensitive enough that even a whiff of it getting out could compromise national security."

"Are we talking about Olivia's cover as Phoenix?" His eyes narrowed. A brief expression of surprise passed through her face. "Ah, I should have known. She and Roth are working out of here."

"When the bioweapon scare happened last year, she showed up and helped eliminate the threat. And now, the Ghost will only talk to her, so even though Olivia wanted to retire from the Agency, she has to be part of this task force."

"But your team shouldn't know this. Only a handful of people are aware of Phoenix. The fact that you do tells me this leak could be disastrous."

"I can vouch for every one of them. They know her identity is highly classified, on a need-to-know basis. And they needed to know last year. But I still don't get why this has anything to do with pulling me off O'Shea. We suspect he might be leaking the info, so shouldn't we be doubling down on plugging this hole?"

She held up a hand. "I don't like it either, but orders are orders. The director believes that pushing O'Shea any harder might force the leak into the open in a way we can't control."

"So, we just let him roam free?" he pressed, pushing his frustration out into his voice.

"For now. We surveil, we collect, but we do not engage."

He clenched his jaw. "And the Ghost?"

She picked up a pen and twirled it between her fingers. "Continue with that line of the investigation, but know your hands are tied when it comes to O'Shea. Unless new evidence mandates a different course of action, we sit tight."

He nodded his reluctant agreement. "Very well—ma'am," he added as an afterthought.

"Thank you." She stood.

He rose from his chair. "Is there anything else?"

"That's it. Keep me posted on the Ghost. And"—she locked her gaze with his—"be careful. By the way, I'm staying at my house."

Right, she was from the area. Much like politicians, she kept a house in her home state and another place up in the DC area.

Her gaze lingered. Was she thinking of the last time they saw each other, before the retirement party? She took a deep breath. "Ron, does it bother you that I'm now your superior?"

He shook his head. "It was a long time ago."

"Yes, it was. Well, see you around." And she walked out.

He stood there, gathering his thoughts before going out to the squad room for the morning briefing. He joined Olivia by the coffee machine in the kitchen. "Got a minute?"

"Sure." She turned. "What's up?"

He pulled her aside, away from prying ears. "I just had a meeting with the deputy director. What's really going on about this O'Shea?"

She saluted him with her cup. "Politics is going on. That's always the case. The Company doesn't want to broadcast there might be a traitor in their ranks. Jay said they had it under control."

"He could be the leak." He studied her micro expression to determine her underlying meaning. "Aren't you concerned who blabbed their mouth to the Ghost?"

She looked around, ensuring no one was eavesdropping. "Of course, I'm concerned. Officially, I can't condone any actions against Adam O'Shea. Unofficially"—her hard gaze drilled into him—"you do what you think is best. Just tread carefully."

"I will." He got himself a cup of coffee while he was there. "About Eva's so-called Uncle Bill. You remember Officer Bill mentioned in Clara's journal?"

"Yes, we think they're the same person. Proving it is another matter."

# CHAPTER 14

## TASK FORCE OFFICE

***KYLE***

After the briefing, Kyle hurried to catch his dad. He'd seen him talking to Olivia earlier. Maybe she found out more new information on Doug. But when he got close, Dad was on the phone with Mom. Once he ended the call, Kyle called, "Sir." He tried not to call him Dad in the office. Sir sounded more professional.

Dad turned around. "Just the person I need."

"That was Mom, wasn't it?" He followed Dad into his office.

"We need to talk about Doug." Dad slid out his desk chair. "Your mom found bundles of cash, in various currencies, and a stack of bearer bonds hidden high up with a gun. She said he commented something about living a double life."

While Dad folded his hands on the desk, Kyle remained standing. "Did Olivia discover something? I thought you said he was a nobody in the intelligence community."

"No, she didn't find anything else. And he was a nobody. However, the cash raises another kind of red flag."

"What do you want me to do?" He bounced on his feet.

"Start by digging into his financials, look for any irregularities or connections to known criminals. Pull up his travel records. See if any of his trips align with significant events or criminal activities. Keep it under the radar."

He nodded. "Got it. Financials and travel. You're not thinking he's a spy, are you?"

"No. Depending on what you find, he may be doing something illegal, but what, I don't know yet." Dad put his reading glasses on. That was a recent addition. For a long time, Dad had refused to wear "granny glasses." He'd finally caved.

"On it." Kyle started to leave.

"Keep me posted."

Back at his workstation, he started digging into Doug's financials. Then he changed course. Financials weren't his forte. He'd start with something easy—the man's travel records. Doug mostly traveled to Europe with a few trips to Asia. Leaning back in his chair, Kyle grabbed his cell phone and called his mom. "Hey, Mom." He frowned. Just how was he going to ask this? Might as well cut to it. "Just wondering if you know anything about Doug's travels?"

"He always has these conferences. In London and Paris, I think. Why?"

Instead of answering, he rubbed his forehead. "Did he ever go to Asia?"

"Not that I recall. At least not during our marriage. What's this about?"

"I'm just checking everything." After promising he'd update her as soon as he knew something, he ended the call.

The man definitely went to Asia a few times. What was he doing in all these places? What was he hiding?

**RON**

A tense anticipation tainted the atmosphere when Ron returned to the office after lunch. Fluorescent lights hummed overhead as he stood in front of a digital screen and absorbed the energy while agents gathered around, shuffling their papers and double-checking their facts before another briefing.

"So, I've got confirmation on the buy." Cooper was the first to speak up, the words coming out in his slow drawl. "It's a low-level deal, not enough to get us the intel we need on Martinez."

Ron folded his arms across his chest. "Understood. We need someone inside to roll over and give us a better shot at the top of the chain. You agree?"

"Yes, sir," Cooper replied.

Tanner set aside his stress ball and took the floor. "Coast Guard intel indicates a shipment's arriving next week. DEA and the Coast Guard are both geared up to seize it. This could be the big fish we're looking to fry."

"Excellent." Ron scratched a finger against his crossed arms. "We'll coordinate with both agencies then, make sure we get everything we need from the bust."

Ana stepped forward. "I'm set to go undercover with one of Cooper's guys for the buy. We're preparing alternate identities, histories, the whole nine yards."

"All right. Let's make sure everyone is on the same page here. This is a joint operation, and communication is key. Mistakes can cost us the case or worse." He scanned the faces in the room to ensure the gravity sank in.

As the team began to disperse, Olivia lingered. Her expression more serious than usual, she approached him. "Can I have a word?"

"Of course." He stiffened at the urgency in her tone.

"I didn't tell you everything this morning. I've been doing some digging of my own."

"On O'Shea?"

"Yeah, and on Eva's 'Uncle Bill' and Clara's 'Officer Bill.'"

She tapped her phone a few times. "I got police sketches from both Eva and Clara." Clara, Eva's aunt, had only recently recovered her memories after twenty years.

Olivia showed him her phone, switching between two images. One sketch depicted a man in his early thirties—brown eyes, short hair, no facial hair. The other was a middle-aged man with thinning hair and a mustache.

With his glasses on, he studied both images. "The younger one is from Clara?"

"Yes. It was twenty-some years ago, so her memory is hazy. The other is from Eva."

He leaned against a cold filing cabinet. "So you think they could be the same person?"

"It's a possibility." She reached across and swiped on her phone one more time. "Here's the age progression AI images. It fits."

He suspected the same. "But I don't get it." The cabinet rattled as he moved. "From Clara's journal entries and her account, Officer Bill sounded like a good guy. Then, when Eva recounted her story with Uncle Bill, he became elusive. And if we now suspect him to be the one to leak your identity, I gotta ask, what changed?"

She grabbed her phone back. "I don't know, but according to Jay, this person suffered some type of tragic event some ten, fifteen years ago. And apparently, he blamed Uncle Sam for the tragedy. I can only surmise that he was ripe for the Ghost."

He ran his fingers through his hair. "Say your theory is correct. You're the spy. How do we ferret out a spy?"

Her left foot was tapping like she was counting beats. "Remember I told you how I thought the fake O'Shea was an operative. I feel strongly this Officer Bill or Uncle Bill is the fake O'Shea. He's been in the game for a long time. And people like that have a knack for covering their tracks. But I'm working on it."

His heartbeat kicked up at the suspicion she'd do something not quite legal. "What are you going to do?"

She was already walking away, but she turned and winked. "I don't think you wanna know."

The next morning, before the briefing, Ron sat at his desk, reflecting on his phone call with Sheila the day before. Should he have been more honest? There could've been an innocent explanation for the bundles of cash in various currencies, but more likely, it was ill-gotten, especially since it was hidden from her. Most emergency monies would be in American dollars. Unless one planned to flee the country, one wouldn't need foreign currency.

"Hey, got a minute?" Kyle tapped on the doorframe.

Ron motioned him in. "What's up?"

Kyle sat in one of the visitor chairs. "So, I did some digging on Doug. His travel history, in particular. Mom thinks he only goes to London and Paris for some real estate conferences, and according to his travel itineraries, he does go to London and Paris a lot. He stays there for a number of days. But when I checked with the hotels, there never were any conferences during his stays. And the concierge said he couldn't find any real-estate-related conference during his stays in town."

Ron massaged his temple. Couldn't he just have one problem at a time? "Have you asked if he was alone?"

"Yes, and I even talked to the security people. They checked the footage for me. Get this. He would check in, go to his room. A bit later, he'd come out and go out. Then he wouldn't come back for a day, two, or three at one time."

"Could he be seeing someone in London?"

"It's possible."

"But that still doesn't explain the money."

"And it doesn't make much sense since this pattern began before he married Mom. If he was seeing someone in London or

Paris, he didn't have to hide then. And he wouldn't marry Mom if he already had someone else. Don't you think?"

He didn't know what to think. Doug wasn't going anywhere. The task force had more important things to take care of right now. "Let's revisit this after the operation. We've got a cartel to bring down."

"Yes, sir." Kyle rose to leave.

Ron followed his son out to the squad room. *What are you hiding, Doug?*

His team gathered around the big screen as soon as he turned the corner. "Listen up, everyone. We're on the eve of a significant operation. I don't have to tell you how important it is that we get this right."

Cooper stepped up next to him. Feet planted wide, hands folded in front of him, he could have been waiting in a fast-food line for all his lack of apparent tension. "Our inside man says that the cartel is getting nervous. They're shifting around their players. Even the low-level guys are tense. The window of opportunity is narrowing, so it's now or never."

"I'm ready." Ana, dressed in street clothes to blend in, squared her shoulders. "Once I get the signal, I'll hand over the money and complete the transaction."

"We're gonna wire you up with earbuds for communication. Hernandez, how are we doing on the tech side?"

Hernandez gave a thumbs-up. "Everything's tested and ready. The transmission is clear, and we've got a direct feed from her earpiece to our van. I'll be monitoring from there."

Ron nodded. "Tanner, Cooper, and Kyle, you guys are on ground support. Keep your distance but stay close enough to move in if things go south. Do we have eyes on all exits?"

"Yes, boss," Tanner confirmed. "We've identified all possible exit routes. We'll have unmarked vehicles at each."

"Good. Ana, remember, your safety is paramount. If you

sense even the slightest off-vibe, abort the mission. We'll pull you out."

"Got it."

Rob turned to Cooper. "DEA's been doing a good job disrupting their supply chain. Now, it's our turn to pull the rug out from under them."

The lanky agent rasped a hand over his buzz cut. "That's the plan. They're already off-balance. This will push them over the edge. We're looking at getting someone on the inside to turn against the higher-ups and hoping this operation gives us that leverage."

"As soon as we confirm the transaction, we move in. No hesitation. Every second will count. We can't afford any mistakes."

With a glance at Ana, Ron let out a slow breath. It had been years since she worked undercover. Time better not have dulled her skills.

# CHAPTER 15

## THE MITCHELL RESIDENCE

*SHEILA*

Sheila pulled into her garage, preparing to end a call through her Bluetooth earpiece. "Fantastic. I can't wait to go over the garden-themed wedding ideas with you. I'll see you tomorrow at 2 p.m."

"Thank you so much." Her client's voice came back, sounding relieved. "You're a lifesaver."

Smiling to herself, she stepped out of her car. Another happy client, another chance to do what she loved. Her job was her refuge, her temporary escape from the uncertainties on the home front. When she walked into the house, the security alarm had already been disarmed. So Doug was home early from his trip.

Carrying her Gucci bag over one arm, she headed into the foyer and placed her bag on the dark cherry antique table that had been in her family for generations. He had always thought it was too old-fashioned, but she loved it. The smell of fresh-cut lilies wafted from a vase on the living room coffee table. He often complained they were too fragrant, but she adored them.

She made her way to the kitchen, braced for more surprising discoveries. "Hey, you're home—"

Her footsteps paused, her gaze frozen on the stark smear of red blood trailed across the white tiles. The shocking contrast sent alarm jolting through her. For a heartbeat, her mind raced, her breath catching in her throat. Then her gaze landed on her husband, sprawled motionless on the floor. Panic propelled her forward. She rushed to his side, her mind clouding.

"Doug!"

A hole marred his forehead.

*No! No! No!* She was dreaming. This wasn't happening.

She knelt near him to feel for a pulse, something. But, alas, nothing. Not even a faint one. His unseeing eyes stared at the ceiling. She stood up and tried to think. Her mind was telling her to call 911, but her body wouldn't obey. Before she could summon her hands to grab the phone, something struck her head. Her legs buckled, and her world plunged into darkness, the kitchen's lights and sounds fading into a suffocating void. The last image that flickered in her mind was Doug's still form on the floor. The haunting sight would linger in the shadows of her consciousness.

# CHAPTER 16

## ALLEY

*RON*

R on sat in the unmarked car with Tanner, his eyes trained on Ana and Rick Sanchez, the DEA undercover agent. From a distance, Ana was almost unrecognizable in her new getup. With a hairdo that screamed "don't-mess-with-me" and makeup that made her look like she belonged in the underworld they were trying to dismantle, she was totally in character.

"She's good," Tanner whispered, his stress ball flexed in a white-knuckle grip. "She could give Hollywood actresses a run for their money."

Ron grunted.

Several unmarked vehicles were also parked around the perimeter, housing other agents and backup officers. A tight operation like this couldn't afford any mistakes.

Ana and Sanchez stepped out of the car and strolled toward the waiting sedan. Thanks to the tiny mic and earbuds, Ron and the others could hear every word exchanged. Sanchez introduced Ana as the buyer, going by the name of "Sonia."

The seller, who introduced himself as Jorge, had his underlings approach them. The goons patted them down, ensuring they weren't carrying any weapons. Apparently satisfied, he nodded.

"Let's see the goods," Ana, or rather Sonia, said.

The boss signaled one of his guys who popped the trunk to reveal bags of presumably uncut cocaine.

"I want to be sure it's the real thing," she insisted.

The man unsheathed a pocketknife and sliced open one of the bags. He offered it to her. Sanchez, the inside man, took a sample, rubbed it between his fingers, and then indicated his approval.

She unzipped the duffel bag she'd brought with her, revealing bundles of cash to make the trade-off. "Here you go."

The moment felt like it lasted an eternity. Ron's hand hovered over the radio, his heart pounding. Then it came—the agreed-upon signal. Sanchez subtly adjusted his baseball cap, an inconspicuous move that screamed "Go!" in the language of undercover operations.

"Move in, now!" Ron shouted into the radio.

Agents and officers swarmed out of their hiding spots, guns pointed, descending on the alleyway like hawks on prey. "Federal agents! Freeze!"

Jorge and his underlings went for their weapons, but outgunned, they surrendered. Soon, they were handcuffed and read their rights.

Ana and Sanchez were also "arrested" to maintain their cover for any onlookers who might be part of a bigger network.

"Good work," Ron whispered as he stepped out of his vehicle, looking at Ana and Sanchez while other agents ushered them into a squad car.

Tanner joined him, both men watching the agents from both agencies process the scene.

"Let's go debrief. We've still got a long way to go." And Ron's mind already raced with the operation's next steps.

The agent nodded. "After that, drinks are on me."

About an hour later, Ron sat side by side with Cooper in the DEA's sterile, cold interrogation room, waiting for Jorge to be brought in. The door finally creaked open, and two guards ushered in the cuffed suspect and escorted him to the metal chair. His gaze darted around, calculating, but he seemed to be at the end of his rope.

They did the routine, telling him the interview would be recorded, identifying themselves and the date, etc., and ensuring the suspect understood his rights. So far, he hadn't asked for a lawyer. Ron would like to keep it that way for as long as possible.

"Let's get to it. You're looking at a lifetime in federal prison, Mr. Rodriguez. Drug trafficking, weapons charges, the list goes on." Cooper slid a file toward him.

Rodriguez glanced at the file, then Cooper. "I got nothing to say. Lawyer."

The agents packed up their files and walked out. "That didn't take long," Ron mumbled as his phone rang and an unknown number flashed across the screen. He answered anyway and motioned for Cooper to head on back to his desk. "Peters."

"Ron! He's… dead…" Sheila started sobbing.

"Who's dead?" He stopped walking.

"Doug. I found him. They don't believe me."

She wasn't making much sense. "Where are you?"

"They arrested me."

# CHAPTER 17

## THE MITCHELL RESIDENCE

*SHEILA*

When consciousness seeped back into Sheila, it arrived like the slow creep of dawn. Her eyes blinked open, each flutter clearing away a portion of the murky haze clouding her mind. She was in their living room, planted in the plush teal accent chair they'd bought on their first anniversary—a chair that was supposed to symbolize comfort and domesticity. Now it felt like a trap.

She shook her head gently, attempting to dispel the fog. The details of what had happened started to assemble themselves into a grim picture. She remembered Doug's eyes, her dizzying descent into darkness. But how did she end up here?

Her gaze darted around, scanning for her husband. She found him quickly enough, and the sight sucked the breath from her lungs.

He was sprawled on the floor, a pool of dark blood around his body. His eyes were vacant, a gory tableau that transformed their peaceful living room into a nightmarish crime scene. A scream clawed its way up her throat but lodged there, stifled by shocked disbelief.

Driven by adrenaline, she started to push off from the chair, intending to rush to Doug's side. That was when she felt the weight in her hand—a cold, metallic weight. She looked down, horror-stricken—What? How? She gripped a *gun*.

How did this happen? Was she being set up? She couldn't— she wouldn't—hurt Doug. She barely had time to register the implications when a loud crash interrupted.

"Drop the weapon!" a voice thundered through the room.

Men in tactical gear burst through the front door, guns pointed at her. Her mind screamed for her to explain, to plead her innocence, but the words wouldn't form.

Hands trembling, she placed the gun on a side table next to the chair. The lead officer, his face stern behind a shield of protective eyewear, signaled to a colleague who moved forward to secure the weapon.

Another officer was already kneeling beside Doug, checking for signs of life. Her eyes met the officer's as he stood up and shook his head. Doug was gone, and judging by the way the officers were looking at her, she was their prime suspect.

As an officer began reading her rights, handcuffing her with grim efficiency, her thoughts swirled into a maelstrom. What had Doug been involved in? Who had done this to them? And most urgently, how could she prove her innocence in a scenario designed to implicate her?

**RON**

"Listen." Ron sucked in a sharp breath. "Do not say anything. I can't leave now, but I'm sending Kyle over. They won't let you make another call, so I'll call Simon. He can represent you for now until we know more."

Lowering his voice, Ron turned his back on Cooper at his desk, chilling. "Remember, do not talk." How was it he was advising a "suspect" not to talk? But above all else, he knew Sheila couldn't harm anybody. And he also knew police tactics. He hung up and called their son.

Though understandably upset by the news, Kyle promised to head over to the station right away. Next, Ron found Simon's number.

After Ron explained the situation, the former senator cleared his throat. "Um, you know criminal law isn't my expertise. You're going to want a top gun on this. It doesn't sound good."

"I know, but I'm in the middle of a case. You're the first lawyer I think of and trust."

"Sure, I'll go and get her through arraignment. If it's okay with you and Sheila, I'll see if Zimmerman is available. He'd be the one you want on a case like this." Todd Zimmerman's law firm handled the Marino family's personal and business affairs. The man himself was a brilliant criminal attorney.

"Yes, please. Sheila would appreciate that." Calm reclaimed Ron. They'd get through this, and they'd have help. But right now, Cooper was motioning for him. "I gotta go. Thanks, bud. I owe you."

Rodriguez's public defender, a young, harried-looking guy with dark circles under his eyes and pockmarked skin, arrived and requested some time with his client alone before the interview. Fifteen minutes later, they were back at it.

Ron began, "We already have enough to put you away, but you can help yourself by helping us. You roll over on your boss, and we put in a good word with the prosecutor."

Before his lawyer could do anything, Rodriguez snorted. "Haven't you heard? Snitches get stitches."

Bracing both hands on the metal table, Cooper leaned in

closer. "You're already in a world of hurt, man." His calm drawl added extra menace to the words. "Don't you want to get out from under this, even a little?"

The lawyer whispered something to him, and Rodriguez nodded. Unfortunately, it turned out that Rodriguez was a low man on the totem pole. They needed to get to Marco, his boss, and continue climbing until they got to Martinez.

They spent the next hour going over names, places, dates—details to help them bring down the cartel. Even though Rodriguez wasn't high enough, he still provided valuable intel.

As Ron exited the room, his mind went to Sheila and her predicament. What was Doug into that got him killed? And why frame her?

# CHAPTER 18

## POLICE STATION

*SHEILA*

Stark and cold, the interrogation room matched the typical sterile setting she'd always seen in the movies—a one-way mirror on a wall, a metal table bolted to the floor, a hard chair under her. Sheila just never imagined she'd ever be in one. Shivering, she shifted in her seat alone on one side, her fingers tapping the surface, anxiety twisting her tummy. Her gaze flitted to the door every time a muffled noise drifted from the corridor.

Then the door swung open, and Detectives Spaulding and Monnin entered. Detective Spaulding, a stocky man with graying hair and a stern face, took a seat across from her. Detective Monnin, a tall woman with sharp features and long sandy-brown hair tied up in a ponytail, sat next to him.

"Mrs. Mitchell," Spaulding began, "the officer took your statement at the scene, but we'd like to ask you a few more questions."

But hadn't Ron said not to say anything? A deep breath helped her push out her response. "I'm sorry, but I'm not saying anything until my lawyer gets here."

Monnin rolled her eyes. "You've been watching too many crime shows."

Spaulding sighed and stood up, telling his partner, "She did invoke."

They opened the door to leave, but the senator stood just outside, poised to enter. This was beyond weird. She was in the police station, being accused of murdering her husband, and the former senator, Simon Roth, whom she'd only met in person less than two weeks ago, was here to represent her.

Senator Roth nodded to her and faced the two detectives. "May I confer with my client?"

Detective Monnin raised an eyebrow, her voice snarky. "Senator, going to the dark side, eh?"

The senator put his briefcase on the table. "Every person has a right to representation, Detective."

Spaulding frowned. "You're here as her attorney?"

"Indeed, I am. So, may I confer with my client?"

"Of course, Senator." His stern expression seeming forever etched in place, Spaulding held the door open for his partner.

As the door closed, Roth sat beside her.

"Thank you for coming, Senator." She sat up, shivers jittering through her, shivers having nothing to do with the stark-cold room.

"You're welcome. And please, I'm not a senator anymore. Just Simon." He pulled some papers from his briefcase. "Before we proceed, let me explain how this works."

He then told her about what to expect and how Zimmerman would likely take over her representation after that. Then he asked her to tell him what happened. And she did. After some counseling, he told the guard outside he needed to talk to the detectives.

They came in and took the seats opposite her. Before Simon was able to say anything, Spaulding said, "Mrs. Mitchell claims—"

"Detective." Simon put his hand up to stop him. "I understand she hasn't been seen by a medical professional yet. She was knocked unconscious. Shouldn't she be checked for a possible concussion? The side of her head has a bump the size of a goose egg."

The two detectives exchanged glances.

"The responding officer didn't say anything about her injury." Spaulding frowned down at the file.

"According to Mrs. Mitchell, the responding officer didn't listen to her. He just cuffed her." Simon stood up. "I understand she hasn't been booked yet. Are you going to charge her now?"

Monnin eyed Spaulding. Neither said anything.

"I didn't think so," Simon said. "We're leaving."

"Don't leave town." Monnin's long ponytail swung when she called the words over her shoulder as they walked out.

Sheila didn't dare ask any questions until she was outside of the police station. "That's it?"

"For now, but Ron will want to find out what happened. You're still the prime suspect." He opened the front passenger door to his Lexus. "Let me take you to the hospital to get checked out."

Only now, she remembered she didn't drive here. She got in. "Is that necessary?"

He came around to the driver's seat. "Yes, we must document your injury. Also substantiate your claim of being struck."

"So, what's our next step? I mean, after the hospital."

He started the car. "Do you have some place to stay? Your house is still a crime scene."

Right, Kyle mentioned that, though she hadn't been paying much attention then. Too many distractions at the police station. "Kyle said I could stay with him. But I'll need some things from the house. Oh, can you find out what happened to Skippy? I just remembered I didn't notice him when I came to."

"Skippy?"

"Doug's tabby cat."

"Okay, I'll find out and arrange for you to get some stuff from your house. And maybe the cat."

His phone rang, and Kyle's contact number flashed on the dash. Simon pressed the key to answer. "Hey, I have your mom here. Heading to the hospital now."

"I'll meet you there. Did they tell you the result of the GSR?"

# CHAPTER 19

## PARK HILLS PRIVATE SCHOOL

***GRACE***

The school bell echoed through the halls, its shrill chime signaling the end of another week. Grace, standing at the front of her music classroom, offered her students a warm smile. "Have a good weekend, everyone!" she called out, her voice rising above the din of excited chatter and scraping chairs.

As the students bustled out, her smile faded into a resigned sigh. Friday was the only day she taught a last period music class, and while she adored teaching, the timing meant her weekend started later than she'd like. But today, at least, she didn't have bus duty, a small mercy she was more than grateful for.

She began to pack up the room, placing sheet music back into its rightful place and ensuring the instruments were properly stored. Her movements maintained a practiced efficiency, a routine perfected over the years. The room soon fell silent, save for the distant hum of the school emptying out.

She lingered, as was her habit, waiting until the last bus rumbled away and the pickup line outside had cleared. She didn't mind the solitude. It gave her a moment to transition from her role as Grace the teacher to Grace the individual.

Having locked up the music room, she made her way through the now-deserted halls and exchanged brief farewells with fellow teachers. Their voices echoed faintly in the empty space, a stark contrast to the vibrant energy reverberating through the corridors during school hours.

She approached the main office, and Jenny, the school secretary, beckoned her over. Jenny's face was a familiar, friendly school fixture, always ready with a helpful word or a sympathetic ear.

"Hey, this letter came for you. Hand-delivered." Jenny edged closer, peering over Grace's shoulder, her tone casual but her eyes betraying her curiosity. Letters for teachers weren't unusual, but they were typically of the mundane, professional variety. And seldom hand-delivered.

"Thanks, Jenny." Grace accepted the envelope. Light, almost weightless, it felt oddly significant as it bore the word *personal* in neat, bold letters, but no return address or sender's name. An oddity, indeed.

Curiosity piqued, she tore open the envelope as she continued her walk to the parking lot. She expected perhaps a note from a parent or an old acquaintance, maybe even a misplaced piece of student work. But she found none of these things.

She unfolded the paper, scanning the neatly printed words. And then she froze, her heart skipping a beat. Who would send such a short note with this clear and chilling message?

# CHAPTER 20

## THE ROTH RESIDENCE

*SHEILA*

"It's only a mild concussion," Sheila said to alleviate the tension in the room with Kyle, Ron, and Simon.

After the hospital, they'd headed back to Simon's place to regroup and strategize.

She sat on a plush ebony leather sofa. From her perch, she could see the open kitchen across the house. Compared to her own house, the décor seemed modest. Well, not everyone was like Doug who wanted to project an upper-class environment. The glass sliding door looked out over a meticulously manicured lawn.

"You need to watch for symptoms of something more serious." Kyle parked himself next to her. "Just like the doc said."

Simon sat on a chair with his laptop on a lap tray. "Before I forget, Sheila, they didn't notice any cat."

"Oh, he must have run out." She wrung her hands.

Simon then turned to Ron. "I gave Zimmerman a heads-up. You or Sheila should call him to discuss details."

"Thanks." Ron sat in the other chair facing Simon. "Now, Sheila, you need to take us through it again."

Ever since Simon found out about the positive GSR test result, he didn't talk much. She didn't know whether it was a good sign or bad. She watched enough TV shows to know that meant she supposedly had fired a weapon. But how could she?

"Mom, you need to tell us everything." Kyle leaned toward her.

"Ah, yes." So she went through the whole thing again. How she arrived home and found Doug on the ground and then got knocked out. How she came to sitting on a chair in the family room—with a gun in her hand. How the police showed up.

"You didn't call 911?" Ron frowned.

"I was going to. Then someone knocked me out. When I came to, I didn't get a chance. They just showed up."

Ron and Kyle exchanged glances. "The killer called. And probably as an anonymous caller."

Simon nodded at Ron's assessment, then tapped on his laptop. "That's good. But did you tell the officer you were attacked?"

"I tried, but the officer apparently didn't believe me. He looked me over. I didn't have any blood on me. The lump didn't start swelling until later."

"What time was that?" Ron leaned forward.

"I don't know. Probably four-ish?"

This was going to be a long night. The men were now discussing time of death, autopsy, and witnesses. At one point, Kyle got up to refill his coffee and brought one back to her.

"Okay, as I told Ron when he called"—Simon stopped the tapping and fixed his light-blue gaze on her—"criminal law isn't my specialty. But I want to help you through this initial stage."

She took a sip, the warmth of the coffee slightly calming her nerves. "What happens now?"

"Now, we investigate." Ron touched her arm. "Kyle can take lead on this. I'm neck-deep in a big case."

"I believe Zimmerman has his own investigators as well," Simon added.

Kyle stood up. "Mom, let's get you to my place so you can get some rest."

She followed her son. As they rounded the corner, she overheard Ron tell Simon about her suspicions and stacks of cash.

"I think we need to dig deeper into—" Ron was saying, but she couldn't hear the rest.

# CHAPTER 21

## M&M ENTERPRISES

*LILY*

Her meeting with Janet yesterday was weird. Why didn't she seem more concerned? And then the Lockwood fellow showed up. Perhaps it was due to her kidnapping ordeal the prior year and her spy mother's influence, but Lily felt something was off. *Think, think!*

Her eyes grew wide at the inspiration. First, she looked up this Trent Lockwood online. She'd already seen the website, but she hit it again. And she frowned. She could have sworn the man's photo wasn't there yesterday, but now the site prominently displayed him with the title of district manager. They had to have updated the website. How very convenient!

She found nothing else on this Trent Lockwood online. Oh, there were many hits for Trent Lockwood, but none referred to the man who'd sat across from her. She drummed her fingernails on her desk. Who should she turn to for help? Mom would ask all kinds of questions and then tell her to stand down. Kyle might resist, citing "not an active case" or some other reason, but then he'd find a way to help her. She called, but he didn't answer. So she texted him.

Now, she prepared herself for the arrival of Toby Filmore, the guy she found so suspicious before the holidays. He was scheduled to check in today.

Around lunchtime, Dylan poked his head in. "Let's go."

She minimized the windows on the screen and got up. Tommy waved when she exited her office. They headed toward their favorite casual dining spot, reminiscent of an Applebee's, located on the bustling retail floor. The restaurant's familiar ambiance, with its cozy booths and the aroma of a diverse menu, offered a comforting retreat.

They slid into a window booth, the menu already familiar in their hands. The waiter, recognizing them, came over and took their orders with a friendly nod.

"Everything okay?" Tommy asked, his voice barely rising above the hum.

She understood the depth of his question pertaining to the ongoing issues with the two LLCs. She exhaled, a finger tracing the edge of her water glass. "Looks like they've sent someone to town." She shrugged off her apprehension. Much better to portray her inner resilience. "It still feels off, you know?"

Despite her outward nonchalance, she wasn't giving up yet. However, she wouldn't share everything.

Shifting the conversation, she furrowed her brow. "Remember Toby Filmore—the guy I suspected was tailing me during the holidays?" She paused, and her chest tightened. "He's supposed to arrive today."

"I thought you and Kyle checked him out and cleared him." Dylan sat back as the server laid down his plate of chipotle chicken avocado sandwich.

She waited for the server to finish placing Tommy's plate of turkey wrap with a side of tomato soup. "We did. I guess I'm paranoid." As always, she ordered a salad. Today, she picked an Asian sesame salad with shrimp.

The food, of course, was delicious. Soon, the conversation veered toward other things, like their plans for the weekend.

"You and Kyle an item now?" Tommy wiped his mouth. "Seems you're hanging out with him a lot."

She stiffened, eager to deny it right away, but then they did go on a few dates. Pointing to her mouth, she exaggerated chewing to buy time to formulate a good answer. When she was literally plucked from Hong Kong to come here, she was stuck with Kyle. At one point, she even thought she was attracted to him. As they got to know each other and especially when they were out on dates, her mind kept wondering what Dylan was doing. Could that be her answer?

She swallowed. "Nah, we're really just friends."

"Oh, cool!" Tommy stood up. "Excuse me—bathroom."

"You know you mentioned you fancied a boat ride?" Dylan dabbed his mouth with a napkin.

She sipped her water. "Well, I mean, these fancy yachts kind of thing, not a ferry ride. I've had those. Like on TV—"

"—with a deck and staterooms." He finished for her.

She nodded.

"Well, let's do it."

She scoffed. "What do you mean? You don't have a boat."

"I don't, but I have access to one or more." He squinched one side of his face. "Not sure."

Now she understood. "I didn't know M&M had boats."

"Me neither, but Jeff said he could have one or however many I want ready when I need it." Jeff was some sort of executive assistant for the upper echelon. "I don't usually use my connections, but if you want…"

With her mouth half open, she gawked at him, and her heart skipped a beat. Did he just ask her on a real date? Finally!

"Hello?" He waved a hand in front of her. "Is that a yes? No? Maybe?"

She chuckled. "Yes, that is so sweet of you. Of course!"

As if on cue, Tommy returned and eyed his buddy. A wide grin split his face, and he slapped Dylan's back. "I knew you could do it."

The server chose this time to leave the checks. They always paid for themselves. On the way back, Dylan promised he'd find out the details from Jeff and let her know. Her day was looking good.

At her desk, surrounded by paperwork, invoices, and the spreadsheets displayed on her computer screen, she contemplated her next step. While the two LLCs were occupying her mind, she had other duties. Now, she tended to those before they all got sidelined or, worse, forgotten.

The notification pinged on her computer, startling her.

*Member Toby Filmore has checked in.*

She chewed on her lower lip, contemplating her next move. If Filmore didn't bother her, if he just went about his business like any other guest, she'd leave him be. After all, the guy was just a regular businessman with no malicious intent—right?

So why couldn't she make herself believe that?

Her spirit soared when her phone pinged with Dylan's text about the boat situation. They could go the following weekend unless they were willing to ditch work a day next week. She chuckled at that and thumbed back that the weekend would be fine. He then told her he managed to score the tickets to Universal Studios for the weekend. Since she arrived last fall, she'd only been to the park once and loved it, especially Harry Potter World. She sent a string of heart emojis back.

During all the texting back and forth, she also finished the report she was working on. Time to pack up. Her laptop pinged with another alert. This time, it was a notification from the security system, confirming Filmore had used his key card to enter his room. Room 214. The name wouldn't let her go. It just kept popping up.

Just as she was ready to head out, another alert came in. With all these alerts in just one afternoon, she might have to change the settings. But her eyes narrowed when she glanced at the notification.

*Rain Tree LLC has extended their stay by another week.*

They rarely stayed longer than a few days. What was different this time?

Another alert!

*New Life LLC made a reservation for the conference room.*

What did they need a conference room for? Trying to look legit? Or would they cancel in the next couple of days? She'd need to watch for that. It didn't look like she was leaving soon, so she'd try something else.

Having a spy mom took some getting used to, but one thing she did like was getting her mom to teach her some tricks of her trade, especially in the cyber world. Now, she opened her own laptop and logged into a database she rarely used, ready to dig deeper into the background of Rain Tree LLC and New Life LLC. Maybe their other business activities would provide a clue. After some persistent searching, she found something curious—both companies had made multiple transactions with a third company that had been flagged for fraud in the past.

# CHAPTER 22

## GRACE'S APARTMENT COMPLEX

*GRACE*

Grace studied the note, hands shaking. If this was the only thing she received, she might have chalked it up to a prank. But given that she felt she was followed, coupled with the inexplicable disturbances at her home, she'd take it seriously and file a police report. Maybe they would do something.

But in her brief and somewhat disturbing visit to the police station, the officer, a bored-looking woman with a no-nonsense attitude, took her statement with a professional detachment bordering on indifference.

"Do you have any enemies?" she asked, her pen poised over the report form.

Grace shook her head. "I don't think so."

"Any other threats? A stalker, maybe?"

When Grace again answered in the negative, the officer folded her hands, her expression unchanging. "Ma'am, I have to tell you there's nothing actionable in this report."

What a polite way of saying they couldn't do anything.

"Ma'am, this type of incident won't be a priority. In fact, it's probably just a prank. One of your students, maybe."

*My students are elementary schoolkids!* Grace held that in, saving her breath, thanked the officer, and walked out of the station. She hurried to her car, the cold night air whispering past. After she slid into her seat, she couldn't bring herself to start the engine. The thought of going home raised her heartbeat. So, she dialed Alex's number, the one sibling who lived close enough to be of any immediate help.

He answered on the second ring. "Hey, Grace. What's up?"

She hesitated, then launched into the story, starting with the first incident of being followed, then things being misplaced or rearranged at home, adding in the note, and ending with her visit to the police station.

"They just brushed it off?" he asked once she'd finished, his voice tight and off-key the way it got with concern.

"Pretty much." She let out a huff. "They said there's nothing they can do unless something more tangible happens. 'Nothing actionable' is what she said."

"That's ridiculous! You're being followed, for goodness sake. Things are happening at your house. And this note… it's creepy."

"I know, I know." Whew! At least someone took her concerns seriously. Why did the validation feel so good? Now what? She hugged her arms around herself, rocking a bit in her driver's seat. Wouldn't it be better to be told she was paranoid and be able to go back to everything being normal? "I just… I don't know what to do now."

After a pause, her brother's voice, firm tand resolute, came through the phone. "Where are you?"

"Sitting in my car in the police station lot."

"Okay, here's what we're going to do. Head home, stay in the car. I'm coming over. I'll stay over, at least tonight, and we'll figure out what your next step should be."

A weight lifted off her shoulders! "Thank you."

A little later, she sat in her apartment lot. She traced a finger over her steering wheel. Her life before the Christmas program was boring, but normal and mundane. She was content teaching music and going to her Bible studies. Her biggest problem, according to her mom, would be a lack of social life or a boyfriend, in particular. And now, someone sent her a creepy threatening note and started gaslighting and following her. *What are you telling me, Lord?*

Before she could dwell on it further, Alex pulled up. They agreed they'd go to the complex office first. She didn't bother introducing him since that would invite unnecessary questions. *Your brother? In their mind, yeah, right? A blond man and a Latina?*

First, at his prompting, she asked if they noticed anybody loitering around or going into her apartment. The manager, seated in his cubbyhole office, the room thick with the odor of chicken soup from a congealing bowl on the desk, cocked his head to one side and rolled back his chair. "We have a big complex, ma'am. We don't keep track of people coming and going." Arms crossed over his thick chest, he nodded out the window. "As you know, each building has its buzzing system. Without a code, you just can't get in."

They exchanged glances. Both knew how to get around that. Most people were honest—not all. But if you pressed enough buttons, someone would buzz you in with a cockamamie story.

"Do you have security cameras?"

"Of course." The man swiveled his chair side to side. "But none point directly to your building's entrance if that's what you're after."

Her shoulders sloped, but Alex rested his hand on the small of her back, thanked the manager, and guided her out. Feeling defeated, she tried not to kick at the pebbles in their path as they headed back to her apartment. She went through the usual routine to check if anything had been moved, especially her piano. Everything was good today.

He dropped off his duffel in the guest room and came right back out. "Let me see that note."

"They took the original. Said it was evidence as if they would do something about it. But I took a picture." She swiped on her phone to show him the note.

*You will pay for her sin.*

With a frown, Alex muttered, "Assuming it's not a prank, whose sin are you supposed to pay for?"

# CHAPTER 23

## DEA OFFICE

*RON*

For once, the good guys had a break. When they arrested all the people in the alley, they had also arrested Marco, a twitchy young man in his mid-twenties with a gaunt face and unkempt hair. They just hadn't known it at the time. The kid was smart—he acted like he was a nobody and let Jorge Rodriguez appear to be the boss.

Fortunately for Ron, unfortunately for Marco, the suspect's fingerprints revealed his identity. And a review of all the surveillance videos showed him doing all kinds of illegal transactions. Now, after some morning caffeine, Ron and Cooper were sitting across from him in the interrogation room.

Cooper braced his long forearms on the table, leaning on them. "We've got you, buddy." That drawl, slow and sweet, coated his words, but likely didn't make them any easier for the kid to swallow. "Red-handed. Drugs, money, the whole deal."

The suspect's darting gaze met Cooper's. "I don't know what you're talking about." His chin may have jerked up a defiant fraction, but the quiver in his voice betrayed his anxiety.

"Look," Ron chimed in. "The DEA has been tracking your gang's movements for weeks. We've got informants, surveillance footage, transaction records. And then there's the stash we caught you with." He spread his hands wide, then gestured to Marco. "You're in deep, and the charges won't be light."

The kid swallowed hard, the weight of his predicament probably sinking in. "I was just doing my job. Just a delivery guy."

"That's not how the law will see it." Cooper's relaxed stance almost appeared bored, but those deep-set eyes flared at the edges as he rocked back on his chair's hind legs. "You're part of the chain. And right now, you're the weakest link."

Ron slapped a folder on the table and dropped a series of photographs before Marco. Pictures of him making deals, meeting with shady figures, even one of him counting a wad of cash. "You see, we've got enough evidence to put you away for a long time. But we're not after you."

The kid's eyes widened, his gaze flickering between the photos and the agents. "Then what do you want?"

"The guy above you." Ron locked gazes with Marco. "We want the big fish, and you're going to help us reel him in."

Cooper jammed his index finger on the table, then smudged a line with it. "You roll on your boss, cooperate fully, and maybe, just maybe, we can work out a deal for you."

The interrogation room door creaked open, and a disheveled-looking man in a wrinkled suit, a public defender badge hanging around his neck, shuffled in and slumped into a seat next to Marco. "Sorry I'm late."

"Glad you could join us." Ron nudged the folder closer to the newcomer. "Your client here was just getting acquainted with the evidence we have against him."

The public defender glanced at the photos, then Marco. "You should seriously consider their offer. It might be your best shot."

The kid bit his lip, his gaze darting between Ron, Cooper, and his lawyer. "What kind of deal?"

Cooper crossed his arms over his chest, still rocking his chair as if this deal didn't mean anything to him. "That's up to the US Attorneys, but we can put in a good word for you. That is, if you give us something good."

Marco raised a pleading gaze at his public defender, seeking some kind of guidance. The lawyer whispered in his ear, and after a few moments, Marco exhaled a heavy breath. "Let me hear what you can give me first. I can tell you who the boss is, what we've got planned, everything."

"Okay, you hang tight. We'll get the paperwork going." Cooper went to contact the federal prosecutor. Fifteen minutes later, he came back in with the paperwork. Once the public defender was satisfied with the deal, Cooper prompted, "Start from the beginning."

The kid licked his dry lips, his gaze flickering to the one-way mirror. "I don't know where to start. It's all so… mixed up."

"Let's start with Nunez," Ron suggested, making sure he had the suspect's full attention.

"Rubio Nunez." Marco rubbed the back of his neck, fiddling with scraggly clumps of hair. "He's the man in charge. Every-thing we did—every deal, every shipment, every payment—went through him or his right hand."

"His right hand?" Cooper shot a look at Ron, obviously already sensing where this was heading.

"Yeah, the guy they call Greek." Marco palmed his forehead as if trying to summon more memories. "He's the real deal. I've seen him do things… things that would turn your stomach."

Ron displayed a picture of a man with an olive complexion, piercing eyes, and an unmistakable scar running from his left ear to his chin. "This him?"

Marco hesitated before nodding. "Yeah, that's Greek. But"— he swallowed hard—"I've heard him use another name. On the phone. Frankie. Said it real casual like."

Cooper and Ron exchanged glances. This was big. Not just a

nickname, but a potential real name. It was like a light in the overwhelming darkness of the investigation.

Ron tapped on the photo. "You're sure about the name Frankie?"

"Yeah. He was pissed. Yelling at some guy for messing up. Kept saying, 'Do you know who you're talking to? This is Frankie!' Like he was someone big."

"All right." Cooper scratched out a note. "Now, back to Nunez. How close are you to him?"

"Not close." Marco scoffed. "I'm just a runner. I see him at the warehouse sometimes, but that's it."

"And where's this warehouse?" Ron bounced his knee under the table, keeping everything above slow and calm.

Marco bit his upper lip, his shoulders slumping. "Off the highway. An old textile factory. But you won't get near it. It's guarded. Cameras, guards, dogs… The whole shebang."

"We're more interested in Nunez's connections with Martinez," Cooper drawled. The front legs of his chair thudded to the floor.

Marco shook his head. "I've never met Martinez. Only heard about him. But if Nunez is involved, Martinez is pulling the strings."

Ron flattened his palms on the cold tabletop. "We believe Nunez is one step below Martinez in the chain. If we can get to Nunez, we can get to Martinez."

Marco paled. "Look, I've given you what I know. Nunez is dangerous, and Martinez… he's a ghost. People whisper his name and vanish. Just like that."

"We're not afraid of ghosts." With the pen and notebook braced on his lap, Cooper rasped both hands over his buzz cut. "But we need everything. Every detail, every name, every location."

Marco sighed, a visible weight bowing his shoulders. "There's a club downtown, El Paraíso. Nunez hangs out there.

Usually in the VIP section. Greek is there too. They meet people, make deals. It's their playground."

El Paraíso—VIP section. Ron's leg jittered faster under the table, its pace kicking up with the uptick in his heartbeat. Now they were getting somewhere. "Good. Anything else?"

Marco hesitated. "Just… be careful. They're not just drug dealers. They're… monsters."

Cooper closed his notebook, standing up straight. "We'll take it from here. And remember, Marco, you keep your end of the bargain, and we'll keep ours."

As Ron left the room, his mind went to Sheila's case. If this were his case, he'd want to know everything. His source had told him the autopsy would be today. Maybe he could find an excuse to attend or at least learn the results—

His phone rang.

"You might want to come down here. The morgue," Spaulding said without preamble.

Reeling from the unexpected call, Ron made his way to the morgue, his quick pace matching his sense of urgency. The facility's sterile, cold air hit him as he stepped inside, a stark contrast to the warm spring day. Detective Spaulding and the ME, a bald and slim man, stood near a stainless steel table where a body lay, thankfully covered by a white sheet. In the corner, an assistant cleaned the tools and surfaces, the clinking of metal echoing in the quiet room.

Ron caught the stocky detective's eye and arched a brow. Spaulding responded by beckoning him over. Ron had been to more autopsies than he cared to remember, but the unsettling feeling never faded. He approached, maintaining a respectful distance from the table.

"Ron, this is Dr. O'Bannon." Spaulding gestured toward the

ME, whose serious demeanor and sharp eyes seemed to miss nothing.

"Nice to meet you." Ron nodded toward the doctor.

The ME wasted no time. "We found something unusual." He held up an evidence bag containing a piece of paper, but it wasn't just any piece of paper. "We retrieved this from deep within the victim's throat."

Ron leaned in, his eyes narrowing as he tried to make sense of the images—two pictures—on the paper, both partially obscured and smeared. They seemed to be candid pictures, as in surveillance. One was of a young woman, judging by the clothing, with long hair walking with purpose to somewhere.

"Hey, does this guy look like an agent? He walks like one." Spaulding pointed to the other picture.

Ron's heartbeat stuttered. The picture looked eerily like Kyle. He could even make out the background of the Fed building. "Yes, I believe he's an agent."

"Is that chick an agent too? I don't see it."

He shook his head. "No idea who that is."

"There are some writings." Spaulding jutted his chin toward the bottom part. "I can't make out anything, can you?"

"Nah. If I could get it back to Deanna—eh, our forensic analyst—she might be able to do something to clear it up and make the words more decipherable." Ron straightened up. "Okay if I sign this out? We can get results faster."

The detective frowned at the paper. "The guy looks like one of yours anyway, so I guess it's okay."

Ron nodded his thanks.

"Before you fine gentlemen run off to catch bad guys, let me show you a few more things." The ME stepped closer to the table. He then showed them the scars and old wounds on the body.

"Was he in the service?" O'Bannon asked.

"Yes, he was in the army." Spaulding waved both palms upward. "Yeah, I checked."

"Maybe that's where he got these injuries. His military medical records would confirm them."

Spaulding made a note of that.

The doc covered the body up. "Show's over."

Ron thanked the ME and followed Spaulding out after he signed the chain of custody for the evidence bag with the paper.

The detective waited for him. "I checked you out."

Ron put the bag securely in his breast pocket.

When he didn't say anything, Spaulding went on. "My partner didn't like the idea of letting you in on this. But, like I said, I checked you out. So, why the bureau? Why not NCIS? You were with the corps."

Ron shrugged. "I didn't want to be assigned an agent afloat. Didn't want the risk. Still don't."

"Ah." Letting out a low whistle, the detective resumed heading out the door. "So, what say you we work together to close this? It appears it might involve one of your agents anyway."

Surprised by the offer, Ron grinned. "Certainly. Let's do it. About that 911 call—"

"Yeah, we checked. An anonymous caller, but that doesn't mean your ex-wife is off the hook just yet." The detective winked and fired his parting shot before he went off.

Seemed Spaulding had written Sheila off the suspect list, or at least moved her to the bottom of the list. A more pressing concern—Why was the paper with Kyle's picture, assuming it was Kyle, and a young woman, in Doug's throat?

# CHAPTER 24

## THE ROTH RESIDENCE

*OLIVIA*

Olivia pushed her chair back, creating some distance between herself and the labyrinth of information spread out before her. After much research, she narrowed her list down to two. Her finger traced the two names she'd circled in red ink on a piece of paper. Each name was like a beckoning doorway, beyond which lay either a treasure trove of answers or yet another maze of questions.

Photos of the men would've been invaluable, but alas, they eluded her search. Instead, she had dates, places, and code names —all jargon from an era gone by. She picked up a separate sheet where she'd handwritten each man's specialties and the various missions they'd undertaken. One was a master at subterfuge, the other an ace in psychological warfare. So, which one could be the Uncle Bill Eva talked about?

Running her fingers through her silky hair, she let out a low breath. Time to make the call. She went through the security protocol to get patched through.

"Phoenix, what fires do you need me to put out now?" Jay asked by way of greeting.

"Come on." She drummed her impatience out through her fingers. "I called to say hello a few times."

A chuckle. "Yes, and then ask for a favor. So, what do you need?"

"Remember I asked you about an Officer Bill?"

"Yes."

"What else can you tell me about him?"

"Nothing."

The answer came too fast. "Jay, please. What do you know?"

His sigh echoed through the speaker. "If you need something to do, find the mole and plug the leak."

"What do you think I'm doing? You said it was an internal security matter regarding Adam O'Shea. Now, I'm working on identifying this uncle or officer Bill."

"It's all connected. That's all I can say. And use that smart brain of yours. Be careful." Click.

Her hand still holding the phone, she frowned. *It's all connected.*

# CHAPTER 25

## TASK FORCE OFFICE

*RON*

The morgue's sterile, chilling air still clung to Ron as he made his way back to the task force office. Inside the building, he went straight to the lower level that housed the lab. There he found Deanna, their forensic guru, in front of her computer and engrossed in whatever was on the screen amid the hum of machines and the odor of chemicals. The lab was her domain, and here, mysteries unraveled under her expert hands.

Kyle stood at her shoulder, hovering. And the tension in his son's posture, the hesitancy, didn't go unnoticed by Ron. They exchanged a brief, acknowledging nod before Deanna looked up as if she had just realized his arrival. "Oh, hi!"

"Something I should be aware of?" he asked.

"Nope." She stood, the screen forgotten.

And Kyle exited.

Something odd here, Ron frowned, but now wasn't the time to pursue the matter. Instead, he presented the evidence bag. "Run whatever tests to make the images clearer and the words decipherable."

She signed the chain of custody with a flourish, then peered at the paper through the bag. "What do we have here?"

He folded his arm on a counter. "It was found hidden in a victim's throat."

Her eyes lit up. "I'll get right on it. Anything specific you're looking for?"

"No." He shook his head. "I need it ASAP."

"Of course." She gloved up and opened the bag.

As he strode away, she uttered, "This looks like…"

He stepped off the elevator, cutting through the squad room to his office.

"Ah, there you are!"

Ron knew that voice and expected it, but he'd hoped it would take a while before word reached the upper echelon. Apparently, the rumor mills still beat the official communication. He grunted and faced the deputy director.

Vera nodded to the team, smiling, then crooked a finger at him. "May I have a word?"

"Of course. I'm just heading back to my office. Please." He gestured for her to follow.

Moments later, she sat across from him, posture stiff. "Really sorry to hear about your ex-wife's situation."

"Thank you. But she didn't have anything to do with it." He pushed the papers aside. "You didn't have to come down here to tell me that."

"No, but I need to remind you to stay out of it."

He braced an elbow on his desk and dropped his chin in his upraised hand. "One—there may be a connection between the victim and the drug cartel we're investigating. Two—there's now evidence there's a lot more to it than murder. Three—he swallowed or tried to swallow a piece of paper with images and words. One image looks like Kyle."

"Is that right?" She arched a brow over amber eyes agleam.

"Deanna is working right now to enhance the images and words. We'll know more."

"And how was he involved with the cartel?"

"We don't know that for sure. Early investigations indicate something strange about his travel patterns. We'll keep digging."

She sat back, chewed on her lips, then exhaled. "All right. Keep me posted. Especially let me know if it is indeed Kyle. It could mean something else entirely." And she stood.

He stood as well. "Yes, ma'am." But his mind kept replaying her words—*It could mean something else entirely.*

And what would it be?

# CHAPTER 26

## FEDERAL DETENTION CENTER

*ROOK*

A prickle of unease tingled Rook's scalp as he navigated the circuitous route to the Federal Detention Center. He adjusted his high-tech glasses designed to thwart facial recognition technology. Today was not a day for taking risks. He had been to see the Ghost before, and something about that last visit hadn't sat right. His intuition—what some people might call a "Spidey sense"—warned him to be extra cautious this time.

After parking at one of his safe houses, he changed his clothes, shed his initial disguise, and slipped out through the back. Then he made his way to another car he'd stashed for occasions like this. It was all a bit cloak-and-dagger, but when you were trying to hide your identity, the theatrics were a small price to pay for staying off the grid.

Finally, after what might've been an unnecessarily complex journey, he arrived at the detention center. As always, he presented himself as one of Marge Beaumont's attorneys, Adam O'Shea.

Minutes later, he was inside the attorney visiting room. The guard closed the door behind him. Beaumont, aka the Ghost, looked up as he entered, her unemotional eyes calculating. "You're late."

"Extra precautions." He slid into a cold seat. "You never can be too careful."

"Indeed. What have you found?" She drummed her fingers on the table.

For appearance, he took out a notepad, preparing to jot down notes. He did have his notes in front of him. "Special Agent Ron Peters and DIA Agent Ana Ruiz are as good as their files suggest—maybe better."

She raised an eyebrow, a subtle invitation to continue.

"I'm sure you're familiar with Peters. Meticulous, not one to leave loose ends, he has an impressive network of contacts and a knack for being in the right place at the right time—or the wrong place, depending on how you look at it."

"I could have told you that. What about that other one? Ana Ruiz?"

"Equally skilled, but more unpredictable. She's a wild card, could go off-script, which makes her dangerous but also potentially useful."

Head cocked to one side, the Ghost locked her eyes onto his as if she could see straight into his thoughts. "Details."

"There's no way to tell from the reports whose shot killed Jade. Both Peters and Ruiz fired their weapons." He held his breath, observing her reaction.

For the briefest flash, the Ghost's eyes narrowed. Ah, so he'd hit a nerve. Jade's death was more than a professional failure—it was personal.

"I see." Her voice trickled over him, colder than ice. "And they will both pay. What's your assessment? Peters can't be turned or manipulated. But Ruiz?"

"Perhaps. She has a few... vulnerabilities that could be exploited." He crossed one leg over the other, holding out on something. "The plan is in motion. However, we've got a... complication."

She clucked her tongue. "Complications?"

He held up a hand. "Nothing that can't be remedied. The original contractor declined the job. We've since secured a second team."

"I take it the original contractor is no longer a problem?"

"That's correct."

"See that it doesn't come back to bite us."

"It will not." He didn't tell her that he had added a personal touch to let the target know why she had to die.

She leaned back, her cold eyes steady. He imagined her brain was like a little computer—all the bots now running different simulations and deciding on the best course of action. She always had a way to see a few steps ahead of everyone else.

"Okay, keep me posted." She broke the silence that had settled over the room. Then she turned and called, "Guard."

"Yes, ma'am." Rook stood up, dismissed. What he didn't tell her was he changed the plan. Was he playing with fire? Would he end up with a hole in his head?

# CHAPTER 27

## GRACE'S APARTMENT

*GRACE*

The morning sun was just beginning to peek over the horizon, casting a soft golden light through Grace's apartment window. She'd always been an early riser, finding solace in the quiet hours before the world woke up. Today was no different. With a stretch and a yawn, she slipped out of bed, her mind set on a refreshing jog to start her day.

As she waited for the Keurig to fill her cup of joe, Alex's door opened, and her brother approached, his hair sleep-tousled.

"Morning. I have cereal in the cupboard." She grabbed her cup and poured a dash of cream in it.

He came around, slid a mug from the cupboard, and got his own cup going. "Morning, yourself. You're going jogging?"

"Yeah, after this." She held her cup up.

"Wait for me." He rubbed the sleep from his eyes. "I'll come with you. Just in case, you know?"

She smiled, appreciating his protective nature, but was it necessary? Since he'd just rolled out of bed, she sat at the table. Growing up, her friends would tell her Alex was hot. And she could never see it. His blond hair and lean and toned body probably contributed to the "hotness." He was four years older, the youngest of three boys, and she was the only girl in the family.

"I'll just be a minute." He downed his caffeine, put the mug in the dishwasher, and shuffled back to the room.

"Brush your teeth!" she yelled.

He soon returned in his jogging gear. Their run was uneventful, the streets quiet in the early morning light. However, as they neared the apartment on their way back, a familiar sight drew her gaze—a truck she thought she'd seen parked near the school.

"What's the matter?" he asked.

"That truck. I saw it at school yesterday." Or had she? Was she imagining it?

He edged in closer, almost shielding her. "Are you sure? Same make and model?"

She shrugged. "I don't know. Same color."

"You'd better stay here. I'll be right back." Then he jogged over to the truck, looked around, and jogged back. "This one has a back bench seat with a car seat on it."

"I guess it's nothing to worry about, then." They headed back to the apartment.

After cleaning up and settling down with more caffeine reinforcement, he brought up a topic that must've been on his mind. "So, I've been thinking. Maybe you should move back home for a bit, you know, until all this gets cleared up."

She nearly choked on her coffee. "Move back home? Isn't that overreacting?" As in way overreacting? "I'm fine here."

Sitting on the lumpy couch across from her recliner, he braced his elbows on his knees, coffee mug held in both hands before his serious expression. "At least consider getting a doorbell camera and maybe one for the balcony too. I'll pay for it if you can't spring it."

She always joked that he won the job jackpot. He was an IT guy with a big company, but he hardly ever went into the office.

Compared to her teaching job, he had it made. He rolled out of bed, didn't have to get dressed if he didn't want to. Of course, if he had a meeting virtually or in-person, he'd have to dress up.

True, a teacher's salary was a pittance, but she had a summer job as an assistant manager at a resort. And she had these piano gigs every so often. She could afford the cameras, but why not take advantage of her brother's generosity? "That'd be great. The cameras sound like a good idea."

He sipped his coffee, seemingly relieved she agreed to one of his suggestions. "All right. Finish your drink, and let's go shopping. Those things are easy to install and set up."

They went on to discuss various security measures, falling into the comforting familiarity of sibling banter. And then he brought the subject back to the matter at hand.

"Whose sin are you supposed to pay for?"

She shook her head. "No idea. I've been thinking of nothing but that. My life's boring. It's not like I know anybody with mafia connections or something like that. I can't think of anyone who has done anything requiring this—or any—type of retribution."

He set his empty mug on the coffee table, quiet but pensive. Long moments later, he exhaled. "We need to figure out who this 'her' is."

# CHAPTER 28

## TASK FORCE OFFICE

*RON*

Ron sat at his desk, staring at a fixed point on the wall. How could he use the task force resources to help find the truth about Doug and his murder? From what Kyle told him, Doug's travel histories were curious. Then there were the stacks of cash and the bearer bonds. He told Vera that Doug had some connections with the cartel—nothing he could prove. Right, so, that was what he could use the task force to do.

He gathered his team, along with Cooper, in the squad room. They centered around the large screen, as usual. Then Kyle pressed the remote, and the screen displayed the pages of Doug's murder book.

"Vic is Doug Mitchell." Kyle started and explained the circumstances of his death.

"We investigate homicide now, boss?" Tanner frowned.

"The local detective has invited us to help." Yes, Ron was exaggerating, but it was close enough.

Kyle went on to detail Doug's travel histories, the lies about real estate conferences, the unaccounted-for days overseas, and the stacks of cash.

"And this is, was, your stepfather?" Ana asked.

Kyle cringed at the word but nodded.

"Aside from the cash, I'd say he was cheating," Cooper drawled.

"Exactly, how do you account for the stacks of cash? If he was cheating, he'd be dishing out money to the mistress, not getting paid bundles," Tanner countered.

"That's why I said—"

Ron held up a hand, redirecting. "Let's agree he wasn't having an affair. What other reasons can you think of for his actions?"

"Well, let's see. He hid his reason for traveling, then disappeared for a few days, and was paid handsomely." Ana chewed her lips. "I hate to say this, but I can't think of anything good. I assume the stacks of cash were payment—it might not be—but if it is payment of sorts, it wouldn't be books. Say, he smuggled something illegal? Diamonds? Drugs?"

Hernandez spoke for the first time. "Has anyone looked at his finances?"

"I'm glad you mentioned that. It will be your assignment," Ron said. "Work with Kyle. Dig deep. And, Kyle, liaise with the detectives. They're doing their part in uncovering the vic's last movements. See what they found. Maybe there's some tangible connection between him and any of the known cartel guys." Then he turned to the others. "Tanner and Cooper, keep working on the cartel angle. Ana, stay undercover."

As his team all responded with a variation of "yeah, boss," he checked his phone, hoping for an update from Deanna. Alas, nothing on the images yet. He was almost positive the image was Kyle, but what did it mean? And who was the other person?

# CHAPTER 29

## KYLE'S APARTMENT

*SHEILA*

In the soft morning light filtering through the half-drawn curtains, Sheila moved around her son's apartment, her actions gentle and methodical, a soothing rhythm borne of years of domestic routine. The clock ticked past eight, a time when most reveled in the leisure of a Saturday morning, but she'd been awake for hours. Sleep had eluded her again, slipping through her fingers like the quicksand she'd built her life on, leaving her with thoughts that churned and twisted in the dark.

Kyle had already left for the office. His dedication to his job as a federal agent reminded her so much of Ron. She remembered those days too well—one reason they parted ways. Now, she only hoped Kyle would have better luck in that department.

Barred from going home—still a crime scene—she didn't know what to do with herself. If only she could do some work, but she had already asked an associate to take over some of the urgent clients' work. Hands settled on her hips, she surveyed the apartment. His wasn't a mess—he was far from a slob—but his relentless work schedule left little time for housekeeping. She'd start with the bathroom, scrubbing and cleaning until every surface gleamed.

Just as she folded the freshly laundered towels, her phone on the bathroom counter rang. Simon's contact lit the screen.

"The detectives want to ask you a few questions," he said after a brief greeting.

"Oh, of course." She walked out of the bathroom. "Do I need to go to the station?"

"My home office will work. I can pick you up in fifteen minutes. Or do you need more time?"

She ran a hand down her sweatpants. She'd just swap the sweats with a business outfit. "That'll work."

"See you in a bit."

Less than an hour later, she was sitting in his simple, yet elegant home office, a more professional space than the living room they used yesterday. When he offered her coffee or tea, she asked for water. She didn't need the extra caffeine. After he handed her a bottle of water, he sat at his desk, backlit by the window. She started to sit across from him, but he waved her over to the chair he put beside him.

"They'll be on the other side," he explained. "They talked to Rachel, the client you were on the phone with just when you were getting home. She confirmed your story. That's good news. The 911 call was anonymous. These and your hospital record of a concussion go a long way in proving your innocence."

He opened his laptop. "Now, they also tracked Doug's last movements. They got him on video at the airport before he drove home. They saw him talk to a few people. They'd like to ask if you've seen or know them."

"Okay." She uncapped and sipped her water.

The doorbell rang, its shrill tone slicing through the quiet.

He glanced at his phone. "That's them. Lucia will let them in."

Moments later, the plump lady he'd introduced yesterday as

Lucia, his part-time housekeeper, showed the two detectives into the office and offered them coffee or tea.

Both declined. They sat in the two chairs facing them.

Detective Monnin, sitting taller, at least a head above her stocky companion, pulled out a folder and got right to business. "We have some photos here." She laid out several photographs across the desk. "Can you let us know if you've seen any of them with your husband?"

Sheila leaned forward, studying each picture—closely. They were all men, a variety of races and ages, all menacing. "I'm sorry, Detectives, but I don't recognize any of these men. Should I?"

"We're not sure yet," Spaulding interjected. "We're pursuing all leads."

"What can you tell us about your husband?" Monnin put the photos away.

Simon nodded to give his okay to answer. She thought about Doug, his kindness and thoughtfulness, then the stacks of cash, bearer bonds, and those cryptic things he said. "What do you want to know?"

"We understand that you approached your son and ex-husband about your suspicion that your husband might be a spy. Can you tell us about it?" The detective slid her notebook out. "What made you think so?"

Again, Sheila saw the nod. So, she explained everything. "But Ron told me he had someone look into it. Doug wasn't a spy. He wasn't on any intelligence database."

"Yeah, we know. Can you tell us about his travels?" Spaulding asked.

Another nod. "He traveled to London and Paris for real estate conferences. That's all I know."

"What about this last trip?"

"He went to London for a conference, like always." She took another sip of water.

"There was no real estate conference at the time he was in London."

"No, no." Jolting, she sat up straighter. "There must be. Maybe not a conference. Could be a meeting with clients or developers." Even as she said it, a twinge pinched her chest. Had she known the man at all?

The two detectives exchanged glances. They mustn't believe her. Then they stood up. "All right, then. That's all for now."

"Senator, ma'am." Spaulding dipped his graying head. "We'll see ourselves out."

As they left, Sheila turned to Simon. "What were they talking about? No conference?"

He sighed. "Ron mentioned that to me. He has people working on Doug's past and travels. He'll find out what he was doing and how it might lead to his being murdered, but for now…"

She didn't hear the rest, focusing on one thing. Was everything a lie?

# CHAPTER 30

## TASK FORCE OFFICE

*RON*

"Best I can do." Those were the first words Ron heard when he stepped into the lab.

Deanna clicked a button and projected the paper onto the big screen on the wall. He stepped closer. The man was Kyle, and the woman was nobody he recognized. Latina, twenties. He pointed to the building in the background. "Is this a school?"

"Yes, I enlarged it. Park Hills Private School."

He frowned. A schoolteacher? Undercover agent? Now he looked at the words underneath. Under Kyle's image was his name, and under the young woman's was the name Grace Benson.

"It's a kill order." Deanna's voice trembled. "It's above the images. Only the bottom half of the letters, targets, showed, but that's what it said. Who wanted him dead?"

And why did Doug have this in his throat? Aloud, Ron asked, "What else have you found?"

"Nothing. Is the vic a contract killer?"

He didn't answer. The idea hadn't occurred to him, but maybe he could have been. "Guess we'll find out."

"Uh, Deputy Director Haskin happened to see this. I was working on it when she walked in. Sorry."

"When did she get here?"

She shrugged. "She came down giving me something to do."

He frowned as Deanna's gaze darted around and her response seemed evasive. "What?"

"Sorry, can't say."

Shaking his head, he headed back up to the squad room. As he walked in, Tanner crossed to him. "Boss, the deputy director is waiting in your office."

Kyle was also in his office. That meant Vera was going to—Ron stifled a groan. This wouldn't go over well.

"Sorry, Ron." She rolled back her chair—his desk chair. "I took the liberty of sitting here. Gentlemen, please sit." She gestured toward the guest chairs.

After they did, she continued without preamble. "I'm sure Ms. Swanson gave the report by now. So, Agent Kyle Peters, you'll be in protective custody until this is over."

"What?" Kyle jerked back in his seat. "I don't understand, ma'am."

"Your father will explain."

Ron gave his report.

"But I'm an agent. I don't need protection," Kyle protested.

She smiled. "We'd all like to think we're invincible. But even agents need protection details sometimes. You're now reassigned to the young woman's protection detail team. You'll report to the team leader, Chuck Torres. Agents are securing the young woman as we speak. And that's an order."

She always worked fast, like in the old days.

"Now." She folded her hands on the desk, her gaze skewering Kyle. "What's your relationship with Grace Benson?"

His son's eyes went wide, a low breath whistled out. "I don't believe I know her. There's no relationship."

She sighed and waved to Ron. "Can you show him the pictures?"

"Certainly." He got up, pressed the intercom on his desk, the one he could have reached if he'd been in his proper seat.

"Yes?" Deanna's voice flowed through the speaker.

"Will you send the images up here, please?"

"Beaming up now."

He clicked the remote, and the images showed up on the wall screen. He thanked Deanna and hung up.

"All right. Now, take a look, agent." Vera rocked back in Ron's chair. "What's your connection?"

Kyle got up to get a better look, then shook his head. "Never saw her before."

"Agent, my experience tells me you and this woman are connected somehow. Someone put out a contract on you and her. The same contract. That means the same client. If there were two separate contracts, there might not be any connection. But since it's not, there is a connection. Get her file, look through it, find the connection. Who knows? You might have run across her without knowing it. Your old cases. Maybe she was a witness. Perhaps you didn't interview her. I don't know. But find that connection."

"Yes, ma'am." Kyle sat back down.

She pivoted the chair toward Ron, her amber eyes flashing a fiery light. "Now, what can you tell me about this Doug Mitchell character? Why did he have a kill order? Was he an assassin?"

"Up until a few minutes ago, we were under the impression he was a real estate developer. His travel patterns have raised some peculiar questions. He had cash of unknown origin. We're in the process of digging into his finances. We suspected money laundering, but given what we've just discovered, we may have to reevaluate."

Her brows furrowed, and her gaze fixed on his desk calendar as if that would give her answers. "All right. Continue to pursue all leads. You're working with the local LEO?"

LEO—law enforcement officer. "Yes, ma'am."

She stood. "Find out why they're targeted. See if it's cartel related."

"Yes, ma'am."

"Thank you for letting me borrow your desk." She walked out. He needed to get used to her being so bossy.

Kyle slammed a fist on his knee. "She reassigned me to babysitting!"

"Calm down." Ron got up and went around to sit at his desk. "Your last babysitting gig didn't turn out so bad. In fact, it was rather exciting, wasn't it?" Of course, he was referring to Kyle escorting Lily from Hong Kong during the bioterror threat several months prior. "You sure you never ran into this woman before? Not a college fling? High school?"

His son turned around to face him, his are-you-kidding-me look reminding Ron of Kyle's teens. "Dad, don't you think I'd have remembered dating a pretty girl like that? I don't know her."

Ron raised his hands in surrender. "Okay. Just trying to look for a connection from another angle. The deputy director is right. There has to be a connection between you and her—and we have to find it."

"What if she is the one connected to the cartel or something?"

"Sure, but that wouldn't explain you. Have you worked on any drug cases before?"

He shook his head.

"There you go."

"I was checking his finances with Hernandez." Kyle finger combed his hair, frustration evident in his jerky movements. "And I'm supposed to—what? Drop it?"

"You heard her. It's an order. Sometimes, that's how it goes. Do your job. Tell Hernandez you're reassigned and call Torres."

"Yes, sir." Kyle stood.

"It won't be long. We'll get to the bottom of this." So many questions, and they were in the middle of the cartel investigation. Not enough hours in a day!

# CHAPTER 31

## M&M ENTERPRISES

*LILY*

L ily sighed at her computer screen, her gaze shifting between the program's billing system and the digital clock at the corner of her desktop. No Filmore sightings since yesterday. Had she overreacted? Maybe the guy was just another businessman going about his day. But something deep down warned her not to lower her guard.

Refocus on the job! She gave herself a little shake. Since the LLCs extended their bookings and reserved a conference room, she'd been awaiting the cancellations. But what could she do if they canceled? Janet didn't seem concerned. Dare Lily go above her?

Her finger was twirling the thumb drive with research from yesterday. Who should she give it to? When would Kyle get back to her about Trent Lockwood?

As if her thought had summoned him, Kyle texted her.

> Nothing much on Lockwood yet. Asked
> Deanna to dig deeper. Will call later.

She texted back her thanks. That didn't help. So, what now?

The chime alerted her to a meeting with all the coordinators. No time to think about this Lockwood fellow or what she found. It would wait.

During the mundane meeting, she asked if anyone noticed anything unusual in their bookings and cancellations, especially the patterns. They all said they hadn't noticed anything, but they'd check and report back.

With that done, she grabbed her purse. Maybe she'd pay an unannounced visit to Rain Tree LLC.

She hesitated, sliding the purse strap over her shoulder. It could be dangerous.

*Oh, be quiet!*

For once, she had lunch by herself. Dylan had a lunch meeting, and Tommy was having lunch with the accounting staff. For a change, she had lunch at the lobby café and ordered a salad. She was scrolling on her phone, waiting for her food, when she became aware of someone nearby. Out of the corner of her eye, she saw a familiar figure stroll by. Filmore again!

At least he wasn't bothering her or staring at her. She had no excuse to tell him to go somewhere. He was a guest. And she was at the lobby café, after all. Thankfully, the server brought her salad. She sipped her iced tea and dug in.

After lunch, she found herself standing in front of a nondescript office building, staring at a plaque that read "Rain Tree LLC, Suite 310." Taking a deep breath, she pushed open the glass door and took the elevator to the third floor.

The door to Suite 310 was slightly ajar. Lily knocked and stepped inside. A young woman, not much older than Lily herself, looked up from her phone and greeted her with a tentative smile.

"Hello, can I help you?"

"I hope so. I'm looking for someone who can discuss Rain

Tree LLC's account with the Program. Is Missy around?" Missy was the name on record.

"That would be me." The girl put down her phone and extended her hand. "I'm Missy."

Lily shook it. "I'm Lily. We spoke on the phone. I'm with the Private Select Program at Marino Hotels and was hoping to chat with you about some irregularities in your account."

Missy's face remained polite but blank. "Oh, I wouldn't know anything about that. I'm mostly here to answer phones, take messages, that sort of thing."

"Is Mr. Lockwood around? Maybe I can speak with him?" No way would Lily give up so easily.

A frown scrunched Missy's face. "Mr. Lockwood? Er, I think that's Trent? He hasn't been in. Last time, I saw him was weeks ago."

How strange. He was just at the hotel the other day. "All right, then. Thank you for your time. I'll leave my card here in case he calls or shows up." Lily dug out a hotel card to give the receptionist.

As she stepped out through the glass door, she saw Missy pick up a phone. The receptionist spoke with furtive glances to the back office. Was Lockwood in the office? But why hide?

Back at her office, Lily tapped a pen against her notepad. The day had been anything but ordinary. An idea came to her. She logged in. The reservations originated from an email address, the same email address for all the bookings. When she cross-checked it against her database, it came back to a Trevor Lang. A search for this guy only yielded social media when she used his email—an ordinary man, thirties, a self-employed carpenter. Hmm, would a carpenter have the need for the rooms? And why would he be making the reservations for those LLCs?

She found and dialed the number. Lang answered on the second ring. She introduced herself and said, "I want to thank you for your support all these years."

"Oh. Uh, thank you."

"On checking your records, I noticed you made several reservations over the last few months, and then you canceled them a few days later. We'd like to know why. Is it our service? We want to do something to make sure you and your company enjoy your stay here." Was that lame? It was all she had on the fly.

"Um, no, it, er, timing just didn't work out. Sorry, but I gotta go. Thanks for calling." Click.

When she tried again, it went to voicemail. Okay, this was officially strange.

Sighing, she glanced at the clock. It was time to leave. She rolled her neck side to side to shake off her anxiety. She could investigate further tomorrow. For now, she had a dinner date with her parents, and she didn't want to be late.

She passed by her boss's office and hesitated. Should she share her concerns? But Janet would dismiss them, wouldn't she? She'd tell her she was reading too much into things. Lily walked on. She'd keep her suspicions to herself, at least for now.

In the dimly lit underground garage, its echoey expanse made her footsteps sound unnaturally loud. With a sense of relief, she approached her car—a reliable silver sedan that had seen better days.

She slid into the driver's seat and started the car, the engine roaring to life. She pulled out of her parking spot and made her way toward the garage exit. With every twist and turn, her mind played over the day's events, seeking an explanation for her unease.

The light ahead indicated a sharp bend, and she eased her foot onto the brake, expecting the car to slow. But it didn't. Her chest tightened, and her heart raced as she pressed harder. But the car seemed to have a mind of its own, refusing to respond.

"Oh no." She gripped the steering wheel so tightly her knuckles turned white. Thump, thump, thump. Heart pounding, she did the only thing she could think of. She aimed for an empty parking spot, hoping against hope that the car would come to a stop. As the sedan sped forward, a rush of thoughts overtook her. Was this an accident? Or was someone trying to hurt her because of her inquiries?

With a screeching of tires and a jolt, the car stopped, the front bumper kissing the concrete wall. Trembling, she took deep breaths to calm herself. She turned off the engine, the silence in the garage now deafening.

She sat there, processing, her mind racing. She needed to get her brakes checked, but the timing of the malfunction was suspiciously convenient.

After what felt like an eternity, she mustered the courage to step out of the car. She examined the brakes, though she was no expert. To her untrained eye, nothing seemed out of the ordinary.

Then she unlocked her phone and dialed her dad's number. "Hey, Dad. It's me." Her voice shook. She swallowed hard to choke down the tremor. "Something happened. I'm okay, but I might be a bit late for dinner."

She explained the situation.

"Call the police!" Mom ordered. Dad must've put her call on speaker.

Lily hesitated. "I was thinking of calling the insurance to report an accident."

"No…" Olivia started.

But Simon said, "We'll be right there."

Hanging up, Lily leaned against the car to steady herself. The feeling of unease from earlier was now amplified tenfold. Whatever was happening, she was in over her head.

The evening sky was turning into a deep shade of blue, its horizon dotted with the early glimmers of stars. Her parents wasted no time getting to the scene. Now, Olivia knelt next to the car without hesitation. She used a flashlight from her purse to inspect the underbelly.

After her observation, Olivia slid out, her expression grim. "Brake line's been cut."

A churning in her stomach brought bile to Lily's mouth. "What do you mean? How would that happen?"

Simon stepped in. "Lily, it doesn't just 'happen.' Someone did this. Deliberately." He wrapped an arm around her and hugged her close, giving her some semblance of comfort amid the realization.

Scared and angry, she stepped away and clenched her hands. "I don't understand. Who would do that? Why?"

Olivia, her expression taut, replied, "We don't know, honey. What have you been doing? I don't usually see this unless someone's trying to send you a message."

Lily summed up what she'd been doing, her suspicions and everything.

Her mom's eyes narrowed. "When we get home, you'll tell me everything in detail. It does sound like you've rattled some cages. But right now, our primary concern is your safety."

"I want to figure out what's going on." Lily's clenched hands tightened into determined fists.

"First, we have to get the car fixed."

Her dad nodded, pulling out his phone. "I'll call a tow truck. We'll get it to the mechanic, and he'll make it roadworthy again. Now, we wait for the cops."

# CHAPTER 32

## PARK HILLS PRIVATE SCHOOL

*GRACE*

Grace's weekend unfolded with a semblance of normalcy, punctuated only by the minor disruption of Alex installing security cameras. The first camera, a sleek, modern doorbell variant, he affixed beside her front door. The second, a more robust model, found its home on the back balcony, its lens sweeping over the other building.

"All right. That should do it," he had announced. "You can check the feed from your phone. Any movement, and you'll know."

They racked their brains to figure out who the note writer was referring to, but they couldn't come up with anyone. They had a distant cousin in jail for some minor stuff, but they had no contact with her.

The morning sun cast a warm glow over the city as she set out for work, the lingering fears from the past weeks somewhat eased by the newly installed security cameras. She left her apartment confident that normalcy had been restored. Alex decided to stay and work remotely.

She immersed herself in the school day, a flurry of familiar routines and lively student interactions. As the final bell echoed through the halls, she began her preparations for bus duty and gathered her belongings, her thoughts already on the task ahead. Outside, the schoolyard was buzzing with the energy of students eager to return home.

She took her position, scanning the crowd for any signs of confusion or distress among the students. She moved with practiced ease, directing the younger ones to their buses and ensuring the car riders found their rides safely. The afternoon sun was warm on her back, a gentle breeze playing with her hair.

Amid the controlled chaos of departing students, a pair of siblings looked a bit lost. She approached with a smile and guided them toward their car. Then she saw *them*—two men in crisp suits strode through the crowd. How out of place they seemed in the casual schoolyard setting.

As they neared, her pulse quickened, and unease shivered over her. The men stopped in front of her, both had their ID pack out. They looked official in a way that didn't fit with the local police or any other agency she was familiar with.

"Ms. Benson?" the taller of the two men inquired, his voice polite but firm.

She nodded, her attention divided between the men and the siblings who were now safely in their car. "Yes, that's me. Can I help you?"

"FBI Special Agent Robert Wood." The taller one tilted his bald head toward the other more rugged-looking man. "And Special Agent Chip Jackson. We need to speak with you regarding a personal matter."

She watched enough TV shows to know badges could be fake. "I hope you don't mind, but I'd like to check your ID for myself."

"Not at all."

She went to the office. The agents followed her.

Jenny glanced at the agents. "Everything okay?"

"I think so." Grace took her phone out, found the local FBI office website, and called. "I'd like to verify if you have an agent Robert Wood and agent Chip Jackson."

After a moment of key clicking, the woman came back on. "Yes, ma'am. Can you give me their badge numbers, and I'll verify they are the correct numbers?"

After getting confirmation, Grace returned the ID packs to the agents. "Thank you. Can't be too careful these days."

"No problem at all." Wood pocketed his pack.

"Do you want to go to the music room to talk?" That should be private enough.

"No, ma'am. We need you to come with us."

At Wood's no-nonsense tone, she bristled. "Why? I'm not going anywhere with you. You need to tell me what this is about now."

Wood flicked a glance at Jenny, stepped away with Grace, and spoke in a soft voice. "There's a credible threat to your safety. It's urgent that we get you to a safe house."

Her heart skipped a beat. A threat to her safety? "Does this have anything to do with the note?"

The two agents exchanged glances. Wood crossed his arms. "We're not aware of any note. Have you received a written threat?"

"I guess so. It was more creepy than threatening, I think. I reported it to the police. They said there was nothing they could do."

"Where is the note?"

"The police kept it, but I have a picture of it." She pulled out her phone. After a few swipes, she showed it to them.

Jackson was tapping on his phone the whole time she was talking with Wood. Then he held the phone to Wood's face. Wood read it and frowned. "Okay, we'll go with you to your apartment. You can pack a few things, and then we'll go."

"Everything okay?" Jenny called.

Before Grace could say anything, Wood yelled, "All good!"

She went to grab her things with them in tow. When she passed Jenny, she smiled to reassure her everything was fine. Minutes later, she headed to her car, Wood following her. When she pressed the fob to unlock the car, he guided her to the passenger side and opened the door. "I will drive you home. Agent Jackson will follow us."

Was that necessary? It was her car, after all. But she shut her mouth, sensing arguing would be futile. She got in and gave him her address once he settled into the driver's seat.

She strapped on her seat belt. "Okay, what kind of threat if you didn't know about the note?"

"I don't know the details. But you're on a kill list. Our order is to take you into protective custody."

The words *kill list* echoed in her mind, sending a chill down her spine. Her knees weakened, her world tilting on its axis. "Kill list? No, I don't believe it. Are you sure? I mean, there must be some mistake."

"We're sure, Ms. Benson. And there's no mistake," Wood affirmed. "Your safety is our priority right now. We need to move quickly."

"But my job... the children's choir," she stammered, her mind racing. "I can't just leave. What will I tell the school?"

"The school will be notified. They'll be told it's a family emergency. It's important that we keep the reason confidential for your safety."

She pressed cold fingers to her temples, in a daze, the reality of the situation barely registering.

"Tell me about the note. Have you received any other threat?"

"Not really, but..." She went on to explain being followed, finding misplaced things at home, and of course receiving the note.

At the apartment building, she punched in the code to open the door. They all trooped up to her apartment. She opened the door, Alex's laptop on the kitchen table.

The guest room door opened, and Alex walked out.

"Hands where I can see them!" Wood and Jackson hollered. Both had their guns out.

Alex's hands shot up. The apple in his hand fell.

If the situation wasn't so serious, she'd have laughed. "Chill! He's my brother."

"Your brother? Your report said you lived alone." Wood holstered his weapon.

"He was staying with me because of the note."

Alex tentatively lowered his hands as if he was still in trouble. "What's going on? Who are they?"

"FBI. They're taking me into protective custody. Said I was on a kill list."

His jaw dropped.

# CHAPTER 33

## THE ROTH RESIDENCE

*OLIVIA*

The aroma of freshly cooked food wafted through the air as Olivia walked into the house with Simon and Lily. It was a little chilly outside, but inside, it felt toasty. They had stopped by a local Chinese restaurant for takeout, and the scent of spices and fried noodles permeated the house.

Sitting down at the dining table, she began unpacking the food, placing bowls and dishes in front of everyone. But her mind was preoccupied, and the rhythmic clinking of forks and spoons against plates did little to ease the tension. She looked pointedly at Lily, her daughter's innocent brown eyes meeting her gaze.

"Lily, you need to tell us everything. Why would someone sabotage your car?"

Lily sulked, mixing some chicken with fried rice. "I haven't done anything to threaten anyone. I mean, I just started the job! What could I have done?"

Simon shook extra seeds onto his sesame chicken. "That's

what we're trying to find out. You mentioned Rain Tree LLC and New Life LLC. What are they?"

She recounted the events of the past few days, detailing her observations about the two companies, a bizarre visit from Trent Lockwood, and her boss's dismissal of her concerns.

Olivia rubbed her temples at the onset of a headache. "Something doesn't add up. An attempt on your life over some companies? It doesn't make sense. Somebody is sending you a message. What have you done that's got somebody very edgy?"

"There's got to be something more." Simon pointed his fork at their daughter. "These LLCs you mentioned, did they have any ties to known criminal activities or shady deals?"

Lily frowned. "Now that you mentioned it, I did find they were associated with a third company that has been flagged for fraud. But I'm not sure. The only suspicious thing about these companies is they would make reservations, then cancel the bookings. When I called the guy who made all the reservations and cancellations, he sounded weird. He got off the phone real quick and wouldn't take my call anymore." She scooped the last bit from her bowl of fried rice, then held the spoon up, frowning at it, before recounting her experience with the front desk girl at Rain Tree LLC.

Olivia sipped her drink, deep in thought. "If these are shell corporations—and it sounds like they are—then they have layers upon layers to hide illicit activities. If someone felt you were getting too close…" She stopped there, the implications clear.

"I just don't see it. It's not like I'm a detective or anything. I was just doing my job."

"But that's just it." Simon leaned back. "Maybe you stumbled upon something you weren't supposed to see or know. Maybe it was unintentional, but now you've attracted unwanted attention."

Olivia drummed her nerves out through her fingertips, the repetitive sound echoing the pulsing in her skull. "This is serious, Lily. We can't just brush it off. Try talking to your boss again. She needs to know something isn't right."

Simon agreed.

Olivia finished her soup. "Be careful. Don't go anywhere alone. And keep us updated on any new developments."

"I will."

Whose cage had Lily rattled?

# CHAPTER 34

## TASK FORCE OFFICE

*RON*

Morning briefing was about to start. Ron stepped into the squad room where the team was already gathered in front of the screen. Cooper was there as well, looking ready to give his update.

"All right, listen up." Cooper adjusted his shirt collar. "We've had a breakthrough."

He had the remote, but after several attempts, Tanner grabbed it from him and pressed some buttons. Photos of Rubio Nunez and Frankie, more commonly known by his alias, Greek, popped up on the screen.

Cooper waved at the screen. "Thanks to Marco, we have intel on these two key players. Greek is our heavy hitter—the guy you call when you want something done, no questions asked." He pointed to a scar-laden face, the eyes cold and unyielding.

"Nunez," he continued, "is only a rung below Martinez. If we get to Nunez, we get a shot at Martinez, the kingpin we've been after."

Ron crossed his arms. "What's our lead on Nunez?"

"That's the interesting part. Marco mentioned a club—El Paraíso. I did some digging. It's not just any club. It's a den for the cartel's operations."

Hernandez chimed in, "I've heard whispers about El Paraíso in the circles. It's not a place you waltz into uninvited."

A murmur of agreement spread around the room. Cooper shifted his gaze to Ana. "You should be the one to check it out. Your history and cover give you an in."

Her lips tightened into a determined line. "I can do it."

"It's too dangerous," Tanner interjected, holding up a hand still gripping his stress ball. "We can't just send someone in there alone."

She cocked her head, her bobbed hair slipping across her cheek, her defiance sparkling in her eyes. "I've handled worse."

Time to mediate. Ron held up a hand. "Tanner's right. You need someone to watch your six. But it can't be just anyone."

Hernandez stepped forward. "I'll go."

That worked. Ron nodded, the words *kill list* flashing through his head. Focus! "It needs to be someone who fits the demographics, who won't draw unnecessary attention."

Cooper rocked back on his heels, and his slow drawl poured out. "Hernandez has the background, and he knows the territory. It makes sense."

With a short, irritated motion, Ana shook her curls away from her face, her shoulders back, head high. But a touch of gratitude cracked her usual calm as she gave Hernandez the nod. "I trust José."

"All right, but we'll ensure you both are equipped." Tanner tossed the ball onto his desk and crossed his arms, his chin jutting out. "We can't take any risks."

"Agreed." Cooper widened his stance, hands folded before him. "We'll set up surveillance around the club. If anything goes sideways, we'll be there in seconds."

Ron cleared his throat, capturing everyone's attention. "Our focus remains on Martinez, but these leads on Nunez and Greek are vital. If El Paraíso is the link, then that's our way in. We need to move swiftly, but cautiously." He eyed both Ana and Hernandez. "You two, prepare, get what you need, and stay safe."

"Understood." The two agents headed out.

Hours later, they were back in the squad room, planning the El Paraíso op. An intricate blueprint of El Paraíso was projected onto the screen, detailing each entrance, exit, and potential vantage point. The club's grandeur was evident from the layout, with its vast main hall, private rooms lining the periphery, and the labyrinthine network of service corridors beneath.

Ana and Hernandez sat together, focus fixed on the blueprint, discussing amongst themselves. Other agents, technical experts, and surveillance personnel filled the remaining seats.

Cooper set up the blueprint on the screen. The DEA agent jabbed a long finger at the blueprint. "Primary entrance. It's the front door, so it's also the most watched. But it's our way in."

Hernandez rolled his chair so he half faced the screen and the others. "It's a members-only club. But I have an old contact who can get us passes."

"Once inside, we'll need eyes on both of you at all times. Thompson and Patel"—Cooper motioned to two techs seated at the back—"you'll be on surveillance. Eyes on screens, tracking every move."

Thompson, a wiry man with glasses, adjusted his headset. "We've got earpieces for Ana and Hernandez, smallest we could find. Virtually invisible. We'll hear everything."

Patel, with her jet-black hair tied in a tight bun, added, "We've also secured satellite visuals of the club's perimeter. We can guide you through if needed."

Ron pointed to a VIP section on the blueprint. "Our intel suggests Nunez and his crew use this area. Ana, your mission is to get close, engage, and extract as much information as you can."

Her focus on the blueprint, she narrowed her eyes. "I'll play the role of a high roller looking to make some… business deals."

Hernandez tapped the service corridors on the blueprint. "I'll use my cover as a supplier for the club. Gives me an excuse to move around, check the back areas."

Cooper leaned in. "Remember, Greek goes by Frankie in his dealings. If we can find him and track his movements, we might get a lead on where Nunez is and what they're planning."

"Folks, remember"—Ron spread his hands—"our primary goal is intel. We need to understand their operations, any upcoming deals, and any hints on Martinez's whereabouts. Arrests tonight are secondary. We can't tip them off."

A door at the back opened, and Deanna walked in, holding a small case. "Got some additional gear for you two." She placed it on the table and opened it to reveal two slim, metallic devices. "These are short-range trackers. They're adhesive. If you get the chance, slap one onto a key player or their vehicle. It'll give us a tail on them for at least seventy-two hours."

Hernandez let out a low whistle. "These are new."

"Latest tech." Deanna smirked. "Just got them in."

Cooper cleared his throat. "We've secured a safe house two blocks from the club. If things go south, that's your rendezvous point. Ron and I will be there, coordinating."

Ron struggled to focus, his thoughts drifting again to Kyle and Sheila. That wouldn't do. "We have a narrow window. El Paraíso is our chance to crack this wide open. We've prepared as best we can. The rest is execution."

"We've got this," Ana said.

Hernandez nodded, his face a mask of focus.

The room started to clear out, agents moving to their designated positions. Ron placed a reassuring hand on Ana's shoulder. "Be safe. And remember, we're always with you."

She smiled, rested her hand atop his, and squeezed. "Thanks, Ron. We won't let you down."

At least one operation better go well. In the back of his mind, there was always that kill list to worry about.

# CHAPTER 35

## M&M ENTERPRISES

*LILY*

The staff lounge was almost empty. The scent of freshly brewed coffee intertwined with the buttery aroma of pastries, creating a comforting atmosphere in stark contrast to the turmoil churning inside Lily.

She sat at a corner table, the smooth leather cool against her skin. Dylan's and Tommy's familiar faces provided a semblance of normalcy, though the undercurrent of her recent ordeal lay just beneath the surface of their casual greetings.

"Morning, Lily." Dylan's voice was even, a touch of concern behind his composed façade. "How are you holding up after last night?"

Taken aback, she stilled, her fork pausing midair. She'd wanted to talk with him last night, but got too tired after long discussions with her mom. "How did you know about that?"

Tommy's chuckle was a warm, grounding sound. "Are you forgetting who he is?" he teased, a playful glint in his eye. "Dylan's got his finger on the pulse around here."

She let out a half-hearted laugh, though the gravity of the

situation was not lost on her. She still marveled at the efficiency of the hotel's information network. "They probably report everything to you."

Dylan shook his head, a gentle correction in his tone. "Not everything. But the usual efficient hotel grapevine does its job well. It happened in the garage, and the cops were called. You know the drill. An incident report was filed. I never would've paid attention to that—except I saw your name on the report."

She recounted the harrowing experience, the helpless sensation of her foot pressing down on the brake to no avail, the sheer panic as she hurtled toward the wall. The guys listened with rapt attention, adding murmurs of shock and concern.

Sinking back in his seat, Dylan crossed his arms, his gaze hooded. "Do you think it has anything to do with the two accounts you've been auditing?"

Her thoughts spiraled. Just how could she connect the dots that seemed scattered and elusive? "I don't know." Thinking about it made her heartbeat kick up the pace. But whether she was mad or scared she couldn't even say. "Mom thinks someone wants to send me a message. Probably to stop what I'm doing. But I don't even know what I'm doing that's so dangerous. I haven't uncovered anything. What reason would they have to harm me?"

Tommy leaned in, his voice dropping to a conspiratorial whisper. "If those companies are up to no good and you're digging into their business—business they want to keep private —you never know what lengths they'll go to."

A shiver ran down her spine, the morning's comfort dissipating like mist. "Now you guys are scaring me."

Dylan offered a reassuring nod, his protective streak coming to the fore. "We're not trying to scare you. We just want you to be aware of the risks. And be safe."

Tommy flashed a smirk both cheeky and comforting. "I'll offer my services as a personal bodyguard. How's that?"

Dylan laughed and cuffed his friend's shoulder. "She knows kung fu, and her mom has been training her in hand-to-hand combat and who knows what else. She should be our bodyguard."

Despite the anxiety gnawing at her, she allowed a small smile. "See, I'm small, and people tend to underestimate me."

As they sipped their coffee and nibbled on breakfast, the conversation veered toward lighter topics, but her mind was never fully present. She replayed the previous day's events like a broken record, each rotation fueling her unease.

"So, when is your big date?" Tommy finished his coffee. "You know, maybe I should start bringing a date to our lunch from now on. Don't want to be the third wheel."

"Has anyone passed the third date yet?" she teased. Tommy had no shortage of girlfriends, but they never lasted.

"Nah, but someday, I'll find the perfect one. Just you wait."

When Dylan circled back to the topic of her mysterious stalker, her heart skipped a beat. "I caught a glimpse of him. That's it. And honestly, I'm not sure what I would do if he approached me." She wrapped her hands around the warm mug, seeking comfort.

"Maybe he's what he said he is."

The day went by without incidents. She didn't see Filmore and forced herself not to think about the two LLCs. Her mom told her to lay low. Said she was working on something right now, but would help her after that. So, Lily spent her day working on other projects. But the LLCs were never far from her mind.

Her phone rang, the sound jarring in the hushed tones of her personal contemplation. She glanced at the caller ID—Missy from Rain Tree LLC. A shiver ran down her spine as she picked up the receiver.

"Hello. Lily speaking."

"Hi. It's Missy," came the voice, chipper and bright like a

morning-show host. "I'm calling for Trent. He'd like to invite you to visit our office. He said he had something to discuss with you."

The words hung in the air, their implications wrapping around Lily like a spider's web. Was this a genuine offer or a lure into a trap she had inadvertently stumbled upon?

"Okay. I'll need to check my schedule. Can I get back to you?" she managed to say, her voice steady despite her thundering heartbeat.

"Of course!" Missy chirped. "We're looking forward to it."

Lily placed the receiver back in its cradle, her hand hovering as she processed the conversation. What should she do? Could the LLC have something to do with her cut brakes?

As the day wore on, the usual office buzz began to simmer down, replaced by the sounds of shutting computers and casual farewells. She was gathering her things when Dylan stopped by her desk.

"Hey, do you need a ride home? Your car is still at the shop, right?" His concern offered a subtle reminder of her precarious situation.

She smiled out her gratitude. "Thanks, but I have to make a sales call." She hesitated. "Can you believe it? Missy from Rain Tree called for her boss to invite me for a chat."

He raised his eyebrows. "Well, maybe they're legit after all. But are you sure you want to go alone? I thought your mom didn't want you to go anywhere alone."

She shrugged, a twinge in her tummy. "Yeah, but it's only a sales call. I'll Uber over to the building."

Quiet, he raked a hand through his dark hair. "I'm heading over to the estate anyway. I can drive you there. It's on my way."

She paused, his offer tempting for more than the convenience. "All right. That would be great. Thank you." She grabbed her purse, relief washing over her.

As they walked out of the elevator to the garage, the evening air was brisk, signaling the end of the day. The sun, dipping below the skyline, cast long shadows across the pavement.

His car was a sleek, unassuming model, its engine purring as they settled inside. Had she made a mistake by accepting Rain Tree's invitation? When Lily called back to say she could stop by this afternoon, Missy sounded upbeat.

"You sure you don't want me to wait? Just in case." Dylan stopped the car by the curb.

"Thanks, but I think I'll be fine. I'll just get an Uber home."

She stepped out of the car, taking a deep breath as she faced the building. The glass doors reflected the fading light. With a final wave to her, he drove on. She was steps away from the entrance when a blur of movement caught her peripheral vision. Then she was knocked off her feet, the air whooshing from her lungs as she hit the pavement.

Sharp sounds of gunfire pierced the air, echoing off the tall buildings, followed by the screeching of tires that faded as quickly as they appeared. Dazed, her mind struggled to process what was happening.

She turned her head, her vision swimming, and stared into the eyes of Toby Filmore. Huh? *Filmore* had tackled her? His body now shielded her from any further danger. "Stay down." He scanned the area for more threats.

She lay there, stunned, her heart pounding, her ears ringing. His presence, once a source of unease, was now comforting.

After what felt like an eternity but couldn't have been more than a minute, he got up, offered a hand to help her to her feet. "He's gone." His brow creased. "He was on a motorcycle."

She accepted his hand, still struggling to catch her breath. "Thank you," she managed to say, despite the tremor in her voice. "But why... how did you...?"

He eyed her, his expression serious. "I've been keeping an eye on you. After the brake-line incident, I didn't want to take any chances."

What? He'd been watching over her, possibly even protecting her? "You were there? I didn't see you."

"I wouldn't be doing my job if you did. Your mom, though, would likely have made me. I was about to show myself before you managed to stop the car. That was good thinking. Let's get you inside." He guided her toward the building. "We need to report this."

"Wait. You know my mom? She sent you?"

# CHAPTER 36
## FEDERAL DETENTION CENTER

*OLIVIA*

The crisp early evening air settled over the city as Olivia sat in her car, parked a discreet distance from the detention center. Clad in a nondescript gray jacket, she wrapped a plain satin scarf around her neck and pulled a cap low over her brow. She'd learned long ago that the best disguises were those that blended into the crowd.

She kept her focus on the detention center's exit, waiting for the fake Adam O'Shea. Her former mentor and handler had been explicit—leave it to the Company. But her instincts, honed over years of undercover work, told her this required a personal touch. And he also said, "It's all connected."

The tracker they'd planted on O'Shea had been discovered and disabled, a rookie mistake that grated on her. Now, she had to rely on the city's vast network of street cameras and a little help from an old friend.

Shadow Shot, a fellow operative currently "in country" for unrelated business, had agreed to assist. They had a system in place, switching surveillance duties to avoid detection. They both knew the risks of tailing a trained asset like O'Shea.

As the detention center's doors swung open, her muscles tensed. O'Shea stepped out, looking both ways before tugging his collar up against the wind. She waited a beat, then started her car, and followed at a distance, her focus never leaving his figure.

Every few blocks, she'd fall back, and Shadow Shot, nondescript on his motorcycle, took over. They communicated via earpieces, a subtle symphony of concise updates and instructions.

"He's heading east on Fifth."

O'Shea's figure became a dot in the distance.

"Got him." Shadow Shot's voice crackled in her ear. "Switching now."

The tail continued like a well-choreographed dance through the city, O'Shea remaining oblivious to the two shadows flitting at his periphery. At least, that was her hope.

Now, he entered a nondescript house in a quiet residential area. They waited, alternating surveillance shifts, but the hours ticked by with no sign of movement within the house.

"It's just like last time," she whispered. "He goes in but never comes out. And we're certain he hasn't left in disguise or a different vehicle."

Shadow Shot's voice came through, tired yet resolute. "We won't know anything unless we get inside that house."

She chewed on her lower lip. "We need a plan—and more intel. I'll make some calls, see what we can dig up on this place."

She glanced at the house, its windows dark, the silence emanating from it almost tangible. They were so close to understanding O'Shea's game, yet the final piece eluded them.

"We'll get it," Shadow Shot assured her. "We always do."

"I can't believe he could disappear like this."

"Do you want to go in?"

Yes. But it wasn't worth the risk. They had no jurisdiction as it were.

"We did it before, and nobody knew we were inside," Shadow Shot said.

"Yeah." She let out a low breath. "But we weren't stateside then. Let's go back to regroup."

A half hour later, she parked in the garage. Simon's car was there, so he was home. Shadow Shot parked his motorcycle in the driveway behind her car. She stood by the garage door to the house, waiting for him.

Simon was putting his shoes on as they stepped inside the house.

"Oh, heading out?" she asked.

"Yeah, I'm picking up Sheila, and we're meeting with Zimmerman."

"Hey, before you go, let me introduce you to a friend." She gestured toward Shadow Shot. And then she realized she never knew his name. They only went by code names.

"Kevin, nice to meet you, Senator." Kevin, offered his hand to Simon who shook it.

"It's Simon. People keep calling me senator even though I left office almost two months ago."

"Well, that's your title for life."

"Sha—uh, Kevin and I worked several cases together back in the day." She couldn't say much more. Most of their assignments were classified. "We need to plot our next steps in, you know, our little op."

Simon's blue eyes twinkled. "All right, then. I'll leave you to it. I'll be back." He walked out after a peck on her cheek. The moment the door clicked shut behind him, a silence settled over the room, punctuated only by the faint ticking of an antique clock on the mantelpiece. Kevin settled into the ebony leather couch, his posture relaxed but his eyes sharp and assessing.

"Is Kevin your real name?" She sat in the armchair.

"Is Jade yours? Or is it Olivia? I only know you as Phoenix."

"It's Olivia." She let out a chuckle. "In our line of work, sometimes we forget who we really are."

He tsked and shook a finger at her. "If we're not careful, we might lose more than just our names."

Having been undercover as Jade for close to two decades, she knew well how easy it was to lose her identity. However, now wasn't the time to dwell on the philosophical or psychological aspects of their profession.

"So…" He scooted forward, elbows resting on his knees. "This fake O'Shea… What's the story?"

She exhaled, the weight of the day pressing down upon her. "The real Adam O'Shea is one of ours—an asset with a lot of value to the Company. Someone leaked information about me, compromising my position. I have a strong suspicion this impostor is connected."

His expression hardened at the mention of a leak. "And the task force thinks it's either this fake O'Shea or someone they're calling Uncle Bill?"

"Yes." Her fingers traced the wood grain of the coffee table absentmindedly. "Uncle Bill is elusive. Even Eva, his contact, can't get ahold of him. He initiates contact every time."

He nodded, his gaze drifting toward the window where the last light of dusk was surrendering to the night. "I've dealt with phantoms before. They can be flushed out with the right bait. And you think following the fake O'Shea will lead you to something? Or are you thinking this O'Shea is Uncle Bill?"

"I don't know what to think. I just know this O'Shea is an operative. Didn't you get the sense he knew the tradecraft?"

"Yeah, but he could be playing for another team."

"That's why I want to find out who he is." She hardened her jaw, then let out a low breath. "Let me back up, though. We suspect Uncle Bill is Officer Bill from twenty years ago. If that is true, then he was one of us, and at some point, he switched sides and became Uncle Bill."

"What did this Uncle Bill do to suggest he's not on our side?"

"For one, he was able to tell Eva, an agent, things that would happen before she knew it. Like she said he told her Ron, head of the task force, would get her an assignment, and it happened. So, he has some way to get that kind of information and is sharing it, which indicates he could very well be the leak. Also, I've combed through our database. No active operative matches his description."

He shifted to stretch his arms across the back of the couch, the leather squeaking with his movements. "It does sound suspicious. He'd have a source inside the bureau, but not the Company, don't you think? He might have been with the Company, but not anymore. A lot of operatives have heard of Phoenix, but only a handful know that's you."

She rubbed the shivers from her bare arms. "I guess you're right. Well then, it only proves he's an ex-officer."

"Likely, but we're still only theorizing. Wait a second, if he was a bureau man, he might know about you, as in Olivia, showing up."

"Yup. Someone leaked that I, Olivia, was here. You think he's a bureau man?"

He spread his arms. "Maybe."

She stood up. "Let's get started."

She showed him to her office upstairs, an alcove just big enough for her desk and multiple monitors and that recliner in the corner. She flipped open a folding chair for him, then went to her closet to retrieve another laptop, and set it on the desk in front of him. "You can use this one."

He made himself comfortable, though with his height he had to hunch when working on the laptop. "We need to find out who the real O'Shea dealt with. His contacts, his assignments. Anything that could tell us more about his impersonator."

"I've been digging into Uncle Bill. If we can find any intersection between him and O'Shea's operations, we might get a lead on who's behind this."

"The fake O'Shea uses real credentials. That means he's likely a Company man, or at least had access to the Company's database." He steepled his fingers. "Your theory might be correct. Our guy has to be a former employee and somehow still had access—"

"Or he could hack into it or bribe someone." She fixed her gaze on the screen as she sifted through encrypted files.

He shook his head. "Those are less likely scenarios. It's not easy to hack our systems, and bribery is risky—it leaves a trail. We should exhaust the more likely scenarios before delving into those."

She nodded, though she remained skeptical. "Jay said this was an internal matter, that I shouldn't be looking into O'Shea at all."

He let out a soft chuckle. "Since when has 'shouldn't' stopped us?"

The corners of her lips twitched upward, a spark of her old fire returning. "Never." She bent back over the computer. "Okay, let's pull up the records on O'Shea's last known activities. Anything suspicious?"

Time passed, the alcove silent except for the occasional click of the mouse and the soft scratch of pen on paper. The digital clock on her desk marched forward, its red numbers a stark reminder of the time slipping by.

Finally, she leaned back, her eyes weary from the screen's glare. "There's something here." She pointed to a series of transactions out of place for the real O'Shea's profile. "These transactions… They were flagged for review, but somehow they slipped through the cracks."

Before they could research further, the garage door rumbled open, and she stood. Simon was back, or Lily came home. "I'll see what else I can find. Maybe more has been 'overlooked' or 'slipped through.'"

He rose as well, his posture still alert despite the late hour. "I'll reach out to a few contacts. See if they can shed light on these transactions from their end."

# CHAPTER 37

## ZIMMERMAN'S LAW OFFICE

*SHEILA*

Sheila's heels clicked on the polished marble floors of the Zimmerman, Townsend & Brown law firm, a rhythmic echo that seemed to match her racing heartbeat. The building's towering glass façade had always represented power and prestige to those who walked the city's streets. Now, as she entered the firm's opulent office, it was a bastion of hope.

Her fingers tightened around her purse strap as she was ushered into a wood-paneled office, where an older gentleman with thinning hair, Todd Zimmerman, stood to greet her. A testament to success, the office displayed shelves lined with legal books, diplomas, and various awards. The desk was tidy, with only a few folders and a laptop.

"Mrs. Mitchell, thank you for coming." Zimmerman shook her hand, his grip firm and his gaze penetrating. "Please, take a seat."

She settled into the plush leather chair across from him, her posture rigid. Simon sat next to her.

Zimmerman wasted no time. "I've been briefed on the basics

of your case, but I need to hear it from you. Everything you can tell me might be important."

She took a deep breath and recounted the events, the discovery of Doug's hidden life, the shocking moment she found his body. As she spoke, the lawyer listened, occasionally interjecting with a clarifying question, his focus never wavering.

After she finished, Simon offered his perspective. "Her ex-husband, Ron, head of an FBI task force, believes there's more to Doug's death than meets the eye. And I agree."

The lawyer nodded. "I understand you've been acting as Mrs. Mitchell's attorney thus far. I'd like you to stay on as cocounsel."

Simon raised an eyebrow. "Criminal law isn't my forte. I haven't practiced for a long time, as you know."

Steepling his fingers, Zimmerman leaned back in his chair. "I'm well aware, Senator. To be honest, I'm swamped. I'm taking this case because of Ms. Marino's and your referral. So, I'll lead if it goes to trial, which I doubt at this point—I don't think they'll formally charge her. I can have one of ours take over, but you're already familiar with the case and the people involved."

Simon hesitated, then dipped his chin. "All right. If you think it'll help her."

"I do." Zimmerman then turned to her. "We'll start our investigation. I have a team of the best investigators who will leave no stone unturned."

"Thank you, both of you. I don't just want to clear my name but also to find out who did this to Doug."

"We need to find out everything we can about your late husband." Zimmerman tapped his index fingers together. "His background, his contacts, his travels—everything may be key to understanding why he's been murdered."

"I always thought he was just in sales." Her voice broke, barely rising above a whisper.

The lawyer looked up, the light catching the silver in his hair, his eyes locking with hers. "Often, what we think we know about a person is just the surface. We need to dig deeper."

Simon shifted. "Doug had secrets. That much is clear. Uncovering those will shed light on the motive for his murder."

"I'll have my team pull financial records, cross-reference his known associates, and check any recent communications." Zimmerman jotted notes as he spoke. "We'll also look into any business dealings that may have been a front for something else."

She nodded, dread mingling with her determination. "I'll help in any way I can. I want the truth to come out."

"Technically, our goal is to clear your name. Finding the truth is optional, but it will be beneficial to our cause since these two things may well be intertwined."

The more she listened, the more she felt like she didn't know the man she married.

# CHAPTER 38

## SAFE HOUSE

*KYLE*

By late afternoon, Kyle approached the nondescript safe house—a building as unassuming as it was secure, nestled in a quiet suburb. Tanner had dropped him off. Protocol required that he not be alone for the duration. Kyle had seen his fair share of safe houses, but this assignment was different. Even though the deputy director made it sound like he was reassigned to protection details, he knew he was being protected as well. And he was supposed to uncover a connection between him and Grace Benson that he was certain didn't exist.

As he entered the safe house, he greeted the agent in charge, Chuck Torres, a man well known within the agency for his meticulousness. The AIC handed over a file. "Everything you need to know about Grace Benson is in there." He tapped it. "I understand we need to find out how you two are connected."

Kyle nodded and flipped through its contents. Grace Benson: twenty-five, five foot five, olive skin, brown eyes, striking features. She was an enigma, though. Their paths had never crossed, and he'd never met anyone like her, let alone formed any significant connection.

Closing the file, he entered the living area where she sat on an old grayish couch, her gaze fixed on the window, her expression a blend of anxiety and annoyance in clear indication of her displeasure over being uprooted. Guess they had something in common.

"Ms. Benson, I'm Special Agent Kyle Peters." He managed a friendly tone.

Her brown eyes slanted his way, a hint of suspicion glimmering in them. "My students call me Ms. Benson. You're too old to be my student. Please, it's Grace. So, you're my babysitter?"

"Not a babysitter, ma'am." At her steely look, he amended, "Grace. I'm here for your protection. And I'm Kyle."

She scoffed. "I don't understand. Whose kill list am I on? And I still haven't heard anything about the note or the people following me or why things were misplaced in my apartment."

He sat on the couch's other end. "Wait. What did you say? What note? You've been followed?"

She sighed. "Don't you guys talk to each other? I told that one agent—what's his name? Oh yeah, Wood. I told Wood everything."

He frowned, stood up again. "Excuse me. Let me get an update from Agent Torres."

About fifteen minutes later, he got the details. Torres had sent an agent to retrieve the original note at the precinct, and Deanna now had it in her capable hands. Dad was aware of the threat and everything Grace experienced since Christmas. Dad would be on top of it. Meanwhile, Kyle still had to figure out when their paths crossed.

He went back to the couch. "Um, Grace, this might sound strange, but... do we know each other? From before, I mean."

Arms crossed, she raised an eyebrow. "Should we?"

"You might not realize it, but we're trying to figure out a connection between us. Nothing comes to my mind. I thought maybe you could help. Have you seen me in my professional capacity at all?"

She stared at him. "Before those two agents showed up, I never saw or met any FBI agent. And I don't remember ever meeting you."

"Okay. Let's try to see if we somehow ran into each other without knowing it."

"How do you suggest we do that?" She uncrossed her arms.

He flipped open her file. "Start by telling me about yourself. Your family."

"Okay, my dad is a pastor. My mom works in the church admin. Three older brothers. Two of them live out of state—Georgia and North Carolina. Alex is the only one in town. He's in IT. Consulting, I think. I'm a music teacher at Park Hills Private School."

"What do your out-of-town brothers do?"

"One is an engineer, and the other is a college professor."

No red flag there. "Any law enforcement in your extended family?"

She gave an eye roll. "My dad's cousins are cops up in New York. But we don't have a lot of contact with them." Her gaze narrowed on him. "How about you? Maybe you're the one who got us on the kill list. After all, you're in a dangerous profession."

"Yes, I agree." He relaxed into his seat. "I've likely made some enemies. In fact, my dad is also an FBI special agent. He's been in this for much longer, so he does have his share of enemies. My mom, uh, well, it wouldn't have anything to do with her."

Technically, it had everything to do with her. Her dead husband had the kill list in his throat. But he couldn't imagine how his mother could be the cause of them being on someone's contract.

Grace threw her hands up. "I don't know. If you ask me, you're the target. Or your dad. I don't understand how I got sucked into this."

Something she said triggered a fleeting thought, he tried to hold onto it, but it just went away. He played back what she said in his mind, hoping to capture that thought. He flipped through her file to the part about her birth. Could it be?

# CHAPTER 39

## RAIN TREE LLC

*LILY*

In the sleek lobby of the Rain Tree LLC building, Lily found herself jittering in a state of shock. What had just unfolded? Filmore, the man she had thought to be a stalker, had just saved her life, pushing her to safety as gunfire shattered the evening calm.

"Hey, you know my mom?" she asked again when he didn't answer.

Acting like he didn't hear her, he went on securing the site and ensuring no immediate threat lurked nearby. Then he pulled out his phone and made a call, stepping a few paces away to speak.

Who was he, really? Did her mom know him?

He ended the call and walked back toward her, his expression unreadable.

"Who are you?" She crossed her arms over her chest.

He smiled, amusement glinting in his eyes. "I thought we covered that when your agent friend accosted me last Christmas."

Heat flushed through her. "I'm sorry. Thank you for saving me. But who are you, really? Are you an agent? A spy? Why have you been following me?"

His smile faded. He didn't answer her questions. Instead, he reached out and tugged her forward. "Are you okay? If so, let's go. Hurry. We need to go before the cops, the press, and everybody else shows up."

She frowned. "Why? Where are we going?"

Then, as if a light switched on in her head, she remembered her original purpose. "No, wait. I'm here to see that Lockwood guy."

"I know, but it might not be safe right now. Whoever was shooting at you might still be around or might have associates. And have you considered this was a trap?" With a hold on her elbow, he steered her to the door.

That hadn't occurred to her. "You think I should leave? What if they had nothing to do with it?"

Sirens were getting closer.

"Now. You can call later. I don't think they'll miss you." He pulled her outside.

"Where are we going?"

"Somewhere safe."

## *RON*

Ron stepped through the lab's sliding door, the familiar chemical scent and the mechanized hum greeting him.

"Hey, boss. I have nothing." Deanna's back was to him, her hands on the keyboard. She must have heard him entering.

"You have to have something."

"The note, right? No fingerprints, nothing. They know how to cover their tracks."

"What about CCTV footage?" He walked closer to the black screen.

She clicked something, and the screen lit up with a video of a street near the school. "I combed through hours of footage. Nothing out of the ordinary, except for the delivery itself."

He leaned closer as a college-aged kid approached the school, holding an envelope. "That's our courier?"

"Yeah. The agents tracked him down. Just a local college kid. Said someone paid him fifty bucks to deliver the note. He had no idea what was in it."

He straightened his stance. "Did he say who paid him?"

She shook her head. "He doesn't know the name. They're getting a composite drawing of the guy."

He sighed, his frustration whistling past his lips.

"Who do you think the writer meant?" She tapped the image on her screen. "Whose sin she's supposed to pay for?"

"That's the million-dollar question. What about her apartment building? Those disturbances? Have you found the culprit?"

After another click on the keyboard, several videos streamed on the screen. "No, they know what they're doing. They ran a loop during a ten-minute time frame the day in question."

"And—"

"I also got the incident report she filed last month. She couldn't see the make and model of the car following her except for the headlights. So, there's no help. By the time the officer came out, the car was long gone. But she did mention a pickup truck. The one in her apartment complex is legit. I found a pickup by the school, but the angle is bad. No plates. Black pickup."

"That means we're nowhere." He rubbed his temples. "Let me know when you have any good news." He walked out, switching gears as he stepped into the elevator. He needed to focus on the operation this evening for now.

# CHAPTER 40

## EL PARAÍSO

*RON*

E l Paraíso, a club known for its vibrant ambiance and shady clientele, was revving up for the evening activity when the team arrived. Ron, along with his team, sat in an unmarked van, monitoring the operation. Ana and Hernandez went inside minutes ago. Thumping music echoed through the agents' mics, and colorful lights flashed in their pinhole cameras.

The two agents split up to cover more ground, each slipping into their assumed roles. Ana's elegance and confident demeanor made her the perfect high roller, while Hernandez, with his rugged looks, blended in as a supplier.

She navigated the crowd while maintaining a nonchalant exterior and ordered a drink at the bar. Soon, a man who matched Nunez's description—suave, with a predatory charm— approached her.

"I haven't seen you before," the man said.

She turned to him, smiling. "A friend suggested this place to do some business."

Good. Ron exhaled. The guy's resemblance to their target didn't escape her notice.

"Yeah? Who's this friend?"

"Marco, you know him?" She sipped her club soda, the movement blurring their visual contact through the camera.

"Ah, Marco, yes." The guy leaned closer. "So what kind of business are we talking about?"

"High stakes." Her tone drifted through the mic, soft and suggestive. "I have a keen interest in lucrative ventures."

The man cocked his head, his interest clearly piqued. "You've come to the right place. I might have what you're looking for."

She kept the conversation flowing.

Meanwhile, Hernandez had made his way to the back room under the guise of discussing supply details. His camera spotted an imposing figure overseeing the operations—Frankie. No mistaking his presence, not when the man exuded authority and danger.

Ron held his breath as Hernandez approached, keeping casual. "Marco told me this was the place for quality supplies. I'm looking to make some connections."

Frankie traced a finger along the scar running from his ear to his chin. Maybe it was a habitual gesture, or maybe it was meant to be intimidating. "Depends on what you're offering and what you're asking for."

"Top-notch stuff and discretion," Hernandez replied.

Back in the main area, Ana kept things going, letting them glean as much as possible. Her contact talked about his operations, but dropped subtle hints that linked him to organized crime activities.

"Let's just say my connections can open doors for you." The man locked his gaze on her.

"This is Nunez." Ron spoke into the mic.

She touched her ear to indicate she heard him. "I'm always

interested in expanding my network. Maybe we can discuss this in a more private setting?"

The man smiled and raised his glass, indicating he liked the idea. "Why not? Let's talk business."

As they moved to a quieter corner, Ron refocused on Hernandez's camera. The agent kept an eye on Frankie, his camera capturing the club's layout and multiple interactions.

Meanwhile, Ana's conversation with the man proved to be more challenging than they anticipated. Every attempt to steer the topic toward his boss was met with evasive or boastful responses. He carried himself with an air of arrogance, talking as if he was the one in charge, the top of the hierarchy.

While maintaining her composed persona, she finished her drink. "So, you're the man calling all the shots, then? No one above you?"

He braced both arms on the booth behind him, smirking. "That's right. I make the decisions. I'm the one people come to for business."

A commotion erupted near the back room—the distraction Hernandez was supposed to create. A fight had broken out.

Nunez's attention shifted. He stood, craning to see what was happening. "Excuse me for a moment."

As the man moved away, she enacted their backup plan. She plucked Nunez's phone from his coat pocket, connected a USB stick to the phone, and waited for the signal—a green light indicating the data transfer was complete.

Ron held his breath, his gaze switching between Ana's and Hernandez's camera footages. Would Nunez return? Would they have enough time?

The light turned green, his breath whooshed out, and she removed the stick, concealing it in her hand as Nunez returned.

With practiced ease, Ana slipped the phone back into his pocket. "Everything all right?"

He waved it off. "Just some idiots causing trouble. Now, where were we?"

She refocused the conversation, navigating around Nunez's bravado. They'd obtained something valuable with the data transfer, but trained agent that she was, she'd maintain the façade longer to avoid raising suspicion.

At last, she excused herself, and Ron shut down the footage as she approached the van.

"Got it." She tossed the USB stick to him and climbed in.

Hernandez followed her and shut the door behind them.

"Let's see what we've got." Ron slapped the bulkhead, signaling the driver, and the van pulled away.

# CHAPTER 41

## FEDERAL DETENTION CENTER

*ROOK*

As Rook entered the attorney visiting room, the Ghost sat at the steel table. After the guard closed the door, he pulled a file from his briefcase as props.

"Report," the Ghost ordered.

"About your plan to avenge Jade's death…" He scribbled gibberish on the legal pad. "Your plan is in play. May I make a suggestion?"

Her finger tapped once. A signal to continue.

"Since we can't turn Peters and Ruiz is a wild card, instead of executing them, it's better for them to suffer the loss of a loved one, much like you lost someone you cared about."

A slow, satisfied smile spread across the Ghost's face, a rare display of emotion. "I like your thinking. It's poetic justice indeed."

He stifled his relief. This was his plan all along. He'd gambled big that the Ghost would go for it. Now, her approval washed over him. "There's more. I've initiated a plan to flush out Phoenix."

The Ghost raised an eyebrow. "Phoenix? Tell me."

"Phoenix gave the US the intel about the antidote last year. It involved a young woman named Lily. I have her under surveillance and expect her to lead us to Phoenix."

The Ghost tilted her head, her expression contemplative. "I remember the girl. She is Olivia's and the senator's daughter. What makes you think she'll lead you to Phoenix?"

"Well, the girl brought the antidote here. Someone gave it to her. And I'm betting that someone is Phoenix. So, there's got to be a connection between her and Phoenix."

"Why would Phoenix still be in contact with her? He is probably still in Asia. That's what they do. They pass the intel—in this case, the antidote—to the courier and move on to their next job."

"Maybe." He continued to scribble. "He picked this girl for a reason. He could have some connection to the senator or her mom. His selecting her is too much of a coincidence."

The Ghost didn't say anything. Her steely eyes held steady, but she'd be thinking and plotting in that brain of hers. Finally, an almost imperceptible shift came, followed by the slightest tip of her head. "Do a deep dive on Olivia. I know they faked her death and hid her. But I've no idea what she's been doing all these years. And now, she shows up here. The way she carries herself… There's a chance she's law enforcement."

He searched through his memories. "If I'm not mistaken, she's a consultant with the FBI. Peters's task force. The one dedicated to you. And since you'll only speak with her, she's now part of it, I believe."

The Ghost lifted a hand as if to slap the table, glanced at the door, and lowered her hand soundlessly. "I know what she does now." Her tone called him a fool. "I want to know what she's done in the last twenty years. Do you have her dossier?"

He fidgeted, gave a subtle headshake.

"Well then, get to it. It would take a strong mother to willingly separate from her child for that long. Make it a priority."

"Yes, ma'am. Do you think this Olivia and Phoenix are connected?"

"I don't know. That's why you need to dig for more information. And what of the Martinez drug cartel?"

Martinez should have learned from Ray Ho's experience. Nobody went against the Ghost. Just because the Ghost was in detention, Ho wanted to retake his territory. Look what it got him —jail! And now, Martinez was foolish enough to try.

"They're still trying, but your task force is dealing with them."

"Good," the Ghost said, her voice cold. "Keep me posted."

As he walked out of the detention center, the tingling sensation of being watched enveloped him. He scanned the whole parking lot, the sky for drones, and the nearby terrain. Nothing seemed to be out of the ordinary. Maybe he was getting paranoid.

## OLIVIA

Olivia sat in her car parked down the street from the Federal Detention Center, her focus on the entrance, her mind a whirlwind. She'd arranged with the detention center to be alerted whenever the man using the fake O'Shea ID visited the Ghost. This time, she was ready for him. Beside her, Kevin sat in the passenger seat, his motorcycle nearby.

As expected, the man they were tracking emerged. Average in build and appearance, he appeared nothing remarkable at first glance, but she knew better. This man could lead them to crucial answers. He paused as he stepped outside. Kevin and she slid down in their seats to avoid being seen.

He got into his car and drove off, with her following. Kevin stepped out and started his motorcycle. He'd wait a couple of minutes, then head out in the same direction. They would do the same tail routine, switching off and on to avoid detection. The chase led them to the same house they'd surveilled before. The man parked in the garage, and just like before, no movement came from inside the house—as if he vanished into thin air.

Kevin's voice crackled through Olivia's earpiece. "He's done the same thing again. No sightings in the back of the house."

She kept her attention on the front, her instincts telling her something was amiss. "I don't see any movement here either."

"Let's check it out."

Kevin's restlessness spurred her on. Still, she hesitated. "We don't have jurisdiction, and we don't have probable cause for a warrant."

"Are you the same Phoenix I know?" he challenged, his tone half-mocking. "Since when have you started worrying about that?"

"Since I'm back stateside," she retorted. But her chest tightened. She wiggled in her seat, torn between her ingrained respect for the law and her deep-seated need for answers.

"Do you hear that?"

"Hear what?" She cocked her head, straining her ears. The street was quiet, save for the distant hum of city life.

"Moaning from inside the garage. Let's go."

She knew the trick well. He was fabricating the sound to justify their entry, but he'd piqued her curiosity. Together, they approached the garage, peering through the window on the garage door. It revealed nothing—just an empty space.

Moving to the side door, they made sure no one was watching while he picked the lock. The door swung open at a touch.

Inside the garage, a musty smell engulfed them. Tools and boxes cluttered the space but offered no sign of the man they had been following.

"Where did he go?" she whispered, scanning the room.

He pointed to a door into the house. "He must've gone inside. But how does he disappear every time?"

She approached the door, her senses heightened. Every instinct told her they were on the brink of uncovering something significant. She tried the handle—it was unlocked.

Weapons drawn, they entered a dimly lit hallway, the interior eerily quiet, the air stale. They moved cautiously, checking each room, but found nothing—no sign of life, no sign of the man they were tracking.

"Something doesn't add up." Kevin lowered his weapon to his side.

No kidding. The house felt abandoned, yet they'd seen the man enter. Where had he gone?

At the end of the hallway, they approached a door ajar. She pushed it open and stifled a gasp.

The room was a sophisticated surveillance hub, with multiple monitors displaying various locations, some of which were recognizably parts of the city. In the center of the room was a chair and a set of controls.

"This is it." Low and soft, she breathed out the words, half hesitant to voice them. "He's watching us."

Kevin approached one of the monitors, his eyes narrowing. "He's been surveilling the whole city. But why? What is he looking for?"

Her mind was racing to connect the dots. "Phoenix, the antidote intel, the cartel—it's all linked. He's been watching everyone connected to the case."

"Who is this guy?"

"And where did he disappear to?"

# CHAPTER 42

## TASK FORCE OFFICE

*RON*

It wasn't usual for Deanna not to return his call. Frowning, Ron walked by the squad room. "Hernandez, have you heard from Deanna?"

"Er, no, boss. The director, uh, deputy director is having her work on something, I think." The agent stared at his computer screen, fingers typing on the keyboard.

"Has she analyzed the USB we brought back?" Ron stepped closer to Hernandez.

The young agent glanced at him. "Um, that's what I'm doing, boss. She started to, but the deputy director—"

"Right, she got pulled." He sighed. What did Vera want now? What was so important? He spun on his heels, heading to the lab to find out.

As the sliding door opened, Deanna's voice drifted out. "I'm going as fast as I can, Deputy Director. If you let José help—"

"No, this is sensitive."

"Okay, but twenty-some years, I'll need a whole lot of

assignments to fill her file." The tech's fingers flew over the keyboard.

"Make most of them classified. Then you don't need to invent so many cases."

He cleared his throat. The swooshing sound of the sliding door should have alerted them, but they must be too focused.

Vera faced him. "We need to give you a bell."

At the same time, Deanna turned around, her eyes wide. "Er, sorry, I forgot to lock the door."

"Just keep going," the deputy director said.

"Want to tell me what's going on?" He stepped closer to the analyst or tried to. Vera kept moving to block his view.

"Vera—uh, Deputy Director—what's going on? Whose file is she working on?"

Vera seemed to be having an internal debate. Then she sighed. "Ms. Swanson, lock the door."

The analyst clicked a button to lock it.

"This goes nowhere." Vera tilted her head to the inner office. He followed her as she slid behind Deanna's desk, her amber eyes hooded and framed in the familiar circles of sleepless nights. "A source alerted me that someone was looking into Olivia's background. We cannot let anyone find out she's Phoenix."

He clattered over a nearby chair and sat. "I thought she had a whole backstory set up."

"Yes, for her legend, her cover, Jade. But not for Olivia. Remember Olivia is dead to the world?"

His temples throbbed. He slowed his breathing. Right, the CIA faked her death. Olivia Tso was dead, but lived on as Jade. Recently, Jade retired from active spook assignment, and Olivia Tso "resurrected." Except for a handful of people with proper clearance, nobody knew about her. In fact, to hide her identity further, she'd be taking Simon's name once they married.

"Ah, so now that she's resurfaced, you need to explain where she's been the last couple decades," he reasoned. "Who's your source?"

She maintained a poker face. "Never mind who it is. We still cannot let anyone find out the truth. So, I'm having Ms. Swanson build Olivia a backstory."

"You aren't gonna have her as a CIA officer?"

"No." She took her reading glasses off and massaged her temples as if she'd caught his headache. "That's the tricky part. She wasn't a citizen until later. And that was part of her—never mind. But I had to fudge the dates a bit. I'm betting nobody will check the official documents. Anyway, no, the story will say she joined the FBI after college—I had to invent that part too—and worked mostly classified ops."

"As long as whoever's checking her out isn't thorough enough to verify everything, she should be good." At least Vera was looking out for Olivia.

"That's the hope. In any case, a lot of her files are classified. So, whoever tries to dig will need to jump through the hoops. And speaking of, I need to speak with her." She stood up, signaling the end of their conversation.

"I can arrange that." He stood as well.

"Deanna, let me know as soon as it's completed." Vera headed toward the elevator.

"Yes, ma'am," the tech genius responded as they walked out.

"Oh, hi, boss." Tanner came out of the stairway, holding an evidence bag with a laptop.

His senior agent followed his gaze and spoke before he asked. "It's Mitchell's laptop. Detective Spaulding agreed to let us process it, much to his partner's dismay. I told him we could get it done quicker. And we probably have better programs."

"Good, but you may have to wait till Deanna's done with her project. Hopefully, it won't take her long." When Tanner raised his hands to activate the sensor, Ron took pity. "It's locked. She's working on something urgent."

"What's so urgent? I thought this and Martinez were our priority."

"Don't ask." Ron pressed the up button. "Wanna run back up or ride the elevator?"

Tanner glanced at the stairs and the open elevator. "I'll ride." He stepped inside. "So, what's she working on?"

"Didn't I say, 'don't ask'? Did Spaulding say anything else?"

"They traced his last movements. He met with some unsavory characters. Facial rec came back on a couple of them. Known associates of the Martinez cartel."

The door opened to the squad room. They stepped out. "That doesn't sound good."

"Not at all."

"Hernandez is busy right now. And Kyle has his own problem. You need to take over digging into Doug's finances. Check the travels first. That's troubling. Laundering money wouldn't need him to travel that much and lie about it."

"Yeah, boss."

Ron headed to Hernandez. Ana was hovering behind him, reading the screen. Ron gripped the back of Hernandez's chair. "Found anything?"

The young agent looked up. "Yeah."

"Beam it up." Ana straightened up and faced the big screen.

Hernandez tapped some keys until text messages showed up on the big screen.

Ana used the pointer to highlight a particular thread. "See this? Who do you think he's communicating with?"

Ron read the texts. The last one clinched it. "It's Martinez. The last line, 'Sí, jefe.' Nunez would only say, yes, boss, to the boss, Martinez."

"So, now we have the connection between Nunez and Martinez." With a satisfactory smile, she sank back in her chair and tapped a pen against the edge of her desk.

"Only if I can trace the phone number," Hernandez said. "It's likely a burner."

"It's something." Ron massaged his left temple. "Keep digging. There may be intel other than who he's communicating with."

Hernandez winked. "Sí, jefe."

Ron started back to his office before Ana's soft voice stopped him. "Everything okay?"

He sighed, running a hand over his face. "Just too many things going on and not enough hours in a day."

"Where's Kyle? Tanner said he was reassigned. What happened?" She walked alongside him.

He explained the hit order found in Doug's throat and detailed the inclusion of Kyle's and Grace Benson's pictures. As he named Grace Benson, her face drained of color, her usual composure faltering.

"What's wrong?" His chest tightened at her reaction.

She took a couple of deep breaths, her gaze darting around to ensure they were alone in his office. "Let me see that picture, please."

He frowned, hesitated, but tapped his phone, swiped to the enhanced image, and showed her.

She sucked in a breath. "She's my daughter."

At her voice, barely above a whisper, the floor seemingly dropped out from under him. He'd known her for years and had no idea. "I–I didn't know," he stammered.

"It was a long time ago, and I was just a kid." She fixed her gaze on the phone. "I wasn't ready to be a mom then. I couldn't give her the life she deserved."

Understanding dawned on him. "Look, you don't owe me any explanation. So, you gave her up for adoption, but you've kept tabs on her."

"Yes." She nodded, and he tried not to react to her obvious regret and longing. "It wasn't an open adoption, but I know who adopted her. They're good people. I don't know if she knows me. She may know of me. I've always hoped she might want to connect, but she never has."

He leaned back in his chair, the puzzle pieces forming a chilling picture. "She's in protective custody now, so she's safe. But the question remains—Why was she targeted?"

Her eyes widened, a gasp escaping her lips. "Are you seeing what I'm seeing?"

He frowned, not following her train of thought.

"Your son and my daughter." Her finger tracked a line between them.

He sucked in a sharp breath, the realization striking him with full force. "But who knows she's your daughter?"

She shook her head. "Nobody that I know of. But, you know, if someone with enough resources is determined enough, they can find out anything. I did disclose it when they did the security clearance check, but they consider it a private matter."

"Still, there would be a note somewhere."

"But why? Why would someone target our kids to get at us? Assuming that's what they're doing."

# CHAPTER 43

## MIRROR ESTATE

*DYLAN*

Even though Dylan had his own apartment in town, he visited the estate often. This was where he learned the truth about his mother's family. Sometimes, the truth came with a burden. Knowing his grandmother was getting on in years, he couldn't just walk away from her. His mother would have wanted him to carry on the legacy. So, here he was at Mirror Estate.

As he entered the drawing room, his grandmother greeted him warmly. Despite her age, she exuded a formidable energy. Not that long ago, she had been plagued with aches and pains and heart problems, but since he came to live with her and work at M&M Enterprises, her health had been on the upswing.

"How's your day?" She lay down the magazine she was reading.

"It's good."

"You still like development?"

Settling into the armchair, he nodded. It was the type of work he liked. Although she wanted him to move up to the management team, the sooner the better, he wasn't ready yet.

"The new marketing strategies are paying off." He crossed one leg over the other and smoothed down his slacks. "We're seeing a significant increase in bookings."

She listened, her eyes sharp. "And how are you finding the business? Is it everything you hoped for?"

He hesitated, thinking of the hidden map and cipher. But those had nothing to do with the business. "It's challenging, but I'm learning a lot. Every day brings something new."

They chatted until dinner was served. When she steered the conversation from business to personal matters, particularly his relationship with Lily, he navigated the topic, not wanting to delve into their relationship.

After dinner, he went to his room to research the old photos and clippings he found. The map was a foregone conclusion since it wasn't the full map, and he didn't have a decoder. He wasn't giving up though, just putting it aside for now.

He didn't know how long he had been looking at the photos, trying to put names on faces. Someday, he'd have to ask his grandmother, but not just yet. His phone buzzed with a text from Olivia. Her inquiry about Lily caught him off guard.

He typed a response, telling her Lily wasn't with him and he'd dropped her off at Rain Tree LLC earlier.

His gut churned. Just why would she ask about Lily so late? He sent another message, asking if everything was all right.

A little later, he was getting into bed when his phone buzzed again—a message from Olivia, reassuring him but asking to be informed if he heard from Lily. He agreed, then stretched out in bed, the day's events replayed in his mind. He was drifting off to sleep when two pop-pops echoed in his mind. He jerked awake. Was that a dream? His mind had to be playing tricks on him. He'd dropped Lily off. Then a motorcycle sped by. Anything else must've been a dream.

The next morning, Dylan pulled into the parking lot of M&M Enterprises, his mind clouded. He hadn't slept well, Lily's safety churning in his mind. A sense of unease had settled over him, exacerbated by Lily's lack of response to his text message. And of course, the text from Olivia.

Stepping out of his car, he approached the building connected to the Marino Hotel that housed the enterprise offices. The morning sun cast long shadows on the pavement, mirroring the shadows in his heart. He'd stop by her office first. But her office was empty, the chair at her desk unoccupied, her computer screen dark. The sight deepened his worry.

Turning to his own office, he ran into Tommy in the corridor. "Have you heard from Lily?"

Tommy cocked his head. "No, why? What's going on?"

Dylan filled him in on her visit to Rain Tree LLC. "I heard some commotion as I was driving away, but when I circled back, I didn't see her anywhere and dismissed it."

Tommy's usually jocular expression turned serious. "Check with her mom."

Dylan dialed Olivia's number as they grabbed coffee from the staff lounge room.

She answered right away, her voice carrying an urgency that matched his own. She and Simon were downstairs, on their way to see him.

His heart sank. This couldn't be good.

He hurried back to his office, Tommy in tow, and waited for them. When they entered, he repeated his account of the previous evening.

Olivia's smooth features tautened. "Remember, her car was sabotaged. And now she's missing." She kept her voice steady, but a glimmer in her eyes revealed her fear. "I should have followed up on that the other night."

"Well, she's an adult," Simon said. "She did text she might be late coming home."

"And that was—never mind." Olivia kept swiping on her phone as if that would summon Lily.

The knot tightened in Dylan's stomach. Tommy looked like he wanted to add something but hesitated. "What is it, Tommy?"

After a moment's reluctance, his buddy spoke. "Have you asked Kyle?"

A rush of bile soured Dylan's mouth, the mention of Kyle heating his blood.

But Olivia spoke up. "Yes, I did. Ron says he's in protective custody. No contact with anyone."

"Why?" Tommy stood up straighter.

"Later." She waved his question away. "We need to check out Rain Tree LLC. Dylan, can you give me the address?"

He recited the details.

"I can't go right now. Need to see the deputy director, but I can meet you there a little later." She stood up and turned to her fiancé. "I'll text you."

"What in the world is going on?" Tommy exclaimed.

"I don't know, but"—Simon tilted his head toward Olivia's retreating figure—"she'll find her."

Dylan didn't doubt that. However, in the back of his mind, a figure kept appearing, taunting him, daring him to defy her wish. Would she be responsible again?

# CHAPTER 44

## THE MITCHELL RESIDENCE

*SHEILA*

Sheila walked into her house and nearly staggered, struck by the sheer magnitude of the chaos. The kitchen and surrounding area looked like they'd been hit by a tornado. A jumble of overturned furniture, scattered papers, and a layer of dust seemed to touch every surface of her once pristine and orderly space. She stood in the doorway, distress physically paining her over the devastation of her former sanctuary.

Upon Zimmerman's recommendation, she'd contacted a licensed cleaning company, one specializing in post-crime-scene cleanup. They were due to arrive this afternoon to restore some semblance of order. And of course, she needed to start the daunting task of making funeral arrangements. With suspicion still shrouding her, maybe she should wait till the nightmare was over before having a service for him.

The doorbell rang.

Thinking it was Simon, she opened the door to find Kim, a neighbor down the street, with Skippy in her arms.

"Skippy!"

"I found him the other day in our backyard." The neighbor presented the cat. "Tried to return him a couple of times, but there was some crime-scene tape here. I heard something about Doug being killed. Is that true? Robbery gone bad?"

Sheila was going to let the cat roam, but the place was a disaster. She got hold of the cat to put him in a room. "Yes and no. Anyway, I can't talk about it now. I'm sorry. And thank you for taking care of Skippy."

"Sure. No problem. You take care now. Just holler if you need anything," Kim offered before turning to leave.

Sheila started to close the door but stopped as Simon's car pulled in with Ron's. She hurried to the guest room, secured the cat inside, then raced back down to the front door.

"Come on in." She greeted the trio, Ana in tow, and stepped aside to let them in. "I must warn you. It's a mess. I called the cleaning company. They're coming this afternoon."

"That's okay." Ron went directly to the front room, away from the kitchen area. "Maybe we should talk here."

They all followed him. She gestured for them to sit on the teal accent chairs or the suede couch. "I'd offer you drinks, but I'm not sure if anything here's still good."

They declined her offer. She sat in a chair, Ron on the couch, Ana in the other chair, Simon standing. "I can't stay," Simon said. "We wanted to update you on a development in the case. And, well, we were hoping you might shed some light on it. I'll let Ron and Ana take over. I'll call you."

Then he left.

"Okay?" Sheila eyed them. Why the seriousness?

"We found something… unsettling." Ron rubbed his hands up and down his thighs, wrinkling up his slacks. She'd forgotten how much unnecessary ironing he'd created. "A hit order with Kyle's and another young woman's picture was discovered in Doug's throat."

A *what?* And did he say throat? Her hand flew to her chest, but a gasp still escaped. "A hit order? In his throat?"

Ana's dark eyes gleamed during her solemn nod. "The woman's name is Grace Benson. Have you ever heard of her?"

Sheila shook her head, her heartbeat kicking up beneath her palm. "I've never heard that name. I can't believe Doug would be involved in something like this. And why would Kyle be a target?"

Ron leaned forward, all business. "That's what we're trying to figure out. Whoever is behind this might have had some interaction with Doug that you weren't aware of."

She fumbled with the buttons beneath her hand, her fingers shaking and her heartbeat racing. "But Doug never mentioned anyone named Grace Benson. And he certainly never gave me any indication that he was involved in… in"—she waved a hand in the air, gesturing toward where she'd found his body—"whatever this is."

"We're not suggesting you should have known. These types of things are often well hidden."

Ana exhaled. When she spoke, she kept her voice steady. "It's possible Doug's involvement in whatever led to his death was deeper and more complex than we initially thought."

Sheila sighed, shivering under a sense of helplessness. "This house, our life… it all feels like a lie now. I don't understand any of it."

Ron's expression softened. He braced his elbows on his knees and laced his fingers by his chin. "We're doing everything we can to piece this together. The discovery of this hit order has given the investigation a new direction. We didn't think it had anything to do with you, but we're covering our bases."

She nodded, trying to process the enormity. "If anything— anything at all—comes to mind that might help, I'll let you know. But right now, I'm as in the dark as you are."

"Can you tell us about his travels?" Ron rested his chin on his hands.

"Like I told the detectives, he would go to London and Paris for real estate conferences. But the detectives said there was no conference on his last trip to London. I just don't know anymore."

"Would it be all right if I looked at Doug's personal items?" Ana stood up, followed by Ron.

"Of course." Sheila pointed toward the kitchen. "His office is on the other side of the kitchen. And our bedroom is upstairs. First door on the left."

They mustn't have found anything in the office. There was no commotion. Now, the two went to the master and searched there.

Meanwhile, Sheila began tidying up other areas. She avoided the kitchen, the memories too raw, too fresh. Instead, she focused on the living room, her movements mechanical, her mind elsewhere.

She paused, her gaze on Doug's favorite recliner. It sat there, innocuous, a silent witness to the man who once occupied it. "Who was he?" she whispered to the empty room.

The man she had loved, had he been a stranger all along?

Why did he have a hit list in his throat?

The questions swirled in her head like leaves in a storm. She tried to recall the day it happened. Was Doug nervous? Did he have that piece of paper with him?

But he'd been out of town. She'd found him home early.

There was no unexplained phone call. It was just an ordinary day, until it wasn't.

# CHAPTER 45

## THE MITCHELL RESIDENCE

*ANA*

Ana paused in the doorway of a spacious, tastefully decorated master bedroom, with a king bed dominating the center and a walk-in closet and en suite bathroom adding to its grandeur. She started with the bed, feeling around the edges and pushing her hands deep into the mattress, searching for any anomalies.

"I'll take the bathroom," Ron called.

"Okay." Finding nothing beneath the bed or within the mattress folds, she shifted to the dresser. The drawers were neatly organized, each containing an assortment of Doug's clothing. One by one, she opened them, inspected their contents, and shut them when nothing unusual caught her attention.

However, as she closed the bottom drawer, a frown creased her brow. Something felt off. She opened the drawer again, her hands moving through the clothing. The drawer seemed shallower than the others.

She dumped the clothing, tossing it onto the bed. "Ron! I've found a false bottom."

He hurried over.

She was taking pictures of the dresser and drawer in situ. She handed him her phone. "Here, record it."

He started the recording with her announcing the date, time, their names, and other pertinent information. Then she pulled at a string on the side of the drawer. The board lifted, revealing a hidden compartment.

Inside, multiple passports bore Doug's photo over different names.

Ron let out a low whistle. "Looks like we've hit the jackpot."

She lifted the passports, examining each one. "How deep does this go?"

He stopped the recording, leaned closer, scanning the various identities Doug had assumed. "This is more than living a double life. This is… this is something else."

They stood there, the gravity of their discovery hanging in the air.

Then he broke the silence. "We need to get these to the team. See if they can trace any of these identities."

She nodded and placed the passports in evidence bags. "Whoever Doug was, he was deeply embedded in something."

"He was more than a real estate developer. Tanner is working on his travel history. This will help."

"The detectives didn't search the house. Can you believe it?" Ana packed up the evidence bags and was ready to go.

"They had no reason to think he was anything but a business-man. Of course, after the discovery of the kill order, Spaulding is looking at this differently." Ron followed her out of the room.

"This still doesn't explain why they target our kids if we're the ultimate targets."

"We need to find out who he really was."

She couldn't agree more.

※

### *RON*

As Ron and Ana prepared to leave, Detectives Spaulding and Monnin arrived. Caught off guard, Ron frowned as the detectives scanned them, then Sheila, who looked equally surprised.

Spaulding broke the silence, his gaze shifting between Ron and Ana. "What are you two doing here?"

Ron stepped forward. "We came here with her attorney to update her on the case." He'd only reveal the necessary details. "And now, if you don't mind me asking, what brings you back here?"

The stocky detective exchanged a glance with his partner before responding. "We wanted to take another look at the crime scene."

Ana raised an eyebrow, and Ron caught her glance. Detectives seldom revisited a released crime scene. "I thought you were finished with your investigation here? The house was released back to Sheila."

Running a hand over his graying hair, Spaulding shrugged. "We didn't know what we know now."

Monnin, who had been observing the exchange, stepped forward, her nearly six-foot frame towering over her partner. "It seems this case is more complicated than a simple murder."

"I thought we had an understanding," Spaulding said. "What have you found? Care to share? I let you have the laptop."

"We do have something." Ron then briefed the detectives on the discovery of multiple passports, each with a different identity.

Spaulding whistled, and Monnin's expression turned thoughtful. "That puts a new spin on things." She started taking pictures of the passports. "Looks like Doug Mitchell was more than just a businessman."

"I had no idea about any of this." Sheila slumped back onto

the couch, frowning at the recliner across the room. "Doug kept so much hidden from me."

It looked like they weren't leaving anytime soon. Sheila was clueless as far as Doug was concerned. Ron told her to carry on with what she was doing. If they needed her, he'd find her. Now that the detectives knew about the passports, they'd be looking at this case differently. There were just too many angles to investigate this. Was Doug in with the cartel? Or was he simply laundering cash for them? Was he a hit man?

And most importantly, why did he have the kill order in his throat?

"What's that about? I heard that was your son's photo. Why didn't you say something?" Spaulding's voice jolted Ron back to the present.

"At the morgue, I wasn't sure. It was only confirmed when our tech got it cleaned up."

"And who's that—what's the girl's name, Bennet?" Monnin asked.

"Benson. Grace Benson." Ana glanced at him. "We have a theory."

"Which is?" Monnin prompted.

They exchanged another glance. He left it up to her. It was her story to tell, if she wanted to.

She took a breath, widened her stance. "We believe we're the ultimate targets."

Spaulding frowned, the expression drawing his stern features even tighter. "How do you figure?"

"Grace is my daughter." Ana let out a long breath. "I'm not sure if she knows, but I believe whoever took out the hit knows."

Nobody said anything. Monnin opened her mouth, then shut it. Spaulding gave in to the urge to inspect his nails.

"So, anyway," Ana continued, "our theory is that whoever did this wants to hurt us badly."

"What a sadistic nutjob!" Monnin mumbled.

"But why? Did you two collar someone? Now, the son is seeking revenge. Something like that?" Spaulding's deep frown lines were showing again.

"We don't know yet," Ron said. "We've got one big enemy. The Ghost."

"But isn't she in jail?"

"She can do a lot, even in jail. Anyway, they're both in protective custody now." Time to steer the discussion back on course. "Let's get back to Doug."

They shared what they learned so far and compared notes. In the end, Ron would take the passports back to the task force office. It would help Tanner with Doug's travel history. The detectives would continue chasing other leads, such as his businesses, as well as known associates of the cartel who were seen with Doug. They needed to find out who the real Doug Mitchell had been.

# CHAPTER 46

## TASK FORCE OFFICE

*OLIVIA*

Olivia walked into the warehouse, aka task force office. Nobody would have guessed this building—appearing decrepit on the outside—housed their elite task force. Apparently, Deputy Director Vera Haskin commandeered Ron's office. Olivia was told to head to their office. As she stepped through the door, the solemnity in Haskin's eyes struck, as did a certain charge in the air. As invited, she took her seat across from the deputy director. Why had she been summoned here?

Without preamble, Haskin leaned forward. "Phoenix, someone is digging into your past. Let me clarify, Olivia's past." As the words hit like a cold wave, sending shivers down Olivia's spine, Haskin continued. "Yes, I'm one of the few who know."

"Olivia Tso is dead to the world. Who's looking into my past?"

"Exactly. I understand you've been looking into the leak. So, I can only assume whoever notified the Ghost of your presence here is the one doing the digging now. Why now? I don't know. How did they know? I don't know either."

"What do you need me to do?" She was ready to be activated again, if necessary.

"Relax." Haskin held up a hand. "I've had Ms. Swanson working on your backstory. Your legend, Jade, has a solid cover story, but when the CIA faked your death, that was supposed to be the end of it. When you decided to retire, or at least out of the covert op, nobody thought about giving you a backstory. Where have you been all these years, what have you been doing, etc.? So, here's what I came up with. Olivia Tso joined the Bureau after college, I know, I know, it's an embellishment. You've been an agent ever since, most of your assignments classified. Pretty close to the truth. Now, you're gonna have to come up with a reason for wanting to fake your death."

She nodded, absorbing the information. As they said, the best lie was based on the truth. As for her death, though... "How about my relationship with Simon? My folks weren't keen on me dating foreigners in general. So, how about we use that? Say they would disown me or something like that. And then, of course, I got pregnant before getting married. That would add to the humiliation."

Haskin tipped her head to one side and tapped a finger on her chin. "Well, we could use that. Work with Ms. Swanson to get something in your file. Classified. Honestly, I don't think it's a big deal. I doubt anyone would check the reason for that, but you never know. Better to be prepared."

She then slid a USB drive across the desk. "This contains everything Ms. Swanson has so far. Study it, memorize it. And make sure your family understands the seriousness."

Olivia picked up the drive, her fingers brushing against the cold metal. "Yes, ma'am. I'll get with Deanna to hash it all out."

The deputy director nodded, signaling the meeting was over.

Olivia stood. Deanna already had the bulk of it done. This could wait. Her mind went to her daughter. Once she found Lily and assured her safety, she'd tackle this problem. *Who are you? You want to play? Well, let's play!*

A little later, she met Simon and Dylan at Rain Tree LLC. Dylan, insistent on being involved, led the way, pointing out where he had dropped Lily off the previous day. The building housing Rain Tree LLC was nondescript, blending in with the other structures on the busy street.

As they entered the office, a young woman at the reception desk, absorbed in her phone, looked up and offered a polite hello.

"Good morning." Olivia took the lead. "We're looking for information about a visitor who had an appointment here yesterday afternoon. Lily Roth?"

The receptionist, identified by her name tag as Missy, frowned. "Nobody came by yesterday afternoon for any appointment."

Dylan stepped forward. "You called Lily for an appointment. You're Missy, right?"

Missy's eyes grew wide, shifted her gaze to the phone. "No, I didn't call anyone named Lily for an appointment. And I don't remember anyone coming by."

"You're lying." Olivia gritted her teeth. Simon's hand touched her, likely to restrain her. "You lured her here. Why?"

"I, uh, well, Trent, uh, asked me to make the call. I don't know anything. It doesn't matter. She didn't show anyway."

"That would be Trent Lockwood?" Dylan clarified.

When Missy nodded, Olivia looked around for cameras, finding none. She gestured for the others to follow her.

"How'd you know she was lying?" Dylan raced to be at her side.

"The way she answered the questions."

Once on the street, she pointed to a security camera across the road. "We should canvas the area. Ask the storekeepers if they saw anything. I'll go check that camera footage."

Flashing her Federal ID badge, she gained access to the camera footage from a nearby store. Within moments, Dylan came running back, Simon close behind. "The shopkeepers heard some commotion, like I did," Dylan reported, out of breath. "But nobody saw anything. Somebody called 911, though, and the cops were here."

"We can get the police report." Simon slid his phone out, probably hoping Ron would get him the report.

"Let's check the footage first," she told them.

The grainy images showed the episode unfolding—a motorcyclist passing by, a gun with what appeared to be a silencer, and a figure tackling Lily to the ground.

Olivia studied the footage closely, her years of training helping her piece together the scene. "They didn't wait around too long after the incident. Split just before the cops showed up." She clenched her fists, pivoting to eye the spot before the building. "But where did they go? And who is this guy? Is he protecting her, or is he a threat?"

They stood there, watching the footage again, trying to glean additional details they might have missed. The motorcyclist was too blurry to make out any defining features, and the Good Samaritan's face was never visible to the camera.

Simon crossed his arms, stepping back. "This is like looking for a needle in a haystack."

"We need to find Lily." Dylan slammed a fist against his thigh. "And find out who this guy is. He could be our only lead to her whereabouts."

Olivia paced, already formulating their next steps as her heeled boots clicked across the tiled floor. "We'll need to widen the search."

As they stepped out of the store, the bustling city street engulfed them. Her phone buzzed in her pocket, drawing her attention away from the conversation. She stilled as the secure line from Jay lit her display. Her heart skipped a beat—calls from Jay were never ordinary.

She excused herself from the men, stepping away to a quieter spot near an alleyway. She went through the required security protocol to answer the call.

"I knew you wouldn't believe a text. Lily is safe," came the familiar voice as soon as she picked up.

She let out a gasp. "How?" He had to have been monitoring the area via store and street cameras. "You have her?"

"Come see me. Alone. And don't disclose anything just yet." The words issued rapid-fire, his voice heavy with unspoken urgency.

She sucked in a sharp breath. How did he get involved? Why was he contacting her about this? And what did he mean by "alone"? She knew better than to ask over the phone.

Instead, she kept her voice steady despite her turmoil. "I'll be there."

Ending the call, she turned back to Simon and Dylan, cautious about what she disclosed. "I have to go." Again, she kept her tone neutral. "Something's come up. Keep me updated on anything you find."

Simon gave her a searching look, smart enough to sense she wasn't saying something. "Everything all right?"

She nodded, masking her anxiety with a practiced ease. "Yes. Just another lead I need to follow up on. Stay safe, both of you."

As she walked away, her mind sped to the meeting with Jay. The relief that Lily was safe warred with the apprehension about the circumstances as she drove to the discreet meeting location.

Who was the guy who saved Lily? If Jay knew she was safe, the Good Samaritan must be one of Jay's operatives. But how did he know to watch Lily? So many questions!

⁕

## *DYLAN*

"What just happened?" Dylan watched Olivia's retreating figure.

Simon shrugged. "My guess is she's been summoned."

"By whom?"

"Never mind. She'll let us know if it's related to Lily. Let's head back."

Dylan walked with Simon. "I'll go do some sleuthing at the office."

"I'll do some checking on my own. She was looking into two LLCs, I believe." Simon pressed his key fob to unlock the door.

They rode here together, so Dylan got in the passenger seat. "Yes, Rain Tree LLC and New Life LLC."

"I'll drop you off and be back home to do some research." Simon started the car.

A little later, Dylan made his way to Janet Reardon's office, each step echoing in the silent corridor. As he entered, Janet looked up.

"Janet, I need information about two accounts: Rain Tree LLC and New Life LLC. Lily had concerns about them."

She paused, her fingers resting on the keyboard. "She did report those companies to me. She thought their activities were suspicious. Irregular booking patterns. They reserved blocks of rooms and then canceled them, but we always received payment. It's not uncommon for companies with headquarters elsewhere to have minimal local staff, but she felt something was off."

Right. Tommy had said Lily's boss didn't take her concern seriously. Dylan's frown deepened.

"Someone from Rain Tree LLC came to see her the other day." Janet's voice cut into his thoughts.

"That would be Trent Lockwood?"

She avoided his gaze but nodded. "I do believe so."

Something about this didn't sit right. He thanked her and

went to the accounting department. He found Tommy at his desk, head swiveling between two monitors. "Hey, got a second?"

Tommy stopped what he was doing and rubbed his eyes before rolling back his chair. "Sure, what's up? Have you found Lily?"

When Dylan tilted his head toward the hallway, his buddy got up and followed him outside. Dylan then recounted what the footage showed, Olivia's sudden departure, and Janet's comments. "You mentioned something about money-laundering code or something like that."

"Anti-money-laundering regulations," Tommy supplied. "I told Lily about that. Why Janet wouldn't do anything, I can't say."

"Okay. Unless you're doing something urgent, please check out those two companies—their bookings, cancellations, billings. Report anything suspicious to Gene." Gene was the EAM, executive assistant manager.

"I can do it. I can access the financial side, but I don't have access to the bookings and cancellations."

"I'll call IT to authorize you. Thanks, bro." Dylan started to walk away.

"Where you going?"

"I need to make a couple phone calls, and I need to see her."

"Wait a minute." Tommy grabbed his arm. "You aren't going to see your aunt."

Dylan turned back. "She's involved somehow. What if she took Lily because I wouldn't cooperate? You said it sounded like money laundering—I know, I know, you haven't checked yet. But if it is, then the companies could well be in cahoots with the Ghost. After all, it's the Marino Hotel. Once upon a time, this was the front of the criminal enterprise. They used the hotel to wash everything."

Tommy sighed. "All right. Just be careful."

"I will." Dylan rounded a corner toward his office. First, he called IT to grant Tommy access. Then he called the corporate lawyer to make the arrangement for him to see his aunt in the Federal Detention Center.

"Just tell them it's her nephew. I'm on the list. Trust me." He rocked back on his heels, bouncing out excess energy. "She'll see me."

Once Zimmerman's assistant agreed, Dylan dropped into the chair behind his desk, replaying everything. When it came to his conversation with Janet, something felt off about the woman. Coupling that with her reluctance to take Lily's suspicions seriously, he decided to look into Janet himself. The employees were all supposed to have gone through some background check, but it was basic, minimal stuff.

After looking up the number, he made a call to an outside security firm on retainer. "I need a comprehensive background check on someone—Janet Reardon, our director of sales and marketing. I want to know everything—her financials, her history, and her significant relationships or affiliations. Anything out of the ordinary."

The person cleared their throat. "Understood, Mr. Roche. We'll begin our investigation immediately and keep you informed of our findings."

After ending the call, he requested her personnel file from HR. As he waited, he rested his head against the back of his chair and closed his eyes. Was Janet directly involved, or was she a pawn in a larger scheme? His gut feeling said something was amiss, and he trusted that feeling.

When he received her file, he pored over it. Her employment record was exemplary, with commendations and positive evaluations. On paper, she was the model employee. But appearances could be deceiving.

His phone buzzed with a message. The Ghost would see him.

# CHAPTER 47

## THE ROTH RESIDENCE

*SIMON*

Since returning home from dropping off Dylan, Simon had been lost in thought, replaying the footage in his mind. Lily had mentioned two companies, and her boss wasn't taking her suspicions seriously. Now, someone shot at her. Who was the Good Samaritan? Was she safe?

Only a few months ago, he'd discovered he had a daughter, Lily. After their joyful, albeit awkward, reunion, he'd committed to making up for the years lost, to building a bridge over the chasm of time. Now, the fear of losing her again clawed at his heart. He couldn't endure that. Yet, he trusted in Olivia. She'd move mountains to find their daughter.

He slid out his cell phone and put a call through to her.

When his attempt to contact her failed, his anxiety only deepened.

Minutes later, his phone dinged, a simple text.

Lily is safe. Keep it to yourself. Later.

Waves of relief washed over him, melting the chill around his heart. He inhaled, drawing in a sense of calm, then stood up from his cluttered desk, his thoughts now shifting to another worry—Sheila. She hadn't been charged yet, and his gut told him she wouldn't be.

In the kitchen, he prepared a fresh cup of coffee to clear his head, then stilled, his attention captured by an out-of-place item—Olivia's notepad left next to the espresso machine. How unusual for Olivia, known for her meticulousness, to leave her notes exposed.

He picked it up and flipped through it, slowing to decipher her handwriting—a complex blend of rapid shorthand and cryptic annotations. Probably why she didn't mind leaving it lying around. He wouldn't understand anyway. But while most of the notes were a puzzle, one name leapt out—Silver Fox.

The name stirred dormant memories. His late mentor, Rifkin, had once spoken of Silver Fox in hushed tones, often in connection with the Ghost. Rifkin had left behind a legacy of secrets and half-told stories that lingered like ghostly whispers.

What was the connection? Was Olivia onto something linked to Silver Fox? She'd been tirelessly working to uncover a leak. So how did Silver Fox fit into this? The notepad, frustratingly, offered no further clues. Yet, the code name set his mind racing, possibilities and past tales intertwining the present mystery with echoes of the past.

# CHAPTER 48

## SAFE HOUSE

*KYLE*

"Thanks." Kyle ended the call and returned the phone to Torres. He had to surrender his cell phone, per protocol. The agent had given them each a burner phone, but using the agent's phone to call his dad was easier since the number would be readily available. So, Dad knew about the adoption, and now, the theory was that Ana and Dad were the ultimate targets. That was wild. Kyle wouldn't have considered that angle. But who would have thought of such a convoluted way to hurt them? And Ana only joined the task force after the bioweapon threat last year. As far as he knew, his dad and Ana hadn't worked together for years.

When he flopped down on the beat-up couch, Grace tapped his shoulder. "What am I supposed to do here? My folks are probably going crazy."

"I share your frustration. Really. But didn't I hear they told your brother you were being taken into protective custody?"

"Yes. He'll let Mama and Dad know, but they'll be in the chapel praying."

"See? They'll let God take care of it, right?" He was around enough Christians to know this was their go-to way to deal with tough situations. "You should relax. What do you like to do?"

She huffed and waved a hand up and down, indicating herself. "I'm a music teacher. What do you think I like to do?"

He got up and spotted a guitar. Probably left by a former protectee who didn't care to claim it. He picked it up and presented it to her. "Do you play?"

She reached for the guitar, then withdrew her fingers as if it couldn't be real. "You guys have musical instruments laying around?"

"Nah, a former occupant must've left it here. It's yours to play now." He pushed it to her.

"I do play." She took it and started strumming. "It needs a little tuning, but it'll do."

Music warmed the safe house, creating a temporary bubble of normalcy. He tried to find a tactful way to ask about her adoption. If she had no knowledge of her birth mother—as Dad seemed to think—and they had no contact with each other, then how would whoever wanted to hurt Ana think to go through Grace? That person would also have to know Ana kept tabs on her child and still cared about her.

"Er, your file has an adoption record," he ventured.

Her fingers stopped. "I was adopted. So?"

He shrugged, playing nonchalant. "Do you know your birth mother?"

Her brows came together. "Yes and no. My parents told me about my adoption a long time ago. I know of her, but I don't *know* her. Like, I don't know her name. She was in college then. That much I know. They connected through the church. Why?"

"So you've never met her?"

A quick headshake sent her rich brown hair swaying. "I've seen a photo of her, though. She was holding me in the hospital bed." Her big eyes blinked at him. "Why are you asking me all this? Don't you know anybody who was adopted?"

"No, no—I mean, yes, of course. I'm just curious. That's all." He'd tell her the current theory. But given her ignorance about Ana, it wouldn't be a good idea. Better to let it rest.

She probably didn't believe him, but she let it go and went back to strumming the guitar. Not a minute later, she paused. "Is there a Bible here?"

"I don't know. Let me look." He searched the house, found one in a nightstand drawer, and brought it to her. "Here you go."

"Thank you." She slid the guitar aside to accept it. "I'm pretty bad. Haven't done a devotional for a while. Now might be a good time to pick it up."

Having never done any devotional, he didn't know what to say. So, he just sat, hoping she wouldn't ask him to participate in whatever it involved. After a few minutes of sitting idle, the agent in him itched for action, for answers. He couldn't actively participate in the investigation while stuck on babysitting duty, but there was another way—the internet.

Aware of the standard safe-house protocol, he was technically in the protective detail, not being protected, so he could go online. He approached Torres. "I need to do some research. I won't contact anyone or reveal our location. I just need to look up some information."

Torres hesitated. "You know the rules. No internet access for security reasons."

"I get it, but I know how to mask my location and cover my tracks online. This is about finding a connection to what's happening. It's important."

After a moment of consideration, Torres relented. "All right, but online activities are being monitored."

With a laptop in hand, Kyle settled in a corner of the living room, his fingers poised on the keyboard. He began scouring the web for possible connections between Doug Mitchell and organized crime. With each search, he navigated through digital spaces discreetly, using various tools and a few tricks he'd picked up from Olivia to mask his online presence.

He burrowed through a rabbit hole of news articles, criminal databases, and forums discussing organized crime. The deeper he dug, the more he realized the vast and complex web of criminal networks that operated in the shadows.

After his hours of meticulous searching, a few threads began to emerge, as did mentions of a real estate developer who fit Doug's description, seen in the company of known organized crime figures. No concrete evidence, but enough coincidental connections to raise suspicions.

If Doug was involved with organized crime, it could explain the multiple passports, the stacks of cash, and perhaps even the hit list. But the question remained—What was Doug's exact role in this network?

# CHAPTER 49

## FEDERAL DETENTION CENTER

*DYLAN*

In the stark, fluorescent-lit visitor area of the Federal Detention Center, Dylan sat and fixed his gaze on the empty chair beyond the plexiglass partition. The space felt both secure and unsettlingly sterile, a barrier that offered not only protection but also a tangible symbol of the chasm between him and his aunt, the Ghost. The only other time he visited his aunt was at her request with Olivia. This time, he came on his own, no federal agent by his side, and since he wasn't an attorney, here he sat.

As the guards ushered his aunt in, his heart pounded. She moved with an eerie—dare he say ghostlike?—calmness, her presence commanding even in handcuffs. When she sat, he picked up the phone, watching her do the same with a detached expression.

"What a pleasant surprise! You should have come with Olivia. We could talk—"

"Where is she? Where have you taken her?" Not caring about her quest for the treasure, he cut her off.

She blinked. "Who?"

"Don't lie! Where have you taken Lily?" His voice rose, edged with frustration.

"Oh, the girl who ruined my plan." She tsked, one finger shaking at him like a pendulum. "I don't know where she is."

His grip on the phone tightened. "You didn't send someone to kill her? Or you didn't send someone to pretend to save her and take her somewhere?"

She paused, her eyes narrowing. "Tell me what happened."

He recounted the footage showing Lily being whisked away by an unknown figure after a shooting.

After listening, the Ghost sat in silence, only her soft breaths coming through the receiver. Then she asked, "What makes you think I'm involved?"

"Lily was investigating two companies for money laundering —Rain Tree LLC and New Life LLC. Someone lured her there."

Her demeanor shifted. "I don't know where she is, but I can look into it."

Everything in him stilled. Something didn't feel right. The Ghost would never offer to help him or anyone. Did she plan to use this as leverage to get him to cooperate to find the treasures? No way would he be foolish enough to trust her. "If you seriously don't know where she is and you didn't give the order to shoot her, then maybe you don't know at all. I'll have to find her myself." He started to hang up.

"Listen, no matter what you do, do not confront those people without backup unless you have a death wish."

He snickered. "I thought you gave an order that nobody was to touch me."

"That would be people in my organization." She resumed her nonchalant expression. "If you wanted to play hero, I won't stop you."

This time, she hung up.

He held onto the phone, debating calling her back and asking her to find Lily. She'd have a way to accomplish that even in jail, wouldn't she? However, would she hold that against him? Would it be worth it?

# CHAPTER 50

## THE BURNS RESIDENCE

*OLIVIA*

Olivia's drive to Jay's house passed in a blur, questions about Lily's safety and the mysterious circumstances surrounding her disappearance cycling on repeat. As she pulled up, Jay was already at the front door. The sight did little to ease the unease churning in her stomach.

Instead of directing her to the house, he gestured to go to the side entrance. Having never been to his house, she didn't know what to expect. She followed him down the steps, had her biometrics scanned, and was admitted to the basement, a SCIF— Sensitive Compartmented Information Facility. Stepping inside, she stilled at the sight of Kevin sitting at a small conference table —one of the few furnishings in the room other than the table chairs around it. Her glance flickered to the door at the other end. Just where did that lead?

"Jay, what's going on? Where's Lily?"

He motioned for her to sit. "Relax. She is safe, but I don't have her."

He didn't have her? Her muscles stiffened. "Who does, then? And why all the secrecy?"

"It's a tricky question." He sighed and sat. "The situation is more complicated than you think."

Kevin remained silent, assessing her reaction.

Jay continued, "Whoever is using the real O'Shea's ID knows he's a vetted Company asset. Not many people have that kind of information. We can't trust anyone right now, not even within the Company."

A chill ran down her spine. She stepped forward and gripped the back of a chair. "What does this have to do with Lily? Who has her?"

He exchanged a glance with Kevin. "The situation is… complicated. She's safe. That much I can assure you."

"That's not good enough."

Kevin finally spoke. "She's safe, Phoenix. That's what matters right now." He leaned forward. "Jay has an asset doing double duty. His cover's boss ordered him to take Lily."

"What!" She tossed the chair aside, leaning over the table into Jay's space. "And you let him?"

Kevin raised a hand. "Calm down. It's under control."

"Sit down, Phoenix." Jay gestured to the chair she'd abused. "The asset is in a position to ensure Lily's safety. He's also trying to uncover why they want her. But the most critical aspect of this operation is to identify the mole."

Her hands braced on the table, she stilled, reeling. "So, your asset is pursuing the mole? Through this abduction?"

"In a roundabout way, yes."

The room fell silent. Seconds passed. Then she righted the chair. She understood the complexities of intelligence work, the need for subterfuge and manipulation. But the idea of her daughter as a pawn in a larger game, a game that involved moles and double agents, chilled her.

She took a deep breath and slid into the chair, hands folded on the table, gaze slicing into Jay. "I want to be kept in the loop —every step of the way. Lily's safety is my priority."

He nodded. "Of course. We're walking a tightrope here. But trust me, we're doing everything we can to keep Lily safe while we root out the mole."

"I want to know everything about this operation. Who is the asset, and who is his cover's boss?"

He merely stared back at her. One breath raised his chest, then deflated it. Again. Again. Then he sighed. "I can't divulge the asset's identity. It's critical for his safety and the operation."

"I can vouch for the asset," Kevin added. "He's a good guy."

She pivoted to him and slapped the table. "You knew about this? And you didn't tell me?"

He held her gaze. "I didn't know the specifics of his operation. And I had no idea it involved Lily."

The conversation continued, with Olivia calming enough to listen to the updates and Jay relaxing enough to explain the asset was in the dark about his cover's boss's identity.

"He never shows his face or talks directly. It's all encrypted texts and dead drops. What he does know," Jay continued, "is that the boss likely works for the Ghost."

Her frown deepened. "But why Lily? Why is she being watched?"

The men exchanged looks.

Then Kevin spoke up. "We think it might be you they're after."

"Think about it." Jay proceeded to hold up one finger for each point. "Lily brought the antidote here. They probably think she got it from someone inside, so they're flushing that someone out. It's my theory."

She nearly shivered at the chilling idea that she was the ultimate target, with Lily being used as bait. "So, this asset... is he supposed to protect her or just observe?"

"The primary objective is observation," Jay replied. "But his secondary objective is her safety. He's been instructed to intervene if necessary."

She let out a slow breath. "So, we're essentially waiting for them to make a move? For this mole to reveal themselves?"

"Essentially, yes," he confirmed. "It's a waiting game now. Meanwhile, we're doing everything we can to track down this mole and ensure Lily's safety."

She stiffened in the chair. "And what about the real O'Shea? What's his role in all this?"

"He has no part in this. If anything, he is a victim as well. He might have known the wrong fellow who took advantage of the friendship and stole his identity, at least for the purpose of visiting the Federal Detention Center."

Olivia folded her hands on the cold tabletop, the weight of the situation heavy in the room and on her shoulders. She knew the risks of her profession, but she'd never anticipated having her daughter caught in the crosshairs.

"I want to be kept informed. Every step, every lead," she reiterated.

"You will be," Jay reassured her. "We're all on the same side here."

As she stepped out of the basement, Vera Haskin's meeting came to mind. On the verge of turning back and letting them know, she hesitated. No. They'd kept her in the dark. She'd wait till she knew something. How did Haskin know someone was looking into her? And now, Jay thought the mole was taking steps to flush her out. Most likely, the person who orchestrated Lily's disappearance was the one who showed this sudden interest in her.

# CHAPTER 51

## SAFE HOUSE

*GRACE*

Grace's world had shrunk to the confines of a nondescript safe house, its walls adorned with nothing more than a faded landscape painting and a clock that ticked away the hours with monotonous regularity. The agents, who were supposed to be her protectors, felt more like jailers, especially Agent Torres, who appeared to be the one in charge.

With her phone confiscated, she sought solace in the guitar and Bible Kyle found her. The strings now vibrated under her fingers, filling the room with melodies that fluctuated between melancholy and hope. Every so often, she paused, her fingers lingering on certain chords before she turned to the Bible to read passages that offered comfort in their familiarity.

Kyle introduced himself as an agent, but he seemed as much a prisoner as she was. Stripped of his phone and other connections to the outside world, he was left to his own devices, which currently involved hunching over a laptop.

She strummed a particularly melancholy chord, her gaze shifting from the Bible to him. His earlier questions about her adoption had been nagging at her, intertwining with the haunting words of the mysterious note. "Hey." She broke the silence. "Why were you so curious about my adoption? Do you think it has something to do with the note?"

He glanced up, his gaze meeting hers before returning to his screen. "Maybe." His voice barely rose above the laptop's hum.

"Whose sin do you think I'm supposed to pay for?" she pressed, her curiosity piqued.

He exhaled audibly, closing the laptop with a soft snap. Dark circles had formed under his tired eyes. "I don't know for sure."

"Take a guess, then." She set her guitar aside and leaned forward, letting her posture display her interest.

"Do you really want to know?" He cocked his head to one side as if afraid of unveiling a truth too heavy to bear.

Did she? She clasped her hands in her lap. "Yes."

He let out another long and heavy breath. "It's possible the writer meant you were supposed to pay for your mother's sin. Your birth mother."

The words lingered, heavy with implications. A chill ran down her spine, the notion more unsettling than she cared to admit. Her birth mother—a woman with whom she had no contact.

"But why? What could she have d–done?" She winced as the tremor in her voice betrayed her rising anxiety.

He shrugged. "That's what we need to figure out. There's a reason we—uh, you—were targeted."

Grace wrapped her arms around herself, vulnerable. Shivers tingled through her. Could her very existence be a consequence of some unknown sin? How terrifyingly absurd! Yes, she'd always known her adoption was a part of her story, but imagining it might be entangled in something so sinister was beyond her comprehension.

"Could it be a mistake? Maybe they got the wrong person?" She clung to the hopeful thought.

"It's unlikely," he replied, his voice low. "The note was too specific, too personal. It was meant for you."

What he said earlier had just hit her. "Wait." She held up a hand. "What did you mean by 'we' were targeted?"

"Nothing. I misspoke."

"No, you did not. I'm a teacher. I can tell you're lying." She gave him the "death stare"—so named by her students.

"I'm on the hit list too."

Her jaw dropped, and her eyes grew saucer-wide. "Did you get a note too?"

"No, but dropping a threatening note at a federal office is a lot more difficult than delivering one to a school."

"What makes you think it's my birth mother?"

He rubbed the back of his neck, ducking his head before peering up at her. "Because my dad and I work with her."

Her, meaning… her mother.

Grace held onto the Bible. "You. Work. With. *Her*?"

He nodded.

"You know *her*? How? I mean, how do you know she's my birth mother?"

"She told my dad."

For the first time in her life, she was genuinely curious about her birth mother. Her parents explained that her birth mother had been young and not ready to be a parent. She'd wanted Grace to have two parents and a good family. So, now Grace had so many questions about this woman, a federal agent to boot. What did this woman—her *mother*—do to cause this?

# CHAPTER 52

## UNKNOWN LOCATION

*LILY*

Lily found herself in an unfamiliar motel, its scarce interior furnished with a pair of double beds, a desk, a TV, a mini fridge, and a bathroom. Compared to the one she and Kyle hid in while they were on the run last year, this was luxurious. After they arrived yesterday, Filmore closed the blinds, and she'd dropped into the desk chair, her mind a whirlwind. So many questions and fears assailing her as the day's events shattered her sense of security.

Filmore, the man who saved her from the shooting, moved around the room checking everything. She watched him, gauging his intentions. She couldn't shake her uncertainty about whether he was a friend or foe. She'd dozed off a few times, worrying he might have sinister intentions. But she needn't have worried. He hardly slept, hadn't even changed clothes or anything. Seemed he lived on caffeine and kept watch.

"Why won't you tell me who you work for?" she entreated again. "And why didn't we wait for the police?"

He tilted his head toward her, his slight smirk irritating. "If I tell you who I work for, I'd have to kill you."

His humor did little to ease her anxiety.

"That's not funny." She crossed her arms, aiming for a tough-chick stance, but not quite succeeding. "I deserve to know what's going on. Why am I here? Why did someone try to shoot me?"

His expression softened. "Look, I promise you I won't hurt you. I'm here to keep you safe. But there are things I can't reveal. It's for your safety."

She stomped her foot in a surge of frustration. "My parents must be worried sick. I need to let them know I'm fine."

He held up a hand. "It's been taken care of. They know you're safe."

"How can you be sure?" she pressed. And Dylan would worry.

"I just am."

His cryptic attitude didn't help. She paced the room, then spun to face him. "Why are we here? What was your instruction?"

He looked at her, his gaze steady. "My instruction was to bring you here, away from any immediate danger. We needed to get you off the grid, so to speak."

"Off the grid?" She stopped right in front of him. "What does that even mean? Who wants to harm me?"

His Adam's apple bobbed. Was that emotion behind his cold blue eyes? "People are interested in you. People who think you have information you probably don't even realize you have. Although the theory is that they are after your mother."

A chill ran down her spine. "My mom? Is this some kind of kidnapping that demands my mom in exchange for me?"

"You watch too much TV. I can't tell you everything because I don't have all the answers myself."

Her knees wobbled beneath the feeling of overwhelm, and

she sat on the desk chair. "This is like some kind of spy movie. Except it's real, and I'm in the middle of it."

He sat on a bed, facing her. "I know this is hard to digest. But right now, the best thing you can do is stay put and trust me."

She looked into his eyes, searching for any sign of deceit. Despite the bizarre circumstances, the sincerity in his demeanor made her want to trust him.

"Okay." She exhaled, her chest deflating in resignation, then rising in determination. "I'll stay. But I need to understand what's going on. I can't just sit here in a void."

He shrugged. "I'll tell you what I can when I can. That's all I can promise."

As the night wore on, she prayed in her heart that this wouldn't bring back PTSD. She didn't want to have to be scared to be alone again. Of course, this time, she felt sort of safe. After all, Filmore did save her earlier. But would he save her just so he could deliver her to another monster? Back in Hong Kong, she led a simple and boring life. She'd even wished her life could be more exciting. Now, it hadn't been half a year since she arrived, and she'd been held captive so many times. Why couldn't it be fun adventures instead of dangerous ordeals?

And what about Dylan? They'd been so excited about their upcoming date, their official date. Oh no! Would he go to Rain Tree and confront them? *Lord, please keep him safe. And my parents too, especially my mom!*

# CHAPTER 53

## THE ROTH RESIDENCE

*OLIVIA*

The evening light was waning as Olivia pulled into the driveway. She'd spent the ride home debating how much she should reveal to Simon. He'd have questions, but how much should she tell him?

As she turned off the engine, the lingering question about Deputy Director Vera Haskin echoed in her mind. Had Simon crossed paths with Haskin during his time in the Senate?

Opening the garage door, she found him waiting in the kitchen. He braced a hip against the kitchen island, in the process of brewing a cup of coffee on the Keurig, and eyed her with a mix of concern and anticipation. The coffee aroma filled the room, a small comfort in their tumultuous lives.

"You said Lily was safe. But where is she? What's going on?"

She hesitated, rubbing the back of her neck. "Yes, she's safe." She crossed the room and touched his arm. Then, as he held her, she told him a simplified version.

"Wait. Let me get this straight." He stepped away, retrieved his coffee, and offered her the cup. "They want to use Lily as bait?"

"Well, not exactly." She accepted the coffee. "Hey, do you know Vera Haskin?"

"Rings a bell. Who's she?" He sat on a barstool by the island.

"Deputy Director, FBI." She sipped her coffee, getting the energy to tell him about her conversation with Haskin earlier.

"Wow!" He shook his head. "Sounds like everything is connected. Someone is looking into you, and Lily was taken because of her connection with you—whether as Olivia or Phoenix. We need to find that leak. Otherwise, we'll never rest."

"I know." She clattered her now-empty mug onto the island countertop. "She wouldn't tell me her source. Who could be her source? How would she know someone was looking into me?"

"I don't know." His brows furrowed.

"Did you know she was read in on the Phoenix operation?"

"People in the Intelligence Committee knew about the operation." He, too, put his cup down. "I'm sure folks in the intelligence divisions of the various alphabet agencies probably know. However, I can tell you that nobody—well, maybe a select few —knew Phoenix's identity. I didn't know."

So, maybe Jay and a select few knew. Then how would Haskin know she was Phoenix? Perhaps now that she had "retired" from the role, more people had access to her identity?

"Earlier, I happened to come across your notes. Why are you researching Silver Fox?"

His voice brought her back to the present. "You know Silver Fox?"

"No, but I heard Rifkin mention the name."

"Tell me what you know. I've narrowed down the possible candidates for Eva's 'Uncle Bill' and Clara's 'Officer Bill.' I assume they're one and the same, but you never know. So, what do you know?"

"I only know he was connected to the Ghost somehow.

Rifkin mentioned that Silver Fox was an intelligence officer once, but in his personal life, something happened to change him. The Ghost took advantage of that and turned him."

"Why didn't anybody do anything about it? I mean, the Company should know who he is."

"Remember this is what Rifkin said. And remember he was proved to be in league with the Ghost. So, this could be something nobody knew about, just him, something he inadvertently mentioned to me."

Made sense. After all, Rifkin had wanted to turn Simon. "Or maybe he was hoping you'd be joining him to serve the Ghost."

He sighed. "We'll never know now."

What Simon said about Silver Fox jived with her research. Would this be the one? Could he be the leak? But who was he?

# CHAPTER 54

## THE MITCHELL RESIDENCE

*SHEILA*

Sheila sat in her quiet living room, the events of the past days swirling in her mind like a relentless storm. The detectives' assurance that the prosecutor didn't plan to charge her for Doug's murder was a small comfort, but it did little to ease her turmoil. Who was Doug, really? The man she thought she knew now seemed like a stranger.

She leaned back in her chair, gripping the teal armrests, closing her eyes, trying to piece together any hint of Doug's secret life. That company picnic they attended last summer… It had been a pleasant day, filled with laughter and casual conversations. But one part stood out now in stark contrast to the rest.

A man arrived late, and her husband's expression changed the moment he saw him—contorting with a fleeting look of concern, maybe even fear. The man didn't mingle. Instead, he pulled Doug aside for a brief, intense conversation.

She pressed cold fingers to her forehead. What else could she remember of that encounter? The man was well-dressed, confident, almost commanding. He'd introduced himself to her. She rocked her head side to side. *What* was his name? It was something Hispanic, wasn't it? Yes, she was sure of it.

She opened her eyes. Could this man be connected to Doug's secret life? If only she'd paid more attention, asked more questions.

After pushing to her feet, she walked to her desk and retrieved a notepad. She began jotting down everything she remembered about that day—the weather, the food, the people, and the mysterious man.

Her hand trembled. The realization that her husband had been living a double life overwhelmed her again. How much danger had she been in without even knowing it?

She set aside the notebook and dug her phone from her pocket, then dialed Ron's number.

"Hey," she said as soon as he answered. "Something I remembered might be important."

"What did you remember?" His voice came through, steady and reassuring.

She described the company picnic, the mystery man's late arrival, and their intense conversation. "His name was something Hispanic, but I can't remember."

"That could be significant. Anything else you remember about him—his appearance, how he spoke, anything at all—could help."

She closed her eyes, sinking back into the memory, summoning more details from that day. "He wasn't that tall, about five eight, dark hair, well-spoken, and he carried this air of authority. I remember feeling a bit intimidated."

"Okay, that's good to know. If you see a photo of him, do you think you'd recognize him?"

Again, she visualized the man. "I think so. Who do you think he is?"

In the silence, she almost checked if they'd lost the connection, but then he said, "If he's who I think he is, then I'm afraid Doug's death is even more complicated than we've begun to think. Uh, I gotta go." Click.

What did he mean? More complicated? As if leading a double life wasn't complicated enough.

## *RON*

Armed with coffee, Ron arrived at the task force office. Yesterday flew by. He managed to check in with Kyle before calling it a night. Other than boredom, everything was a-okay at the safe house. But Kyle did mention what he found on the internet—a possible link between Doug and the Martinez cartel. This new info dovetailed with the detectives' findings from the airport footage where Doug was last seen mingling with known cartel associates.

The sliding door whooshed open, announcing Ron's entrance to the lab's occupants. The soft, electronic sound disrupted the rhythmic tapping of keys and the low hum of machinery. He'd expected to find Deanna immersed in her work, perhaps still entangled in the deputy director's project. He hadn't expected to see Olivia there too, working alongside the analyst.

They barely glanced up as he stepped in, their focus on the data sprawling across their screens. He gripped the back of a chair, leaning over their work. "Olivia, I didn't know you were here."

"Just want to help her finish up." She responded without tearing her attention away from her screen. "We're all good. In fact, I'm about to leave." An underlying tinge of the seriousness of their situation belied her casual tone. It was a small gesture, her being there, but it spoke volumes about Vera's "project." Olivia pushed back her chair, pivoting his way. The dark smudges under her eyes added more weight to their project. "Any news on the situation with Kyle and the teacher?"

He shook his head. "Not yet. But we'll find something." He wasn't just assuring her. He placed his confidence not only in words but also in an unspoken belief in their team's capabilities. No doubt, his son would remain safe.

"I'd help, but I have got plenty on my plate. Sorry." She grabbed her stuff and headed out.

"I understand. You've got enough." He watched her exit, her departure swift yet unobtrusive, like a shadow slipping away unnoticed. He then turned his attention to Deanna, who had been observing their exchange. He waved to her desk. "Tanner managed to give you the laptop?"

She nodded, eyeing him before refocusing on the laptop screen. "I'd only just started, and she came in... so, nothing to report yet."

He pushed his palms harder against the chairback, sharing her urgency, their race against time, the puzzle being pieced together under the pressing thumb of urgency.

"You need to take it apart. Recover what's hidden, deleted, etc. Use all the tricks you've got. I must see what he's got in there."

"Yeah, boss, I know. You want it done yesterday. You'll know when I have something." She turned her focus back to the screen. "I can tell you this. He's got a couple of hidden folders in here. When I know, you'll know."

"Hidden folders?"

"Yes, but I'll *un*hide them. Standing here watching me isn't going to make it go faster."

He had to smile. Her stress was showing. It took a long time to get Deanna to work comfortably with the team. She worked alone—very efficiently—and during a crisis, she reverted to the Lone Ranger. Knowing not to bother her now, he stepped out.

So many questions remained. He needed to get someone to take a six-pack with Nunez and Greek to Sheila. Maybe one was the mysterious Hispanic fellow she saw.

# CHAPTER 55

## M&M ENTERPRISES

*DYLAN*

After a restless night, filled with a jumble of thoughts and concerns, Dylan arrived at M&M Enterprises earlier than usual, the first rays of the morning sun barely touching the horizon. Preoccupied with Lily's whereabouts and his perplexing conversation with his aunt, he strode inside and nearly tripped over the potted plant.

He'd texted Olivia, expecting some concrete information, but received a cryptic reply saying Lily was safe and not to worry. When he pressed for details, she, well, ghosted him, leaving him more anxious and confused. If Lily was safe, why would Olivia cut him off? And could he rest just because Olivia said Lily was safe?

At his desk, he opened his email to the security firm's background report he'd requested about Janet. He scanned the pages, each line and number adding to his growing suspicion. His gut reaction spurred him to confront her, but he hesitated. He needed a second opinion, someone to assess the situation objectively.

He printed the report and called Tommy. "Hey, you have a minute? Can you stop by?"

When Tommy arrived and slid into the chair across from him, Dylan handed him the documents. He laced his hands in his lap, his focus on his friend's gaze now moving over the figures and findings.

His buddy finally lowered the report. "These large deposits in Janet's account are curious. But there could be a number of legitimate explanations for them."

Dylan then pointed to specific sections of the report. "I thought the same, but the investigator found no evidence to back up these payments. No inheritance, no spouse or relative with a trust fund, no side business, not even a hint of an investment."

Tommy sank back in his chair, rubbing his chin. "That does raise some red flags, especially if there's no clear source for this money."

With his friend's concurrence, Dylan's resolve hardened. He needed to talk to Janet, but he would approach the matter delicately. Accusations without solid proof could backfire.

"By the way, did you find anything suspicious?" He put the file in his drawer and locked it.

"I'm still looking, but Lily's right. Something isn't kosher. Janet should have reported it or at least looked into it." He nodded to Dylan's drawer where he'd stowed the file. "Then again, if she was on the take, as they say, that would explain it."

Dylan let out a slow breath, his every muscle still taut after yesterday. He could perhaps talk to her and see what she had to say about those companies.

"So, how did it go with your aunt?"

His taut muscles tightened further as he related their conversation, how she claimed she had no knowledge of it.

"Do you believe her?"

"I don't know." He drummed his fingers on the desk. "Guess

what? She offered to help find her if I wanted. Can you believe it?"

"That is strange. She's not one to do anybody any favor. Or if she does anything for you, then she owns you."

"Yeah, and the weirdest thing is, she said something like, 'Unless you have a death wish, don't go confront them without backup.'"

"Who? Rain Tree?"

"Yup."

"Wow! Maybe you ought to listen to that. You've been quite a magnet for trouble these days." Tommy stood up. "I've got a meeting in five."

Dylan followed him out and found Janet in her office, her posture one of concentration as she worked on her computer. "Excuse me." He stopped in her doorway. "Do you have a minute?"

She looked up, a hint of surprise in her eyes. "Of course, Dylan. What's up?"

He took a seat. This would be a good moment to choose his words carefully. "I wanted to ask you about Rain Tree LLC and New Life LLC. You said Lily reported some irregularities, but you didn't think they were worth checking out."

There it was—a subtle but noticeable reaction. Her eyes flickered, and a small, almost imperceptible sigh slid out. "Right. I can check them out, but I'm not sure if there's anything suspicious."

What an evasive response. "I see. All right, thank you."

Back at his office, Dylan clicked through the report on her again and Tommy's reports and Lily's findings. He thought back to Reardon's reaction. Tommy had cc'd Gene, the EAM. Still, Dylan met with Gene and Kirk, the general manager, to go over everything, putting it in their hands. They'd know what to do.

While they took care of the business end, Dylan needed to find Lily. He replayed his conversation with the Ghost. Then, after double-checking his agenda to be sure he had nothing urgent to do, he locked up. He grabbed a quick sandwich from the café downstairs and headed to Rain Tree LLC, the company apparently at the center of the unfolding mystery.

Arriving at Rain Tree LLC, he paused outside the ordinary building. He pushed open the double glass doors, took the elevator to the third floor, stepped outside, and found the suite. The door was open, but no receptionist. The lack of a Closed for Lunch sign and the open door seemed odd.

He called out a tentative hello and ventured further into the office. The place had an abandoned feel, with empty desks and silent phones. His footsteps echoed in the hallway as he moved toward the only sign of potential occupancy—a closed office door at the end of the corridor.

As he reached the door, his hand raised to knock, the door swung open. Taken aback, he found himself face-to-face with a Hispanic fellow and his imposing bodyguard, a scar tracing the left side of the man's face. The surprise in the man's eyes was brief, replaced by a cold, calculating look.

Dylan's gaze, however, was drawn to the most chilling detail —the gun in the bodyguard's hand, a silent but unmistakable threat. The air in the room felt heavy, charged with tension. His mind raced, calculating his options. He needed to keep the situation under control, to extract information without escalating the danger.

"Hi," he started, his voice steady despite the adrenaline coursing through him. "I was looking for Mr. Lockwood. I can see he's not in. I'll just let myself out." He made to leave.

The man's expression remained unreadable. "Not so fast." He flicked a hand, and the bodyguard grabbed Dylan.

"Hey!" he protested.

But the bodyguard ignored him and started to search him like in the movies. The guy was thorough. He found the little pocketknife in Dylan's secret pocket.

"He's clean, except for this." The goon showed his boss the knife and then pocketed it. And he offered his boss Dylan's wallet, which the man examined.

"Dylan Roche. Ah! You're the nephew. What fortune!"

Nephew. So they were in the Ghost's network. He breathed a little easier. "Well, so you know you can't touch me."

The man ignored him. "What are you doing here?"

"I told you. I was looking for Mr. Lockwood. Just following a lead that might lead me to Lily."

"Who is she? Your girlfriend?"

Who was she to him? Really? Girlfriend? Yeah, sure. "Yes, but that's all right. I see that she's not here. I'll be going now if I could get my wallet back, please." They likely wouldn't give him the pocketknife back.

"Sure." The man handed him the wallet.

But when he turned to leave, the cold barrel of a gun pressed against his back.

# CHAPTER 56

## THE VIEW RESTAURANT

*ROOK*

In the dimly lit ambiance of The View, an upscale restaurant, Rook sat at a table adorned with a white linen cloth and an array of fine silverware, and with little effort, he exuded his well-honed calm and collected persona. The low hum of conversations from surrounding tables filled the air, creating an atmosphere of casual sophistication.

As he enjoyed his meal with his wife and a couple they socialized with on occasion, the vibration of his encrypted phone broke his focus. He glanced at the caller ID, a code name flashing on the screen. With an apologetic smile to his dining companions, he excused himself and stepped away to a more secluded spot near the restaurant entrance.

Ensuring privacy, he answered the call. "Report."

The voice on the other end, distorted for security, relayed the latest developments. As he listened, he stood perfectly still, the only movement being the subtle tilt of his head.

After the caller finished, he spoke, his voice low but clear, the voice distortion app masking his natural tone. "Continue monitoring the situation. Keep watch. There must be a connection between Phoenix and the girl. Report back as soon as Phoenix takes the bait."

The caller acknowledged the instruction and ended the call. He stood for a moment longer, mulling over the information, his confidence in the connection between Phoenix and the girl, Lily, growing.

He brushed against a man as he returned to the table, then shifted seamlessly back to the composed and charming individual he presented to the world. The man didn't look back. Good. His heartbeat settled. Paranoia was a fact of life in his profession. To stay alive, he needed to trust no one.

"Everything all right?" his wife asked.

He gave a nonchalant nod and settled back into his seat. "Just a minor business matter. Nothing to worry about."

As they resumed their dinner, his mind was partially elsewhere, calculating his next moves in this intricate game. The Ghost had assigned him this task. If he could uncover who Phoenix was, he'd be indispensable to the Ghost. While she was in jail, he could run her criminal enterprise and eventually take over. Ironic that she had basically done the same to her mother. Drugging the woman to smooth her way to take over the enterprise. Officially, Mrs. Beaumont had succumbed to heart failure, but rumors had it that the Ghost had been responsible.

The evening progressed with an exchange of pleasantries and discussions on benign topics. Yet, beneath the casual dinner conversation, his thoughts focused on this mission. His other operation was minor, and he already delegated that to a team. He only needed Phoenix to take the bait and show up. But would he? Surely, the legendary Phoenix would risk exposing himself to save the girl.

⁂

## *RON*

"You're sure?" Ron held the phone with one hand, and with the other, he pressed the intercom to summon Ana to his office.

"Yes, I'm sure that's the man I saw with Doug," Sheila said.

"Okay, thank you. Let me talk to the agent, please." When she handed the phone to Agent Flynn, he thanked her and instructed her to return to the office.

At a knock on the doorframe, he beckoned Ana to sit. "Sheila identified Nunez as the man she saw with Doug."

"This is the break we need!" Her face lit up. "Now, we can connect Doug to the cartel."

"But we still don't know for sure why Kyle and Grace are on a hit list. And what was Doug's role in all this?"

Another knock. This time, Tanner peered around the door.

"Boss." The senior agent stood where he was. "It may be easier to show you on the big screen."

"All right." Ron stood up. So did Ana. They followed Tanner out to the squad room and gathered around the giant screen.

"José, beam it up."

At Tanner's instruction, Hernandez tapped some keys on the keyboard. Then a couple of slides showed up on the screen.

"On the left is the vic's travel history. On the right is what we've curated from Interpol, Europol, and our alerts. We've highlighted the common dates."

Ron frowned at the dates. "Okay, what are the alerts?"

"Five missing, thirteen high-profile deaths."

"What kind of deaths?"

"Seven homicides, four undetermined, two accidental deaths."

He rubbed his jaw, taking a moment to process this—this clear implication that Doug had been a hit man. "How was he doing that? He traveled to London and Paris. But the deaths and missing are all over. Ah, the passports!"

"Yup, boss," Hernandez chimed in. "We matched the dates to his various passports. So, he would fly to London or Paris, check in, disappear for a few days, and come back to check out. During those days, he'd use whatever passport he needed to get into the country he needed to go to and do the job."

"What did he do for the army?" Ana asked.

"Special Forces. Most of his missions are classified."

"Was he honorably discharged?" Ron asked.

"OTH."

Ah, an other than honorable discharge. "Do you know why?"

Tanner scooped up his stress ball and gave a firm headshake. "Nope. Classified."

"Let's put that aside for now," Ana said. "It seems he was a hit man. He had training, having been in the special forces, and he was connected to the Martinez cartel. Very possibly their hit man."

Ron nodded. "Assuming he was their hit man and assuming we're the ultimate targets, why would the Martinez cartel want to hurt us? I've not had anything to do with them."

Ana sighed. "Neither have I."

"And may I ask? Why did he try to swallow the order?" Tanner asked.

"We don't know if he tried to do that or if it was forced into him. And either way, very good questions. Now we need the answers."

The View Restaurant, with its elegant décor and panoramic city views, was bustling with the evening crowd. Ron scanned the room, sighting Vera laughing with another couple. The light from the chandeliers cast a warm glow on her face. That, coupled with her casual attire, gave her a softer look.

He approached the table, his heart pounding, his focus on the empty chair beside Vera, but before he could sit, she stood, her expression shifting from relaxed to guarded.

Without a word to him, she excused herself from her friends, her polite smile not reaching her eyes. They moved to a quieter corner, away from the other diners' curious glances.

"You have the nerve!" Her sharp words cut through the ambient restaurant noises.

He took a deep breath, steadying himself. "Vera, I wouldn't be here if it wasn't important. There's been a development in the case."

She crossed her arms, her expression skeptical. "I'm listening."

He briefed her on the situation: Sheila's identification of Nunez, the possible connection to the Martinez drug cartel, and the unnerving fact that Doug could be the cartel's hit man.

"Your ex-wife's dead husband was a cartel hit man. One for the books." She regarded him with the same intensity he remembered from when they once worked together. "You couldn't wait till the morning?"

"Well, there are certain things that your title would help."

"So, you need me to let you work the case with the local detectives officially."

"They kind of invited us to work with them, but it's always good to have your blessings."

She smiled. "All right. Go get them."

"Yes, ma'am."

Vera nodded, turned to head back to the table, then spun back around. Something flashed in her amber eyes. "Ron, be careful."

"Always." With a final nod of understanding, he started to leave and absently brushed against a bald man. Something about that man tickled his brain. What was it?

# CHAPTER 57

## SAFE HOUSE

*KYLE*

K yle's latest discovery was significant. This time, he'd stumbled upon pictures on social media—not on Doug's profile, but in posts where he had been tagged. These images showed Doug in close association with Nunez, a known second-in-command in the Martinez drug cartel. But when he called to report his findings, Dad had already connected Doug with Nunez.

While he talked on the phone, Grace's soft singing filled the air. After he hung up, he moved to her side. "I've never heard these songs before. They're kind of relaxing and, uh, peaceful."

"These are popular worship songs." Her fingers stopped strumming. "Yes, some are upbeat, and some are… soothing. You don't go to church?"

"Not really." He slid onto a lumpy couch cushion beside her. "I've been to different churches over the years, but I don't really believe."

"Oh." A strange expression twisted her features. What was

it? Pity? Sadness? "Well, you should visit my dad's. His sermon is funny, sometimes."

"I'll keep that in mind."

The doorbell shattered the tranquility. Everyone in the safe house snapped to attention, the agents' training kicking in as the mood shifted from relaxed to high alert.

Torres touched the mic. "Jackson, report."

Kyle touched his earpiece just to make sure he had it on, but he still hadn't heard anything. It couldn't be good.

Torres motioned for Kyle to take Grace to the bathroom, then gestured to the other agent, Wood, to go to the other side of the door.

"Who's it?" Torres called out.

Kyle couldn't hear a response, only an ominous silence that seemed to thicken the air. He kept his hand on the holster.

He heard footsteps, the creak of the door opening, followed by a string of curses from Torres. Wood called out, "Clear!"

Then he and Grace were ushered out of the bathroom, to a macabre scene. On the doorstep lay a dead dog, a chilling message pinned to its lifeless form with photos of them both. The handwritten note read, "You're next."

Wood went to grab the animal. "Wait, it's fake. A life-size balloon." Laying the figure inside, he kicked the door shut.

At the sight, Grace gasped and raced to the fake animal. "Oh, wow!" she cried. "This looks just like Boomer."

Kyle had read about Grace's family pet in her file. "That's her family pet," he told the other agents.

The symbolism was clear and terrifying. Their safe house had been compromised, and whoever was after them had escalated their threats to a horrifying level.

Torres was on his phone, calling in the situation and awaiting further instructions. The directive came—they were to relocate to another safe house. Meanwhile, Wood did a perimeter to find Jackson.

"Your family is safe. Agents have eyes on them," Torres reassured her.

Wood came back in with Jackson, who didn't look too well. "Jackson was tased."

"How did they find us?" Torres mumbled while motioning everybody to move. They were going to another safe house.

# CHAPTER 58

## TASK FORCE OFFICE

*RON*

Ron had barely stepped into the bustling task force office when Ana approached him, and her sense of urgency put him on alert. The office, always a hive of activity with agents moving about, phones ringing, and computers humming, faded into the background.

"I have a revelation." She offered him a cup of coffee.

He accepted it and thanked her. They walked together toward his office.

She took a deep breath, squaring her shoulders. "Someone is targeting our children. Kyle, I understand—he's an FBI agent and your son. It's known. But Grace… Few people knew about her existence, let alone her connection to me, before yesterday. And there's no apparent link between Kyle and Grace other than being our children."

He sat and, using his coffee cup, waved her on. "We've established that. We could be the targets."

"Exactly." She turned her coffee cup around in her hand,

frowning at the logo on its side. "But I'm not sure if we're the primary targets or if the aim is to hurt us through our children."

"What do you mean? Like the plan was to kidnap them in exchange for us?"

"Not quite. I was thinking more about who our enemies are." She sipped her coffee.

"That would be a long list."

She gave him a pointed look. "I agree. Individually, the list would be quite long. But together? Remember, we only reconnected last year during the bioweapon threat. Before that, we were with our respective agencies and simply worked together on ops. And that was years ago."

She had a point. "Right. We arrested those goons involved, but I don't see them as about to orchestrate something like this."

"True. But you're forgetting the congressman and what happened at his house." Her lowered voice added gravity to her words.

He scowled at his reflection in the black coffee. "We had to kill Olivia. I mean Jade, her undercover persona. But we only faked her death."

"*We*"—she tracked a finger between them—"know it's fake, but the world thinks she's dead. So, who would miss Jade?"

"Enough to seek revenge." His coffee sloshed over the rim as he slammed the cup onto his desk. Now it was starting to make sense. "We need to talk to her. She might have more insight into this than we realized." He was already dialing the number.

"Need to ask you something. You have a minute?" Ron said as soon as Olivia picked up.

"Yes?"

He explained their theory and asked who she thought would want to avenge Jade's death.

Silence. He glanced at Ana and back at the phone. Still nothing. He hadn't lost her. The call was still going.

"The one person who'd want to do that would be Marge Beaumont."

"The Ghost?"

"She'd be the only one who cared about Jade enough to mourn her."

He drew in a slow breath, taking a second to absorb the news. "O–kay. I guess I'm not understanding your relationship with the Ghost."

"It's complicated." A sigh whispered through the speakers. "I, Olivia, don't have a relationship with her. But Jade did. You can say they had a connection."

He dabbed at his spilled coffee. Too bad they couldn't blot out the past that easily. "Oh, well, it's neither here nor there. Do you think she'd orchestrate something like this to avenge Jade's death?"

"Totally, although she'd delegate it to a trusted lieutenant. Very likely, the one I'm looking at right now. Er, I gotta go." She hung up.

"I don't know how she did it for so long." Ana kept shaking her head. "I'd have lost myself and gone nuts."

He tossed the napkin in the trash. "I don't know either. Jade must've had a good relationship with the Ghost. Had to be. Otherwise, she wouldn't want to avenge her death. But then, Olivia despises her. Thinking about it is giving me a headache."

"It's almost like she's got a split personality."

"Let's refocus." He slugged his coffee. "The more I think about it, the more it makes sense. If the Ghost is behind this, then it's retribution for what we supposedly did."

"Right. She cared about Jade. Now, she's trying to take out the ones we care about."

"I'm thinking out loud here. Assuming she's the one behind it, how did Doug get involved? We can assume he was a cartel hit man. So, is Martinez in cahoots with the Ghost?"

"If that's the case, why did she give Olivia the name? She wanted us to eliminate Martinez."

"So who gave Doug the order? If not the Martinez cartel?"

"And why did he try to swallow it? And how did they find out about Grace?"

"We need more answers." He stood up. "And now, we need to get out there for the morning briefing."

They walked out to the squad room where the team had already gathered. The morning briefing was a ritual, a time when the team converged to share updates and strategize. The atmosphere always fluctuated between intense focus and the underlying camaraderie of a group united. Now, the low murmur of agents discussing their latest findings and theories buzzed into the hall.

As Ron walked in, Cooper stood, ready to give his update. He stopped in front of the screen and clicked through to the relevant slides as he began.

"We have eyes on Nunez." He pointed to a surveillance photo of Nunez and another figure. "He's been seen with Greek, aka Frankie. We're keeping a close watch, hoping they'll lead us to Martinez."

The team members nodded, their attention fixed on the screen. The connection to Martinez, the linchpin in the network they were trying to dismantle, was crucial.

Tanner took over next. "Street intel suggests Martinez is getting antsy. We might see him make a move soon."

Hernandez added, "We've also been tracking communications. There's chatter, but it's coded. We're working on cracking it."

As the updates continued, the team's strategy took shape, each member contributing a piece to the complex puzzle they were assembling.

Amid the briefing, a chime broke the concentration. Cooper's cell phone pinged with a message, and then Ron's phone chimed. They exchanged a glance, both reaching for their devices.

As Ron read the message on his screen, Cooper tapped his phone, syncing it with the big screen to display the incoming images. The team members gathered around, their expressions turning grim.

The images showed Nunez and Greek with a third person, clearly in a compromised situation. Before he could provide commentary, Ana's sharp eyes identified the captive. "Is that Dylan?"

Ron, who had been preoccupied with the message on his phone, now focused on the screen. "Yes, that's Dylan," he confirmed Ana's fear.

Dylan's involvement added another layer to an already intricate operation. The stakes were getting higher, and the dangers more personal.

As if on cue, his phone call further heightened the situation. A threat had been made on Kyle and Grace in the safe house. They were being moved to another location.

Kyle's voice came through the phone. "We're getting ready to move now. She's afraid they might go after her family and the family's real dog."

"Agents are watching her folks' house. So, tell her not to worry. Her folks and pet will be safe. Dylan has been taken. Things are escalating."

"What! Dylan was taken?"

"You get back to your protective duty. We'll take care of this. Stay safe."

Cooper, meanwhile, continued to analyze the on-screen images to glean additional information to aid their operation. "We need to find out where this was taken. Any clue could lead us to Dylan."

Ana stepped closer. "Let's enhance these images, check for backgrounds, anything that can give us a location."

Ron, despite the personal turmoil, maintained his composure and directed the team with a steady hand. "Keep working on these leads. We need to find Dylan and ensure Kyle's and Grace's safety. We're dealing with a multifaceted threat here."

"Got it!" Hernandez announced, tapping some keys to send the images to the big screen. "If you focus on the window, you'll see the—"

"Just tell us the location," Ron interrupted.

"Yeah, boss. This building houses a few companies. One of which is Rain Tree LLC."

"Let's go!"

A half hour later, he sat in the back of a mobile van unit speeding toward Rain Tree LLC. His team obviously shared his sense of urgency. Everyone was ready for action when Cooper's phone rang. He answered.

"We've lost eyes on Nunez," the agent announced. "He was last seen with Greek and Dylan, heading toward a garage on the east side."

"Pull up the footage from the surrounding areas," Ron ordered.

The team sprang into action, tapping into the city's CCTV network. The screens flickered with images from various cameras, providing them with a bird's-eye view of the city's streets.

"There." Ana pointed to a black SUV on one of the screens. "That's got to be them."

Ron leaned in for a closer look. The SUV matched the description of the vehicle they were tracking. When they zoomed in, the driver bore a striking resemblance to one of Nunez's known associates.

"They switched cars," he noted. "Keep tracking that SUV."

Then they lost visual again. After a few more tries, he called it. They would have to return to the office and use more sophisticated equipment to track the SUV.

All the while, he couldn't figure out how Dylan got involved in this. And someone leaked the safe-house location. This was getting out of hand. Nunez and Frankie took Dylan. Grace and Kyle targeted. The Ghost could be the one orchestrating this, but she had to use someone. Who?

# CHAPTER 59

## FEDERAL DETENTION CENTER

***ROOK***

Rook's footsteps echoed in the Federal Detention Center's sterile corridors, the rhythmic sound mirrored the urgency pulsing through his veins. This was an unusual visit, one made without the standard cloak-and-dagger precautions to avoid surveillance. The Ghost's message had been terse but unmistakable.

Stepping into the attorney visiting room, he approached the Ghost, who was already seated, her posture rigid but exuding a controlled intensity. He sat, brought his briefcase up, and took out some papers while watching for the guard to exit the room.

As the guard left, the heavy door closed with a definitive click, sealing them in a bubble of confidentiality. They dispensed with their usual charade of him posing as her attorney. Time was too critical.

The Ghost leaned forward and spoke in a soft voice, almost whispering. "You have eyes on the girl, Lily. Where is she?"

Lily? He didn't expect her to ask about Lily. "She's secured."

"So, you took her." It was not a question.

"Well, Martinez tried to kill her. We saved her."

She sat back. "To lure Phoenix out."

"Right."

"What about Olivia? What have you found?"

"She was recruited about twenty years ago. By the FBI. Her assignments are mostly classified. Ordinary."

She seemed to digest the information. "What made her give up her daughter?"

How would he know? Why would that matter? But he didn't say any of that out loud. "Er, I don't know. Maybe she's one of those career-oriented women."

"Yet, she's here, reunited with her daughter and the senator."

"Well, I don't think it said anything in her file about that." What could he say? Who cared?

"Hmm… Look out for Dylan. He might do something stupid now that you took the girl."

"What do you mean?"

"He came to see me. Wanted to know if I had anything to do with Lily's disappearance. Then he mentioned Rain Tree LLC."

Now he understood. "He might go confront them, and Martinez might take him."

"Exactly. Make sure he's safe."

He wanted to object, to outline the myriad of complications this would bring, but he bit back the words. Facing the Ghost's unwavering gaze, he knew better than to voice his concerns.

"We'll handle it," he said. "But if we have to go in guns blazing, it'll be war with the Martinez cartel."

The Ghost's eyes hardened, a glint of steel in her gaze. "So be it. I've been to war with cartels before, and I've won. Nothing —absolutely nothing—can happen to Dylan."

He nodded, the severity sinking in. But first, he'd better update her on his other assignments. "Jade's situation has hit a snag, but it's under control. And Phoenix? Lily's the key to unmask him."

The Ghost listened. After a moment, she leaned forward again, her voice taking on a sharper edge. "This is more than just another task. Dylan's safety is paramount. Do whatever is necessary."

The weight of her words, a heavy mantle of responsibility, settled on his shoulders. "I understand. Dylan will be back—no matter the cost."

As he walked out, he couldn't help but wonder why the sudden interest in Olivia. The Ghost was too complicated for him to understand. Why did she want to protect Dylan if she wanted to reclaim the Marino throne? Oh, well, he needed to check on Lily and find out about Dylan.

His phone rang while he was driving. His mole in the Martinez cartel reported that they had the Ghost's nephew. Rook swore. This wasn't supposed to be so complicated. Why did the kid have to stick his nose where it didn't belong? The whole idea of using the task force to do their dirty work was so they didn't have to go to war with the Martinez cartel. And now, they might have to—unless… Yes, he could make an anonymous call to the task force and let them rescue the kid. Then again, the Ghost had told him, "Do whatever is necessary." And the Feds would have all those rules of engagement. If Dylan was taken hostage, then it would be a long-drawn-out drama with a hostage negotiator. More often than not, the hostage got hurt or killed.

He couldn't risk that.

He started making phone calls, ordering people to prepare. His mind was so preoccupied he'd forgotten to check for a tail.

*OLIVIA*

Olivia tossed and turned throughout the night. With the first light of dawn, she reached for her phone and dialed Jay for an update on Lily and the other assets involved in the operation. Her voice thick with worry, she inquired, "Anything new on Lily?"

"Nothing yet." Jay's voice came through, steady and calm. "We're still waiting on actionable intel."

She ended the call. Before she headed out to the Federal Detention Center, Simon asked her about Lily.

"You'll be the first to know when I hear anything." And she was out. The guard from the Federal Detention Center called. "O'Shea is here to see the Ghost." She thanked the guard and stepped on it.

Jay had warned her that her inquiries into the fake O'Shea had stirred up trouble. But he remained tight-lipped about the identity of the mole within their ranks or any suspicions about the impostor's true identity. That left Olivia to her own devices.

As she arrived at the detention center, a different vehicle pulled up. She jotted down the license plate number, then called Hernandez back at the task force office. "I need a registration check on this plate."

While waiting for Hernandez's call back, she got a call from Ron. His theory that the Ghost was behind the kill order on Grace and Kyle had some merits. And the obvious go-between would be this fake O'Shea. She was about to explain, but her mark emerged from the detention center. She hung up. O'Shea seemed agitated, hurried, a clear sign of pressure. Instead of heading to his usual haunt, he stayed in the car and drove on.

Her phone buzzed with a return call from Hernandez. "The car's registered to a William Hunt." He then provided an address.

The way O'Shea had been driving made her think he was either too distracted or too preoccupied to drive his usual SDR (surveillance detection route). She followed the car, but it didn't head toward the address Hernandez had given. Instead, it parked in a nondescript motel parking lot.

What was he doing here? Was he meeting someone? In the open parking lot, it would be too risky to check it out. So, she stayed in her car and watched.

# CHAPTER 60

## WAREHOUSE

*DYLAN*

Dylan's pulse hammered in his ears as he stood in the cavernous warehouse, the dim lighting casting long, ominous shadows. It was mostly empty save for the people and the stacks of cartons against the wall. They were in a corner office with minimum furnishings—just a desk, some chairs, a cabinet, and an impressive high-back chair where a Hispanic man sat. His small stature didn't preclude him from exuding an aura of authority. He got up to scrutinize Dylan with a gaze that seemed to pierce through his defenses.

"Nunez, who is this?"

So Nunez, the man whom Dylan had thought was the boss, had another boss. He stepped forward now, his posture stiff with respect. "Jefe, this is the nephew, Dylan Roche. He showed up at the office uninvited."

The boss, an imposing figure despite his height, studied Dylan as if examining a rare specimen. "Bueno, bueno, the nephew. Why was he there?"

"I can speak for myself." Dylan flexed the hands they'd

bound behind him. "I was looking for Lily Roth. The Lockwood fellow lured her to the office, and now she's gone."

"You do not talk unless you are summoned." The scarred bodyguard's voice was as menacing as that scar he kept stroking. He turned to the real boss. "Found a pocketknife, but no wire on him."

"Lockwood?" The boss looked at the one he called Nunez.

"He's a local hire."

The boss nodded.

"You can't touch—"

The bodyguard punched Dylan's face. "I told you—"

"Let our guest speak," Bossman ordered.

Dylan tasted blood, but his teeth and nose were still intact. "You know my aunt is the Ghost. You can't touch me."

Bossman smiled. "That would be correct if she was still in charge."

Heart pounding, Dylan frowned. What did he mean? Of course the Ghost was in charge. "Just because she's in jail doesn't mean she's not in charge."

"My young friend, the Ghost may still control some parts of her empire. But you know what? Her empire is falling apart, slowly, but surely. Once upon a time, I abided by her rules. Not anymore."

Could he be telling the truth? *Could* his aunt lose power? It seemed she had people in high and low places. She didn't appear fearful or worried when he talked to her.

Bossman turned to Nunez and spoke in rapid Spanish. From Nunez's and the bodyguard's expressions, they didn't like what they heard. Then the bodyguard took Dylan to the back of the boxes and sat him down against the wall.

What did Bossman say? Did he not want to kill him right away? Ah, they must be holding him hostage as leverage for something.

# CHAPTER 61

## MOTEL

*LILY*

Lily sat on the motel bed, her gaze fixated on Filmore—or whoever he really was—as he stood at the room's far end, phone pressed to his ear. The room, with its faded wallpaper and faint smell of disinfectant, felt like a cage. Outside, traffic sounds created a distant murmur, a reminder of the world she'd been cut off from.

Filmore's voice was low, his words muffled. So she strained to catch snippets of his conversations. "She's safe," he said at one point, and her heart skipped a beat. He must mean her. The rest of his conversation was cryptic, filled with "yes sirs" and noncommittal grunts.

Then his phone buzzed with a text message, and he shot her a sharp look. "Be quiet," he ordered before slipping out of the room.

Curiosity piqued, she crept to the window and peered through the blinds. He stood outside, talking to a man whose hat and sunglasses hid his face. The conversation seemed intense, but she couldn't make out any words.

When the man walked away, Filmore returned to the room.

Seeing his obvious agitation, she squirmed. "What's up?"

He shook his head, his brows knitted together. "Not good. Looks like your boyfriend is in trouble."

Her frown deepened. Boyfriend? "Dylan?" A knot clenched her stomach. "What happened?"

He glanced at her, his eyes guarded. "He dropped you off yesterday, correct? That's the one."

She bit her lip. "Why can't he stay out of trouble?"

Filmore's hard features softened. "Don't worry." His tone was anything but reassuring. "I'm waiting for a call. Then we'll head out to rescue him."

"Why is he in trouble? What did he do? What happened?"

He sighed, running a hand through his salt-and-pepper crew-cut hair. "I don't have all the details. But it seems he's gotten himself tangled up with the cartel. We need to get to him before they decide to do him harm."

"What are you going to do? What's the plan?"

"The plan doesn't concern you."

"But—"

"No but. These are dangerous people. I need to keep you safe."

The room felt even smaller now, the walls closing in on her. She hated feeling so helpless. Her abduction experience taught her to look out for herself in situations like this. But what could she do? Filmore, if nothing else, did save her earlier. Could she trust him?

*Oh, God, please keep Dylan safe! Help us!*

**OLIVIA**

Olivia's heart pounded as she sat in her car, parked at a discreet distance from the motel. She kept her focus on the man she knew as the fake O'Shea. Through her binoculars, she observed him meeting with another man who emerged from one of the motel rooms. Both men had their backs to her. The exchange was brief and seemed charged with urgency.

She cataloged what she could of the new man's characteristics—average height, nondescript clothing, cautious demeanor. The kind of person who blended into a crowd. If only she had brought along more sophisticated surveillance equipment. Being able to listen in on their conversation would have been invaluable.

As the fake O'Shea ended his brief meeting and made a couple of calls, she mulled over her options. The new man could be a key player in whatever O'Shea was involved in, but following him meant losing sight of O'Shea. What a gamble either way.

The fake O'Shea got into his car, so she had to make a decision—fast. Should she try to uncover the new man's identity or continue tailing O'Shea?

After a moment of hesitation, she stuck with the fake O'Shea. He was the one she had been tracking so far, and deviating from that now could mean losing all the progress she had made.

As she started her car and began to follow O'Shea from a safe distance, she couldn't shake off a sense of unease. Had she made the right choice? The world of espionage and undercover work was fraught with such decisions, and the wrong one brought serious consequences.

She kept a steady eye on O'Shea's vehicle, blending into the traffic. But who was the man O'Shea had met with? Something about him seemed familiar, but what was it? If only she could've seen his face. What was their conversation about? And most importantly, what was O'Shea's next move?

## *ROOK*

The night was dense with almost tangible tension. Rook, known for his meticulous planning and unyielding resolve, found himself in a precarious situation, racing against time. The Ghost's orders were clear—retrieve Dylan unharmed, at any cost. This was no ordinary mission. This demanded swift, decisive action, a brute-force approach in stark departure from his usual orchestrated strategies.

After being informed Dylan had been taken, he'd formed a crude plan. First, he needed to check with Filmore. Phoenix might still make contact with the girl. They needed to be ready. But since Filmore was also his most experienced asset in tactical, he'd have to improvise.

Instead of taking his usual precautions, he only donned a hat and a pair of sunglasses when he met Filmore at the motel parking lot. He told him Dylan had been taken by the Martinez cartel. "The Ghost's order is clear. If we must go to war with the Martinez cartel, we will. It appears we will hit the Martinez compound, and I need your expertise."

His asset ran a hand over his hair. "It's too short a notice. Storming the compound is risky."

"I'm aware. But we don't have the luxury of time. I'm getting a team ready." A direct assault on the heavily guarded Martinez compound would be no easy feat. But they had an element of surprise, and he'd use it to their advantage.

"We strike fast and hard." He showed Filmore a rough map of the compound on his phone. "We don't have much time. Martinez doesn't know we're coming yet."

Filmore leaned over the map, his eyes tracing the lines and markers. "It's a fortress. Even with the element of surprise, it's going to be a bloodbath."

"I know. But we have no choice." Rook met his asset's gaze. "Dylan's life is on the line. I'll send this to you."

They had a hasty, albeit dangerous plan, but it was all they had.

"What do you want me to do with her?" Filmore jerked his thumb toward the room.

"Figure it out." Rook started to walk away. "Wait for the call."

As he was about to get in his car, his phone rang. Team Bravo had located the safe house and planted the scare. And they had eyes on them.

At least, something was going right. And Filmore would oversee the operation. Much like the Ghost, Rook didn't like getting his hands dirty. Now, he had to establish his alibi should it become necessary.

# CHAPTER 62

## TASK FORCE OFFICE

*RON*

Ron stood in the squad room, still rattled after the call about the safe-house attack. The situation was critical, and Kyle was involved. His paternal instinct screamed to ensure his son's safety, but he had to trust Kyle's training and focus on the larger picture.

Hernandez mentioned the name William Hunt, interrupting Ron's thoughts. Why did that name strike a chord in his memory? Unable to place it, he walked over to the agent's station.

Peering over Hernandez's shoulder, he frowned as an address on the registration details jogged his memory. "Who was that? Why were you looking into this registration?"

Hernandez's head jerked up. "Oh, boss. I didn't hear you come over. It was Olivia. I'm not sure why. She just asked me to look up a plate number."

Ron pressed his lips together, his frown deepening. Olivia's request didn't fit into the current situation. What was she on to?

Stepping away from the workstation, he pulled out his

phone. As it rang her number, he paced the room. The safe-house attack, Kyle's involvement, and now Olivia's mysterious inquiry into William Hunt—all these pieces had to fit together somehow.

"Olivia," he said as soon as the call connected. "You asked Hernandez to run a plate. What's going on? Is this related to the safe-house situation?"

"I'm following a lead. Don't know anything about the safe-house situation. I'm tailing the fake O'Shea who might lead us to some answers."

His grip on the phone tightened. "I thought we weren't supposed to do anything about him."

"Well, you know me. And I'm technically still with the Company. It's internal."

"But what's William Hunt got to do with this?"

"He's driving a car that belongs to Hunt. Might be stolen. Who knows?"

"All right, be careful."

"I will." She ended the call.

Unease lingered. Her response had been guarded, almost evasive. Once a spy, always a spy. He could never get a straightforward answer from her. He didn't have time to ponder this further, however, as Cooper approached.

"Is everyone ready?" Cooper's voice cut through the buzz of the busy office. "I just got confirmation of Dylan's location."

Ron's attention snapped to the present situation. He moved to grab his gear. "Where is he?"

"We've traced him to an old warehouse on the city outskirts. HRT is on standby, waiting for our go."

The hostage rescue team's involvement indicated the situation's seriousness. His adrenaline surged as he and the other agents began to prepare for the operation. The atmosphere shifted to a focused intensity while everyone geared up with bulletproof vests, firearms, and other tactical gear. Dylan's safety was paramount, and their operation's success could hinge on the smallest details.

"Remember, we need to approach this with utmost caution," he reminded the team. "We don't know what we're walking into. Stay sharp and stay safe."

The team members nodded, everyone obviously mentally preparing for the task ahead. Ron checked his equipment one last time before heading out. The drive to the warehouse was tense, each agent lost in their thoughts, running through scenarios and strategies.

They arrived to the HRT already positioned. The warehouse loomed ahead, a dilapidated structure that seemed to hold more secrets than it did goods.

He communicated with the HRT leader, finalizing their entry strategy. "We go in quiet, assess the situation before making any moves. Our primary objective is to secure Dylan and any other hostages safely."

The team moved into position.

# CHAPTER 63

## SAFE HOUSE

*KYLE*

In the new safe house, as bland and nondescript as the first, Kyle wrestled with his emotions. Furnishings were at a bare minimum, the walls seemingly closing in, suffocating him with the monotonous silence that had become their companion.

He replayed his conversation with his father, a loop of frustration. He ached to be part of the takedown operation, not a bystander in his own story. But since the attack, Torres was adamant—no internet, no outside communication. He'd effectively cut them off from everything.

For the first hour or so, Grace was quiet. He noticed her mouth moving at some point, but he couldn't hear what she was saying. And then, he saw the Bible on her lap. She must have grabbed it when they had to move. Now, she was finding solace in whatever she was reading. Huh, maybe she was praying.

Earlier, he walked around the house and didn't find a guitar, but he found a small keyboard. Almost like a child's toy. He showed it to her. "Do you play? Not sure if it works."

"Yes, let's see." She put it on the dining table, turned it on, hit a few keys, and declared, "It works." She'd turned the volume down and started playing.

"Do you always memorize the songs you play?" he asked after a while.

She looked up, her hands still moving in rhythm. "Some of them, yes. But others, I just… let them flow."

Wow. "So, you compose your own music?"

"Yeah." She smiled, her dark eyes soft with memories. "Ever since I was little, music has been my way of expressing what I can't put into words."

"That's incredible." He moved closer, the music drawing him in like a siren's call. "I had no idea you were so talented."

Her smile widened. "Nah, but thanks."

Their conversation flowed more freely after that, the music creating a comfortable space for them to open up. He shared his life story, the highs and lows that shaped him into who he was. She listened, her fingers straying to the keyboard to punctuate a poignant moment with a soft chord. He even mentioned Lily—how he was frustrated not knowing if she wanted to move forward with their relationship.

"Have you always wanted to be an FBI agent? Or is it because of your father?"

"I don't know." He shrugged. "Never really thought about it. I guess in some way, it's because I wanted to be closer to my dad."

She stopped playing, got up, and returned to the couch, clutching the Bible. "I get that. But we have our own parts to play in this life, our own paths to forge. As my dad would say, God has a plan for each of us. We just need to listen."

Right, her dad was a pastor. She opened the Bible and started reading. Well, if it would give her peace, good for her!

"Would you like to read with me?" She patted a gray worn-out couch much like the one in the last safe house, inviting him to sit next to her. "Here is a good one if you need guidance and direction."

Uh-oh. This was getting into strange territory. Lily's godmother was a nun, yet she never talked to him about religion or her faith, although she did invite him to church once. He had, of course, declined. Oh well, there was nothing to do anyway. He sat next to her. She told him it was a psalm, read it, and asked him what he thought.

In the middle of their enlightening discussion, the hairs on the back of his neck stood up. He held a finger to his mouth, signaling her to be quiet. Then he got up and peered through the window. Torres was signaling to Wood. They had an intruder on the perimeter.

She watched him with wide eyes, her expression a stark contrast to the relative calm they'd been enjoying. His training kicked in, and he patted his holster to be sure his gun was in place.

"What's happening?" she asked.

"We might have an uninvited guest. Stay behind me." He guided her upstairs, toward a back bedroom closet, a makeshift but secure hiding spot.

Once at the closet, he spoke in a reassuring tone. "Stay here until an agent comes for you, okay? It's the safest place right now."

She hesitated. "Where are you going?"

"Not going anywhere. I'll be right outside."

After she nodded and stepped into the closet, he closed the door before turning his attention back to the unfolding situation.

His gaze then shifted to the window, and through it, Torres motioned to him. Expecting to be called into action, Kyle was surprised when the agent in charge gestured for him to stay put. "Stay with her," Torres mouthed, pointing first at him and then back toward the closet.

Torn, Kyle hesitated. His instincts screamed for him to join the fray, to confront the danger head-on. But the agent's instructions were unambiguous. With a nod of understanding, he stepped back from the window and stationed himself in front of the closet.

"Grace, I'm here," Kyle whispered through the door. "We need to stay put and let the agents handle this. Just stay down and stay quiet."

From inside the closet, her muffled voice came through. "Okay, be careful."

"I will." His hand tightened around his gun. "We're going to get through this. Just stay hidden, and I'll make sure we're safe."

The agents moving outside served as a stark reminder of their precarious situation. This was a new safe house. Did they find them already? How?

# CHAPTER 64

## ON THE ROAD

*OLIVIA*

Olivia's focus was laser-sharp as she trailed the car. Had she gotten lucky, or was the guy's head somewhere else? The fake O'Shea seemed oblivious to her pursuit. Since leaving the motel, he had been navigating the city streets with an urgent haste, yet his destination appeared to be an ordinary suburb.

What had Hernandez said? "The vehicle's registered to a William Hunt." She'd input the address into her GPS. Now, as she followed O'Shea's car, the electronic voice of her GPS guided her through unfamiliar streets. The fake O'Shea might be William Hunt since the destination seemed to be Hunt's address.

How odd. The flurry of activities, the carelessness with which O'Shea had been operating, all pointed toward something significant unfolding. Yet here he was, heading toward what appeared to be his home. It didn't add up.

And when things didn't add up, there was more to them than met the eye.

She kept a safe distance. The car ahead took a left turn, and she followed, scanning the surroundings for any signs of a trap or lookout. The neighborhood they entered was quiet, almost idyllic, with rows of well-kept houses and manicured lawns.

"Continue for half a mile. Then your destination will be on your right," the GPS intoned.

As she drove, she flexed her grip on the steering wheel, pent-up energy coursing through her. "Why would he come here? What's at this address?" she muttered to herself.

The fake O'Shea's car turned into the driveway. Instead of stopping, he continued down the driveway and into the garage, the door closing behind him, cutting off her view. She drove past the house and found a spot to park a safe distance away, far enough to avoid drawing attention but close enough to keep an eye on the house.

From her car, she surveyed the quiet suburban street of a typical neighborhood with kids playing in yards and neighbors going about their routines. Nothing seemed out of place, except for the nagging feeling that something significant was happening in the innocuous house she was surveilling.

Earlier, she had assumed the car or the plate was stolen. So, perhaps that wasn't the case. Her heartbeat picked up and her knee jittered, keeping pace. Could it be? Could the fake O'Shea be William Hunt? Had she uncovered the mole's identity?

## *LILY*

Lily's heart pounded while Filmore's car sped through the dimly lit streets. Her mind raced with worry for Dylan as an uncomfortable silence, broken only by the occasional hum of passing traffic, overtook the car.

"Why did they take Dylan?" She twisted her hands in her lap, her white-knuckle grip betraying her anxiety. She stared at him, seeking answers in his stoic expression.

He kept his focus on the road, his jaw tightening, his hands gripping the steering wheel perhaps a little too tightly. "I don't know."

Her brows furrowed. She needed to understand these mysterious circumstances. "Who exactly do you work for, Filmore?"

He remained silent, his gaze fixed ahead. His lack of response only fueled her growing unease.

Whoever he worked for—he saved her once. So, he had to be a good guy, right? He knew her mom. Could he be a spy like her mom? Then who was that guy he was talking to back at the motel parking lot? And why wouldn't he let her go?

As they approached their destination, the nondescript warehouse loomed ahead. He didn't park near the building, choosing a shadowed spot some distance away. He turned off the engine, and the car plunged into darkness.

He reached into the glove compartment and pulled out a zip tie.

A soft gasp slid out as her eyes widened. "I'm not going out," she said quickly. "You don't have to do that. Besides, what happens if someone comes to investigate? I need to be able to run or hide."

He turned, his eyes searching hers in the dim light. "I hope you know I'm trying to keep you safe."

Was his voice softer than before? Could she trust him? A man about to bind her? "Why are we here? Is this where they took Dylan?"

"You need to stay here—for your own good. Sorry."

He grabbed her hand and fastened it to the steering wheel. She protested to no avail.

Then he opened the car door, stepped out into the night, and disappeared into the shadows. Dylan had to be here. But where was this place?

She repositioned her bound hand, her nerves fraying further with each passing minute. Approaching vehicles periodically shattered the stillness, causing her to duck down. A surge of anxiety roiled her each time a car passed, her mind racing over what could be happening inside the warehouse.

She searched the glove compartment for anything to cut the zip tie. Nothing. After a few wiggles, she realized it wasn't that tight. She tried tugging her thumb close to her hand and kept maneuvering her hand in the right angle to slip out of the tie.

"Ow." Her hand was free, but her skin was scraped.

Then the unmistakable sound of gunshots rang out. Her heart leapt into her throat. All she could think about was Dylan's safety. The urge to know what was happening inside was too strong to resist. Despite Filmore's instructions to stay put, curiosity and concern propelled her out of the car.

She approached the warehouse, the area eerily deserted. Reaching a slightly ajar door, she pushed it open and stepped into terrifying chaos. Several bodies lay scattered across the floor, some groaning in pain. Others remained ominously still. But she didn't see Filmore or Dylan.

Hard fingers encircled her arm and pulled her backward. An accented voice said, "Welcome to the party!"

A gun barrel pressed against her back. Using her as a shield, he shuffled back to the door.

"Stop! You're surrounded." Filmore appeared from behind some boxes. "Let her go!"

The man continued to move backward.

*Remember your training! You can do this!* She heard her mom's voice in her mind. Taking a deep breath, she said a quick prayer and recalled her mom's instructions. Stay calm. Assess the situation. Tipping her head, she made sure it was a gun. When he tried to make her back up further, she stopped and twisted out of the gun's aim while using her right arm to shove the gun away. She then planned to scoop his gun hand with her arm and wrestle the weapon from him. But before she got to finish the series, the man fell backward, several holes in his body.

And then she saw Dylan lying on the ground. She gasped. Her heart dropped to the pit of her stomach.

She ran to him. *Please, Lord, help. Don't let him die, please!*

# CHAPTER 65

## THE HASKIN RESIDENCE

*ROOK*

Rook pulled into the garage, noted her car. She was unusually early. As the deviation from routine piqued his interest, he strode into the house, calling out to his wife. She greeted him with a smile from the kitchen, offering wine. "Sounds good, but I'll be right back." He headed to his home office to retrieve her birthday gift—a delicate necklace. When he returned, he found her still in the kitchen, lost in thought. He slipped his arms around her and planted a tender kiss on her cheek, wishing her a happy birthday. She handed him the glass of wine.

As he sipped, a sudden onset of an allergic reaction caught him off guard. His hand went to his pocket for his EpiPen, but it wasn't there. Panic surged as his breathing became labored.

"Vera, my EpiPen…" he choked out, voice strained. "Call 911."

She didn't move to call for help. She just watched him, her smile unsettling. "You're not having an allergic reaction. It's a paralytic agent in the wine. I know who you are, Rook."

His mind raced as her eerily composed voice repeated itself in his head. No, she couldn't have known. He slid to the floor and gasped, each breath a battle. "What do you mean?"

She knelt just out of reach, her amber eyes flaring with fire. "Do you think I'd be so gullible to fall for you? You inserted yourself into my life. Granted, for a while, I was fooled. After all, any woman will find it nice to have someone paying that much attention to her." Her smile turned to something different, something feral. "You're the mole. I've suspected it for a while now. I've noticed your late nights, your secretive calls, your mysterious trips. Thank goodness you decided to look into Phoenix. Your sniffing around my files for Phoenix gave you away. Until then, I couldn't prove it."

His heart pounded, each pump sluiced the fear and disbelief deeper through him. He couldn't move. He tried to focus, but it was like swimming in a haze. "Listen to me. You're misunderstanding—"

But the words were hard to find as his throat tightened.

"No, you listen, traitor," she interrupted. "How despicable! You wormed your way into my life, so you could steal intel for the Ghost. I'm careful, so don't think I didn't notice your stealth intrusion into my files. You swore an oath to defend this country against all enemies, foreign and domestic. Yet, you collude with the Ghost. I can't prove it, but I know you have a hand in the bioterror last year."

His thoughts swirled, growing hazier. Did she know everything? "You… don't know… what the… government did to… me and my family."

"Oh, but I do. It was an unspecified threat. You know we have to prioritize a lot of things. You were in a mission-critical op. The Company alerted the Bureau. They had eyes on them. They just couldn't prevent the accident. Learn to face the truth. A drunk driver killed them. The accident had nothing to do with the threat."

No, no. He'd never believe that. It was not a drunk driver. "You're wrong. Help… me. You… are… a sworn law enforcement… officer. You can't—"

"But I can." She leaned forward to whisper. "It's a sanctioned kill. We don't need any more negative press." She straightened up, took a syringe out of her pocket, and pushed the needle into his vein. "Don't worry. We're humane. Here's something to relax you, and you'll just go to sleep."

## OLIVIA

Olivia sat in the car, debating checking it out. Too bad she hadn't called Shadow Shot to join her. She resorted to doing some research. Frustrated with the vagueness of online search results for William Hunt, she retrieved her tablet with enhanced capabilities. A moment later, she pulled up property records. Whoa. The house belonged to Vera Haskin and William Hunt. A jolt zipped through her. That would be the FBI deputy director, with whom she recently had a meeting. Or… maybe it was someone else with that name?

For clarity, she dialed Ron. The phone rang once, twice, before his voice, brusque and distracted, answered.

"Do you know where Vera Haskin lives? Your boss, the deputy director?"

He muttered a vague response about the area but admitted he didn't know the house number. His tone remained rushed, his words clipped. "Can't talk now, on the way to rescue Dylan."

Concern flickered, arching a brow. "What happened? Do you need help with that?"

"No, it's under control. Just—"

She cut him off, not wanting to distract him further. "Okay, one more question. Do you know if she's married? Husband's name?"

"Yes, don't recall the name. She kept her own name, so hubby has a different last name. Really gotta go." He ended the call.

According to GPS, she was in the general area of where Ron had said Haskin's house was. So, it appeared Haskin and Hunt were a couple. And this was their residence. Haskin warned her about someone looking into her background. Would it be her husband? No, that didn't fit. Haskin wouldn't have alerted her if she was in league with the impostor and the Ghost. How did Haskin fit into this?

After another thirty minutes of waiting with no movement, she got out of the car, closed the door, and walked toward the house, out of the door cam's view. She felt it before she heard the blast. Before she had a chance to take cover, the shock wave knocked her over. And her world turned black.

# CHAPTER 66

## SAFE HOUSE

*KYLE*

From the gunshots, the situation outside must be deteriorating. The agents' chatter became increasingly distressed. Kyle surveyed the house. Then, making as little noise as possible, he slid open the closet door and gestured for Grace to come out and go to the bathroom. She did with him in tow.

The soft, deliberate footsteps of someone outside, not an agent, padded across the porch as he evaluated their options. The bathroom, their temporary refuge, had one advantage—a large window. Although the bottom sash was frosted, obscuring a clear view, the window itself offered a potential escape route.

He approached the window, taking care not to make any noise, and peered through the upper part of the glass. There was no sign of a large group, which could mean the intruders were focusing on another part of the house.

He beckoned Grace over. "We need to get out of here. Through the window."

Her gaze went from him to the window and back. "You want us to climb out here?"

"Yes, it's not that high."

She took a peek out the window. Without another word, she pulled the bottom half of the window open and slid out. She stepped to the left, extended her arms, and seized a nearby sturdy tree branch. Then, in a breathtaking display of agility, she swung from the branch with a rhythmic, flowing motion. For a moment, she seemed to defy gravity, her body arching through the air in a flawless flip. As she approached the ground, she tucked her body and stuck the landing. He'd have applauded if the situation wasn't so dangerous.

Now that she was safely on the ground, he motioned for her to head toward the next house while he prepared to jump. His landing was nowhere near as graceful as hers, but he made it without twisting an ankle or worse. He was about to join her when a masked man rounded the corner. Thank goodness he had been practicing his draw. His gun was in his hand in no time.

"Freeze!" he ordered.

"Don't think so!" The man pointed his own gun at him. "You're surrounded. Your buddies are in no position to save you."

It didn't sound good. Neither of them backed down. Then Grace emerged from behind the tree. *Go away!* But her gaze was focused on the man's head. Her arms rose high with a potted plant in her hands. Then she slammed it down.

"Yes!" she exclaimed.

"Shush!" He put his finger on his lips and whispered, "We don't want to draw attention. And thank you."

"You're welcome."

He searched the downed man, grabbed his gun, and took his phone. He needed to call for help. He didn't know where the other agents were or what their condition was. If he didn't have to protect her, he'd have searched for the others.

"What now?" she whispered.

He scanned the area. "We need to move. Stay low and follow me."

As they were walking away from the safe house, he called the task force office—the only number he knew by heart—and asked to be patched to his dad. He got his voicemail. He called again, and this time, he asked to be connected to anyone on the team. Ana answered. He gave her a rundown of the situation.

"On my way!" She hung up.

## GRACE

What an exhilarating experience. Grace never thought she would feel this way when she hit someone's head with a potted plant. But when she saw the two men facing off, it was evident Kyle wouldn't shoot first—she watched enough crime shows to know that. She needed to do something to break the stalemate. And she spotted those pots. One looked too bulky and heavy. She picked a smaller, but still good-sized pot. The man was too busy pointing the gun at Kyle, fumbling for something in his pocket to notice her.

"Help is coming."

Kyle's voice brought her back to the moment. They were closing in on the next house when he yanked her back and urged her to run to the backyard. Confused, she looked back toward the neighbor's house and gasped. More masked men with assault rifles were stomping out of the house. She ran. The backyard was hilly, but they were going downhill. Before long, they approached a stream. Unsure of what to do, she looked at him with questioning eyes. He gestured for her to keep running along the stream away from the house. This was a nice place. If the situation wasn't so dire, she would've loved to stay and enjoy the tranquility. Even the air smelled fresh. But they were running for their lives.

Rat-tat-tat. Rat-tat-tat.

He tackled her to the ground. But then they weren't being shot at. A series of heavy gunshots were happening back at the two houses. He kept her down, probably not wanting to risk exposure. The gunfight didn't go on long.

"Kyle! Grace!" a woman was bellowing. A few other men joined her, all yelling for them.

Kyle stood up, waved, and hollered, "Down here!"

A Latina woman and several men in outfits that made them look like giant bugs came running toward them. The men still had their rifles up and kept scanning the area. After they removed their helmets and other headgear, they looked more human.

"You all right?" the woman asked.

"Yeah, we're good." Kyle helped Grace up. "You got the SWAT team. Thanks!"

"Well, your dad got the HRT over at the warehouse. I had to borrow SWAT from the local PD." The woman was speaking to him, but her gaze was on Grace.

He must have noticed that. "Oh, sorry, this is Ana, er, Special Agent Ruiz. She's our DIA liaison." To Agent Ruiz, he said, "This is Grace Benson."

She smiled. "Nice to meet you, Agent Ruiz. And thank you!"

"You're welcome."

Something seemed familiar about the woman, but Grace couldn't figure out what. Perhaps she was another Latina? Wait. Didn't Kyle say he worked with her birth mom?

"Place is secured, ma'am." One of the SWAT guys reported to Agent Ruiz. "Should we book them, or do you want to take them? The ME has been notified about the others."

"Just give me a minute. I'll have a chat with them. Then you can take them in."

"Yes, ma'am."

Agent Ruiz marched up the hill with the man in tow. Grace and Kyle followed. With her suspicion, she watched Agent Ruiz. Should she ask him? Not the time, anyway. He was busy.

"Have you found Torres, Wood, and the others?" Kyle asked Agent Ruiz.

"Yes, don't know who's who, but we got one dead, three injured. Hanson, did you get the ID?" She directed the last part to the SWAT guy.

"Yes, ma'am." He got his phone, swiped, and announced, "Jackson is deceased. Torres, Wood, and Wheeler are injured."

Her birth mom, a federal agent, Grace tried to think about it. Agent Ruiz saved them, after all. A woman who wielded guns and gave orders to the SWAT team. Kind of cool.

Another SWAT guy came running toward them. "Ma'am, your Agent Torres wanted me to tell you, 'Jackson sold us out.' He was adamant I tell you right away. As soon as I agreed, he passed out."

Kyle swore. "So that's how they knew where we were!"

"But wasn't he the one who got tased?" Grace asked.

"Yeah, that's a good way to deflect suspicion."

"Well, he got what he deserved, then," Agent Ruiz said. "Now, we need to find out who hired them."

# CHAPTER 67

## MARTINEZ COMPOUND

*LILY*

Lily scrambled toward Dylan, her heart pounding. "No, he can't be dead. He'll be fine," she whispered to herself.

Filmore rushed over. "I told you to stay put!"

She didn't care what he said. "What happened to him? Help him!"

"He's fine. Just got knocked out. He'll come around." The heat in his voice seeped away. "The brute pushed him to the wall. He might have a concussion, but that's probably it." He knelt and checked the back of Dylan's head, fingers probing. "No blood. Just a bump."

She wasn't sure she believed him. But then, she felt the pulse herself. Gently, she shook his shoulder. "Dylan, can you hear me?"

Filmore left her kneeling beside Dylan. She was vaguely aware of him checking on the wounded and the dead, making calls. Then, somewhere, sirens blared.

First, a soft moan came. Was she imagining it? She shook him again. "Wake up, Dylan."

His eyelids fluttered. Then he opened his eyes.

She breathed out her relief. "Are you okay?"

"Yeah, I don't know. I had the weirdest dream. You were in it." He had a goofy smile. "You told me you wanted a big wedding."

She frowned. Was he delirious? "Are you sure you're okay?"

He closed his eyes again.

## *RON*

Ron tried to slow his rapid breathing as they sped toward the warehouse. The puzzle pieces were all there, but fitting them together seemed too complex. The phone call from Olivia earlier, that uneasy feeling he couldn't shake off, the address Hernandez had pulled up—it all led to one revelation. He didn't lie to her. He really didn't recall the house number, but he did know the address Hernandez had found was Vera's.

Olivia had been tailing the fake O'Shea, a man driving a car registered to William Hunt. His instincts screamed that Hunt was Haskin's husband. Could the fake O'Shea be William Hunt? No way was Haskin working with the Ghost. But how could she be married to someone associated with the Ghost?

His mind kept circling back to the leak. Haskin knew about Olivia/Phoenix, so her involvement couldn't be ruled out. Yes, the pieces were coming together, but they formed an unsettling image.

As they arrived at the warehouse, he braced for a heated confrontation. The entry went unchallenged, everything eerily quiet as they moved inside, weapons drawn.

Dim lights unmasked the aftermath of a brutal encounter. Bodies were strewn across the cold concrete floor, a harrowing testament to the recent violence. On the dead, lifeless eyes stared into the void. Others, injured, groaned in pain, their moans echoing in the cavernous space.

Was that Lily? And Dylan lying before her?

*Oh no! What happened?*

Ron rushed over. Focused on Dylan, she didn't seem to realize he was there. The young man said something, but then his eyes closed again.

She swiveled her head, surprised to see him. "Why doesn't he stay awake?"

Not being a doctor, he didn't have an answer. And then he noticed a faint smile on the kid's face. *Oh, Dylan!*

"Dylan, nap time is over," he commanded.

Sure enough, his eyelids popped open. "Hey, Agent Peters."

"You'll go to the hospital to get checked out. Then I'll let her deal with you." He walked away, giving the young couple some privacy.

Cooper and Tanner were rounding up the injured. Ron told them they'd have to interrogate them separately once they were deemed stable enough.

"Is he okay?" Tanner tilted his head toward Dylan.

"Yeah, whatever it is, it's not serious."

"I didn't know they took her too," his agent said as he went to help Cooper.

Now that he thought about it, why was she here? How did she get here?

"Agent Peters," Lily called.

He walked back over to them.

"Where's Filmore?"

He frowned. Did he know that name? "Who's he?"

"He was just here. I don't know who he is, but he saved me a couple days ago."

So many things happened these last few days, could he have forgotten this bit? No, not possible. "Saved you from what?"

"Someone was shooting at me."

"When?"

"Hmm, yesterday—no, two days ago."

"Your mom knows?"

She shrugged. "I assume."

"Yes, Olivia knows," Dylan spoke up. "We were all at Rain Tree. Got to see the footage of the drive-by shooting and the Good Samaritan tackling her to save her. Then they walked away."

"Why didn't Olivia say anything to me?"

"No idea. She got a call and took off. But Simon later texted that Lily was safe. I thought they found her, but no, and they wouldn't say anything else."

"And you took it upon yourself to find her." Ron glared at the young man who didn't seem to understand the word *danger*.

"Anyway, where is Filmore?" she asked again. "He brought me here. Said he was supposed to keep me safe."

"By leading you to a gunfight?" He arched his eyebrows.

"No, no, he tied me to the steering wheel and told me to stay put, but I managed to get loose and come in." She clutched Dylan's hand. "I know, I shouldn't have. But I heard gunshots. I wanted to see if he had trouble getting Dylan."

Ron sighed. Why did these two always put themselves in danger? "Wait. This Filmore was coming to get Dylan?"

"Yes, that's what he said."

The paramedics arrived. Ron directed them to check Dylan first. He helped Lily up and walked with her to the ambulance. "Okay, start from the beginning. What happened a couple of days ago?"

# CHAPTER 68

## THE HASKIN RESIDENCE

*OLIVIA*

Fog shrouded her thoughts. Olivia had a vague recollection of being in her car, focused on a house the fake O'Shea or perhaps William Hunt had gone into. Right, she was walking toward that house when the world around her erupted. The memory of the explosion hit her as vividly as the shock wave itself had.

As her eyes adjusted to the evening light, she noticed the familiar sight of Shadow Shot, or rather Kevin. But wait. This wasn't an operation. Why was he here? The lines between past and present blurred, making it difficult to distinguish reality from the remnants of her former life.

"Welcome back. Are you okay?"

His voice broke through to her, though it seemed to be coming from afar when he was right there. She pointed to her ear and tried to get up, ignoring the pounding headache.

"I know," he continued. "You didn't have ear protection. And I'm already yelling. Give it some time. Your hearing will return to normal. I don't think anything is broken, but you'll need to tell me. I don't feel blood on your head just a bump. Will probably grow though."

"I'll live." She tried once again to get up, only to be pushed back down by Kevin.

"Don't rush it! You might have a concussion."

She took a few deep breaths. She was lying on the grass. "Why are you here? The deputy director? Fake O'Shea or Hunt?" As soon as the words left her mouth, she knew. "Jay had you follow me. I'm losing it. Should have spotted you."

"For once, you're wrong. I'm here on Jay's order, but not to follow you. He'll fill you in. Haskin is fine. Hunt, not so much."

"What happened?"

"We got everything. Get her out of here now. Cops and the media will be here in minutes." A familiar voice floated from somewhere.

Olivia looked around as Haskin—at least she thought it was Haskin—disappeared into the night.

"Yes, ma'am," Kevin said. "All right, let's go." He helped her up. Together, they hustled back to her car. He helped her into the passenger seat and ran around to the driver's side.

"Don't argue! You're in no condition to drive. I already called Jay. He'll have someone pick up my motorcycle." He pushed the button to start the engine.

"And you didn't even ask for my key fob."

"No need." He glanced at the map on the dash display and drove on.

"So, where are we going?"

"Hospital. I didn't text Simon. Not sure what you want to tell him, and I don't have his number."

"I don't need to go to the hospital."

"Sorry, SOP. Jay said you needed to get checked out. He wasn't happy you were there."

Of course, Jay would insist on standard operating procedures. She'd talk to Simon later. Now she wanted to know what went on. "Yeah, so what's new? If he didn't want me to screw things up, he should have told me everything. Now, you tell me. Everything. Why did Jay order you there? Did you set the explosives? No, that's not your specialty. Jay has someone else. What kind of an op is this?"

He glanced at her. "Haskin is one of us."

She whipped her head toward him. "She is? But she's the deputy director of the FBI?"

He shrugged. "Maybe she's like one of those embassy attachés."

A lot of the embassy attachés were cover jobs for Company operatives. "Oh, but we're back stateside. And we're talking about the Bureau."

"I only know so much. Jay said to go there, report to Haskin. When she gave the word, I helped her move things in place. And get out of Dodge. But then she screamed you were heading to the house. I made a mad dash to scoop you up like a football. End of story."

"Thank you for saving me."

"You're welcome." He followed the sign to Orlando Hospital. "Reminds me of Capri."

"You're forgetting London. I saved you." She looked out at the stars in the sky and remembered the times when her cover "Jade" was on vacation, but in fact, she would be on assignment, usually in Europe. "Most of the time, you just sit behind your rifle and take the shot. I am the one who needs to take the risk."

"Who's counting?"

Her mind went back to the fake O'Shea. "What happened to the fake O'Shea? Or William Hunt? You said he died. How? Explosion? I don't understand."

"That, you'll have to wait for Jay to explain." He pulled into the hospital emergency bay. "And here you get to flash your badge. Maybe you'll get VIP treatment."

# CHAPTER 69

## ORLANDO HOSPITAL

*RON*

R on finally got the full story from Lily. Who was this Filmore fellow? Was he a good guy or a bad guy? Before he had time to contemplate further, he arrived at the hospital with Lily. He parked at the closest spot and hurried into the hospital with her. As they entered the ER, the familiar scent of antiseptic assaulted his senses. A man was at the counter. Simon? How'd he get here so fast?

"Dad!" Lily called.

Simon rushed over and enveloped her in his arms. "Are you all right?" He pushed her out to arm's length and studied her. "Your mom said you were safe, but she wouldn't say anything else."

"It's a long story, but I'm okay. Where's Dylan? How do you know to come here?"

They were in the way of stretchers going in and out. Ron guided them to the side as Simon was saying, "Dylan? I don't know. Why would he be here? What happened to him? I'm here for Olivia."

"Olivia? What happened?" Ron cut in.

"I'm not sure. Something about an explosion. But Kevin said she was fine."

"Who's Kevin?"

"He's—uh, never mind. Let's just go see her now. She's in room 8. And what's with Dylan?"

Lily started repeating her story to her dad as they walked toward the room.

Ron stopped by the desk to ask where Dylan was.

The nurse tapped the keyboard and said, "Roche is going to room 5."

He thanked her and headed there. The curtain was closed. That must mean Dylan was being examined. Ron veered to room 8. Olivia looked tired, but otherwise well.

"I'm not staying," she was saying.

"Why don't you listen to the doctor? They want you to stay at least overnight for observation." Simon sat in the bedside chair, holding her hand.

"You almost got killed, Mom." Lily, standing on the other side, evidently noticed him. "Oh, Agent Peters, did you find out where Dylan is?"

"Yes, room 5, but the curtain is closed right now." He shook a finger at Olivia. "I look forward to your report."

"You'll have it as soon as I get out of here." Her gaze then returned to her fiancé and daughter. "I'm fine. Just a little sore. No broken bones. I can go home. Really."

He wanted to ask who Kevin was, but before he could, his phone buzzed. Ana. "Sorry, folks. I need to take this." He stepped out. "Yes?"

"They're safe and heading to the hospital just to get checked out. Should be there any minute now, along with the injured agents and suspects. I'm heading back to the task force office."

A commotion arose when a crowd of medical personnel rushed to the emergency door. Stretcher after stretcher rumbled past with paramedics calling out, "Male. GSW!" and so on. Ron got out of the way, leaning against the wall. "I think they just came in. So, our theory?"

"I think so, but let's talk back at the office."

"Of course, I'll see you there." He ended the call.

Lily was coming out of room 8 when he turned back.

"Mom is stubborn. She's going to win. She'll get the doc to release her. I'm going to see Dylan." Lily told him as she walked down to room 5.

"I'm not surprised. She's one tough lady." He followed her to check on Dylan. The curtain was parted now.

"Hey, Lily. Sorry I scared you." Dylan sat up straighter as he spotted Lily. "Oh, Agent Peters. You rounded up all the bad guys?"

He nodded. "How did you end up unconscious?"

"I'm not sure." Dylan frowned. "I was sitting on the floor against the wall, my hands tied behind my back. Then there was all this noise. Something was happening. I heard gunshots. But I couldn't see what was going on. They put me behind a huge stack of cartons. And then this guy, the one who saved her the other day, came around and untied me, all the while chewing me out for playing with fire. My legs were asleep after sitting for so long. I'd just gotten up when this big dude came out of nowhere and shoved me to the wall, I guess. Then I don't know anymore."

"Yeah, I saw Filmore after I disarmed the boss," Lily joined in. "Well, I didn't finish the sequence. Somebody shot him once I was out of the way. Then I saw Dylan on the floor."

"Wait. Go back." Dylan held up a hand, his interest obviously piqued. "You disarmed someone? Seriously? How'd you do that?"

"He tried to use me as a shield. Mom made me practice that sequence many times."

"Whoa. You've got a cool mom. I need her to teach me some—"

Ron cleared his throat. "What you two need is to learn not to put yourselves in danger again. Now, what did the doctor say?"

"I was looking for Lily," Dylan protested. "I wasn't looking for trouble."

"How was I supposed to know it was a trap?" Lily added her own protest. "It was supposed to be a sales call."

Ron put his hands up. "Okay. What did the doc say?"

"I'm good. Mild concussion. They want me to stay overnight for observation."

"You'd better listen. I need to go, but I'll check in with you again." He walked out and searched for Kyle. Hopefully, his son would have some answers to his many questions.

He found them just outside of room 15. They might've come out of a mud bath, but neither looked injured, though a bandage wrapped up the girl's arm and Kyle's face showed a sign of a bruise coming on.

"Hey, Dad."

He hugged Kyle. It was always a relief to see him in one piece after an op. Kyle introduced Grace Benson. Ron didn't need that. He could see Ana in her. He started, "Your parents—"

"Grace!"

A blond man hurried toward her with an older couple, likely her parents, in tow. They enveloped her in a giant hug. They all talked at the same time.

"Are you all right?"

"You need to call your other brothers."

While she was busy with her family, Kyle gave him the broad strokes of his days in the safe houses. Then Ron, in turn, updated him on recent events.

Then he heard his name. Grace was doing a quick introduction. The blond man whom he took for a boyfriend turned out to be her brother. Her head swiveled as if searching for something. "Where is Agent Ruiz?"

"She's heading back to the office," he said. "I should be

going too. Very nice to meet you all. An agent will contact you for your statement."

"Should I go with you?" Kyle asked.

"No, you rest and write your report." Ron walked away, eager to wrap it all up. His phone buzzed again. This time, it was Tanner.

"Boss, Deputy Director's house exploded. She's safe, but her husband isn't so lucky."

Was that the explosion Olivia was involved in? Too much of a coincidence. Why Vera's house? Of course, she'd been a spook. But she was with the Bureau now, or was she?

"Er, boss, you still there?"

"Yeah, yeah. Okay. You heard from her?"

"Not directly. She was on TV imploring the media hound to respect her privacy to mourn her husband. A gas leak, they said. The talking heads speculate—"

"I don't care what the talking heads think." No way was it a gas leak. But surely, a gas leak would be what Olivia's report showed. She was following the fake O'Shea to the house. The car was registered to William Hunt. Now, that had to be Vera's husband. So, the fake O'Shea was William Hunt. Following that, Hunt was the leak. Was Vera supplying him with the intel? Or did he steal it somehow? Could Vera be the leak? But she knew who Phoenix was, and she was trying to prevent Olivia's identity from exposure. If she had been responsible, she could have told Hunt that information. No, she wasn't the leak. Would she kill her own husband?

"Boss, have I lost you again?"

"I'm here. Anything else?"

"Uh, yes, Deanna is anxious to see you. Said it was important. And Tommy, Dylan's sidekick, is also asking for you. Also urgent."

"And you told him I was here?" He almost ran into the young man.

"No, boss."

"Never mind." He hung up.

"Agent Peters, is Dylan okay? You saved me a phone call." Tommy braked right before he smashed into him.

"He's fine. In room 5. Lily is in there, I think. What do you need? I gotta get back to the office."

"I'll email everything to you. I just need your email."

He gave it to him. "What is it you're emailing me?"

"Oh, reports on Janet Reardon. Our reports. The security firm's reports. She's about to be fired, but you'd better arrest her before she skips town."

He shook his head. "Who is she? Why am I arresting her?"

"Director of sales and marketing, soon-to-be-former. I'm sure the GM or legal will notify the cops, but I don't know how quickly they work. Anyway, it's all in the reports. Basically, she's part of a money-laundering operation with ties to the drug cartel. Martinez, I think."

"Dylan has been sniffing around a money-laundering operation?"

"Well, not exactly. Lily started—"

"Never mind." Ron held up a hand. "I'll read the reports."

Those two would be the death of him. How did this money-laundering operation tie in to the Martinez cartel?

# CHAPTER 70

## ORLANDO HOSPITAL

*KYLE*

After his dad left, Kyle wanted to check on Dylan and Lily. He caught Grace's eye to let her know he'd be right back. Instead, her eyes were imploring him to help as her family bombarded her. So he approached them. "Excuse me. Grace, you have a minute?"

She extracted herself from her folks. "Yes, of course."

"Wanna meet the heir to the M&M Enterprises?" he asked softly.

"They own the Marino Hotels, right?"

He nodded.

Her eyes grew wide. "For real? Yeah, when?"

"Now, let's go."

"Wait. I'm not dressed. I need to clean up and change."

He waved a hand. "Nah, he won't mind. It's a long story, but he's not one of those spoiled brats or rich playboys. He grew up poor. Come on."

She squinched her eyes, obviously uncertain, but followed him.

"By the way, I didn't know you were a gymnast. You did that flip thing like the Olympians do." His finger did a circle to illustrate.

"Hardly. I started young, but I quit in junior high. I wanted to focus on music."

As they approached room 5, Tommy came out. "Yo, what happened to you? Were you in that raid too? Wait. Olivia said you were in protective custody."

"I was. This is Grace Benson. And Tom Rivers."

"Everyone calls me Tommy. I gave up making them call me Tom." He shook her hand.

"How's he?" Kyle jerked a thumb toward the room.

"A mild concussion, but he's fine. Lily is giving him a hard time. He scared her half to death faking his injury more serious than it is. She was telling him she thought he was going to die. Well, anyway, I didn't want to feel like a third wheel in there."

His heart sank. Yep, she cared more about Dylan than she did him. Tommy said goodbye. Kyle stood by the door, hesitating. Did he want to make the situation awkward? Or should he just bow out?

A hand touched his arm. "I don't need to meet him now if you're not comfortable. That's Lily, right? It sounds like…"

He sighed out his resignation. "I know. Doesn't sound like they want any interruptions." He turned around and headed back toward her family.

"I'm sorry." She followed him. "Look on the bright side. Now, you know. No need to be frustrated anymore."

He glanced at her and smiled without wanting to. "Guess you're right. She's happy. That's good."

"Kyle!"

He turned toward the voice. Ana was striding toward them.

"I thought you were at the office."

She shrugged. "I was heading back there, but Wood is in critical condition. I hope to talk to him, that is, if they let me."

"Agent Ruiz, I'm so glad to see you. Meet my folks." Grace motioned for her family to join them.

"I, er, probably should, er, go see Wood," Ana stammered.

"Mom, Dad, this is Agent Ruiz. She's the one who saved Kyle and me. She brought in this team of SWAT guys." Grace looked from her parents to Ana. "What's the matter?"

"Ana Ruiz," Mrs. Benson whispered. "It's been so long."

"Mrs. Benson, Pastor Benson," Ana greeted them.

Grace's gaze moved from her parents to Ana, and then she grinned. "I knew it."

Alex was quiet, but Kyle saw him doing the same. The brother figured it out. Kyle stepped back from the unfolding family drama.

# CHAPTER 71

## TASK FORCE OFFICE

*RON*

The task force office's fluorescent lights cast a sterile glow over the squad room as Ron stepped in, his mind set on unraveling the threads of Tommy's emails among other mysteries. He had barely taken a few steps toward his office when Deanna intercepted him.

"Boss, I got something. Well, many somethings. What do you want first?"

Her usual chirpy voice hit him like a blast of caffeine. Man, he needed a cup of whatever she'd had. He sank into one of the chairs. "Just give them to me."

"I did the deep dive on Trent Lockwood—"

"Who's he?"

"Oh, a small-time player, but he's been working for the cartel. A front man."

Was he this tired? Why was he not remembering this name? Or his connection to the cartel? He frowned at Tanner. "Who's this Lockwood?"

"No idea, boss."

Hernandez and Cooper both shook their heads.

"Kyle asked me. For Lily," Deanna said.

Lily again. Tommy mentioned Lily started the investigation. Ron stood up. "Okay, I'm gonna need to read Tommy's emails first."

"But, boss—"

He held up a finger to check an incoming text from Ana. She was stuck at the hospital but would be back as soon as possible. His lips pressed into a thin line, a silent acknowledgment of the ever-present unpredictability of their line of work. He addressed Deanna now. "Give me a few minutes with Tommy's emails. Let me see if there's any direct link to the cartel's financial movements. As soon as Ana's back, we'll regroup."

"Yeah, boss."

Twenty minutes later, he sat at his desk, staring up at the ceiling. Lily noticed a couple of suspicious accounts and started investigating. Trent Lockwood was the front man for Rain Tree LLC, also the front for the Martinez cartel. Janet Reardon, their soon-to-be-ex director of sales and marketing, was in the cartel's pocket and facilitating the money-laundering scheme.

Someone lured Lily to Rain Tree and attempted to kill her. What for? To prevent her from exposing them? Who was that Good Samaritan? What was his name? Filmore. How did he know to save her there? Why did he keep her?

Of course, there was this explosion and the hit order. Time for more caffeine stimulation. He went to the kitchen to grab some coffee. On his way, he passed Ana walking in. The coffee machine clock indicated 8:47 p.m.

Coffee in hand, he gathered the team in the squad room. Before he started the briefing, he bent toward Tanner who was still seated at his desk. "I just forwarded Tommy's emails to you. Send them to White Collar. Have them follow up with the local LEO. Get eyes on the woman before she tries to rabbit. And round up what's his name, the guy who does the reservations. It's all in the reports."

"On it." Tanner picked up the phone and started calling.

Five minutes later, everybody was up and ready. Ron started, "I know it's late. We all want to go home. Let's do a quick debrief. Cooper, you first."

The lanky DEA agent checked his notes. "Martinez is dead." He hurried the words, the languid drawl barely noticeable. So *now*, the guy was amped up? "We don't know who shot him. Happened before we got there. Nunez and Frankie are both injured and in custody. They're expected to recover fully. The others are either dead or injured. I don't have the numbers here, but we recovered all the drugs in the cartons. Mostly opioids, the usual, fentanyl, oxy. All in all, in the millions."

"A big win for the DEA!" Tanner high-fived Cooper.

"Thanks for all your help." Cooper gave a nod. "If you all don't mind, I need to head back to the DEA office to drown in the paperwork."

That got a few chuckles. They thanked him for his help in the Martinez operation and said good night.

"Related to the cartel…" Ron went on to explain the money-laundering scheme, the front for the cartel, and Lily's and Dylan's investigations.

"So, that's why Dylan was there?" Tanner asked.

"Who shot at Lily?" Ana asked. "And who's that Good Samaritan?"

"I believe his name is Filmore, but beyond that, no idea," Ron said. "He disappeared when we got to the warehouse."

No need to tell them Lily told him Filmore was supposed to keep her safe. From whom? She didn't know. But because he also took orders from someone Ron now suspected might be the fake O'Shea or Hunt, he still didn't know if he was a good guy or a bad one. Although his gut told him he was CIA.

"According to Agent Torres," Ana spoke after a beat. "Agent

Jackson was in the Ghost's pocket. He was summarily executed by the gang. Guess they didn't want him to make a deal and flip on them."

"Who hired them? Who ordered the kill?"

"The one dude who is flipping for a deal said Silver Fox. I have no idea who Silver Fox is. But he hired them to take out Kyle and Grace."

Deanna shot her hand up like she was in class.

"Yes, Deanna?"

"I know who he is." She beamed.

"Don't keep us in suspense now!" This came from Tanner, of course.

She grabbed the remote, pushed a few buttons, and sent some images up on the screen. "I did the victim's laptop. He communicated with Silver Fox on an ongoing basis. After some digging, I found this." She highlighted a photo of two men with a big fish in between them. "See, this is the victim. And this is Silver Fox, or CIA Officer William Hunt."

"Wait. Did you say CIA Officer William Hunt?" Ron needed to be sure.

"Yes, boss. The deputy director gave me access to, um, some files and databases. I found his information in the CIA database."

How did Vera have access to the CIA database? Was she still a spook? Questions for another time. "Is he—I mean, was he —active?"

"That is unknown."

Whenever an operation involved the CIA, Ron didn't have much confidence in getting a straight answer. He'd shelf this for now.

"Wait. Is this William Hunt the same as the deputy director's husband?" Hernandez asked.

"Yes," Deanna affirmed.

"We got sidetracked. Let's refocus on the kill order. So, Silver Fox or William Hunt ordered it."

"Why?" Tanner asked.

Ron glanced at Ana. "We suspect it's a retribution for Ana and my killing of Jade last year."

"If we can tie Hunt to the Ghost, then there's no question about it." Ana glanced at her watch.

Tanner rolled his stress ball around in his grip. "We still don't know who killed Mitchell."

"Or why he had a note in his throat," Hernandez added.

"I'll touch base with the detectives. See where they are on the case. Let's call it a night. We'll tie up any loose ends and update again tomorrow afternoon."

# CHAPTER 72

## THE BURNS RESIDENCE

*OLIVIA*

Olivia convinced the doctor to release her the night before. A night of rest in her own bed had her feeling much better. After Shadow Shot dropped her off at the hospital and notified Simon, he took off but gave her a phone. She'd examined the phone and the only number programmed on it, Jay's.

Last night after Lily recounted the events, Olivia wanted to confront Jay. He'd promised to keep her safe, but that Filmore fellow allowed her to get away and be held at gunpoint. Still, Lily—amazing girl that she was—stayed calm and remembered how to disarm the assailant.

The phone vibrated while they were in church with Simon. A text to summon her. After Mass, she texted back to say she'd be there. She needed to go home and get her car once she assured Simon she was good to drive.

A half hour later, she was on her way to the SCIF alongside Jay's house. After the scan of her biometrics, the door opened to a regular basement enhanced to shield everything. Two men sat nursing coffee mugs at the only table. Shadow Shot—or rather, Kevin—and a man introduced as Officer Troy Fletcher. She sat facing the men, and then Jay joined them with his own cup of coffee, sitting at the head of the table.

"Your daughter knows me as Toby Filmore," Fletcher explained. "You've trained her well. She almost disarmed Martinez, and she would have if I hadn't shot him first."

Fortyish, five ten, medium build, wavy hair—yep, he fit the Good Samaritan's description. "Thank you for saving her."

"You're welcome."

Jay cleared his throat. "All right, Phoenix. Nothing you hear now leaves this room."

She nodded, acknowledging his gravity. "Understood."

"I hatched the plan since you reported Lily's identity was compromised last year. Nobody was supposed to know of her existence. Naturally, I suspected a mole within our ranks. Unfortunately, I can't tell you the details of the op since you're not on the need-to-know list."

"What?" She jolted, her knee nearly slamming the underside of the table. "Why?"

"You wanted out, remember?"

"Yeah." This was crazy. Was he forgetting— "*I'm* the one they want to flush out, right? Shouldn't I be in the loop?"

"All the more reason, no. As it is now, you're already out of the covert op. Look at your ID, a standard CIA credential."

She schooled her features to contain her wince. "Are you saying I lost my clearance?"

"Not all of them. After all, you know too much as far as the Ghost is concerned."

"Okay." A deep breath settled her. "Tell me everything— everything you can, that is."

He deferred to Fletcher who said, "Jay had me infiltrate the network. I had my sources. Shadow Shot here helped. Anyway, I got assigned to watch Lily. Rook—or call him Hunt or the fake O'Shea—believed Lily had a connection to Phoenix. And he'd be right. Nothing happened until she started investigating that River—er, Rain Tree—a front for the cartel. And Rook took advantage of the situation and expected Phoenix to show to save Lily."

She waved to Jay. "That's why you wouldn't tell me anything about it. You knew I'd go get her."

"What can I say?" He lowered his coffee mug enough to show a smile, then saluted her with the mug. "You gave up the work you love for your daughter. Of course, you wouldn't let it rest had I given you even a hint. And you'd play right into their hand. Don't try to deny it. You love this."

If she was honest with herself, she did miss the excitement, the thrill, but she had already lost two decades with her daughter and Simon. She had to put them first now.

"Okay, so what now?" She spread out her hands. "And, Kevin, what was your involvement?"

He shrugged. "Did some investigating. Mostly kept you occupied and—"

"And you reported everything I did to Jay."

"It's on me," Jay said. "I needed to know what you were up to. We couldn't take the risk of exposing Phoenix."

Okay, now she understood the plan. But her investigation also led her to the leak, William Hunt or the fake O'Shea. "What about the house with all the video surveillance?"

"It's been swept clean. And now, it'll be put to good use. We recovered a lot of juicy stuff there." Jay sipped his coffee.

"I followed Hunt to Haskin's house. He never came out. When I came to, I think I saw Haskin. According to Shadow Shot, she is one of us. Explain the explosion."

Jay exhaled a heavy breath, the scent of coffee growing stronger. "She *was* one of us. For this op, she offered her services since it was personal to her. She felt bad for falling for a honey trap, but she came to her senses soon after. Unfortunately, she had no proof. Just gut feelings. So, she waited. In the meantime, she also set up digital traps. And she caught him searching her files for any mention of Phoenix."

"So that's why she got herself assigned here. And that's why she knew he was looking into me?"

"Yes, she did come here for this op. No, she got that from me, courtesy of Fletcher."

"I don't understand. You said he was searching for Phoenix."

"Phoenix, yes, but not you, Olivia. Don't forget they're two identities."

Easier said than done. She almost rolled her eyes. For so long, they were one and the same to her.

"I think he got that order from the Ghost," Fletcher added. "After one of his meetings with the Ghost, he asked me if I heard of Olivia Tso. My legend has me as a former FBI agent. I said no, but that didn't mean anything. He asked me to check with my former contacts, dig up whatever I could on you."

"But Haskin had Deanna make up my whole backstory. If you were the one—"

"We couldn't assume he wouldn't ask another operative to dig," Jay cut her off.

Right. Made sense. "So, what happened? Was he renditioned to a black site? The explosion and a body to cover that?"

He sighed. Shadow Shot eyed his hands. Fletcher found the wall fascinating. Finally, Jay said, "Haskin presented her evidence to the directors of various alphabet agencies. They all agreed to terminate and run it up the food chain. The order came down to terminate, with prejudice."

A sanctioned kill. "And Haskin did it?"

"She volunteered."

The explosion was to cover up the execution. Olivia sat back, absorbing the revelation. The world of espionage and undercover work was a labyrinth of moral ambiguities and harsh realities. Now more than ever, she was glad she decided to get out before she became as cold as Haskin. Then again, if she were in Haskin's shoes…

# CHAPTER 73

## POLICE STATION

*RON*

Ron had called his team in today for a quick briefing. While he gave them the morning off to allow for religious observances or family obligations, he started the day early. Evidently, the detectives worked on Sundays too when they had a case. The police station was abuzz. Too bad criminals couldn't be considerate of weekends.

Now, he sat in a starkly lit room across from Detectives Spaulding and Monnin, the air tainted with the scent of stale coffee and the buzz of fluorescent lights. He wanted to hear what they found and disclosed what he could that wasn't classified.

In turn, Spaulding and Monnin shared their findings. "The DEA was nice enough to let us interview Nunez. He took a deal to point the finger at Frankie and the others," the stocky detective revealed, his voice grim. "He confessed that Mitchell was their hit man. Rook was the link between the cartel and Mitchell."

"Who's Rook?"

"He doesn't know. That's the only name he knows. And we haven't found anything yet. According to Nunez, he's the Ghost's trusted lieutenant."

Monnin's long ponytail swayed while she reached across the table. "Before the Ghost was captured, the cartel was under her control. But since her incarceration, Martinez was trying to break free."

Spaulding then showed Ron a video of their interview with Nunez in the hospital room. On the screen, Nunez, his hand cuffed to the bar and his posture defeated, detailed Rook's plan to take out Kyle and Grace in revenge for Jade. Ron watched intently, reeling from the revelations.

"Nobody knows who Jade is." Monnin raised a brow, a perfect lead-in for added detail.

When Ron kept his mouth shut, the practiced mask of neutrality on his face, Spaulding continued, "Mitchell had told them he wanted to retire. Martinez and Rook agreed, but only after one last job. But when he realized the target was Kyle, he refused. He said he couldn't do it."

"The decision then came from Rook to have him eliminated," Monnin concluded. "They couldn't risk anyone knowing their plans."

Ron sat back with a huff. "I guess no honor among thieves."

"That's the name of the game. If they don't roll over on each other, we wouldn't solve a lot of our cases."

"I didn't hear him say who killed Mitchell."

"It was Frankie aka the Greek. He is their enforcer, so he pulled the trigger. But it doesn't matter. Rook ordered the kill. Our prosecutor thinks the Feds will have first crack at him. But she's happy to charge him with the murder and fight to prosecute him here. As for Rook, she told us to find him, then we'll talk." Expression stern as ever, Spaulding gathered up the papers.

"If you have any idea of who Rook is, we're all ears." Monnin stood up.

Ron rose as well, prepared to leave. "Wish I could help."

But he suspected the fake O'Shea was Rook. Could he prove it? And if the fake O'Shea was Rook, then Rook was Hunt. And Hunt was killed. Poetic justice!

# CHAPTER 74

## TASK FORCE OFFICE

*RON*

After meeting with the detectives, Ron grabbed a quick bite to eat, then headed to the task force office. He wasn't the first one there. Apparently, Ana beat him to the office. In a casual top and jeans, she was just coming out of the bathroom.

"Did you just come from church?" He nodded to the dress draped on her arm.

"Yes and no." She was all smiles. "It's been a while, but I went to church with Grace. And then we had brunch."

His eyebrows rose. "I didn't know you two were so friendly."

She frowned. "Didn't I tell you? Maybe not. I had to book it out of here last night to have a drink with her and her folks. Her parents are so gracious. She figured it out just because Kyle said we worked together. You know what? She said I was cool. She couldn't thank me enough for saving her and Kyle, but it wasn't just me. Those SWAT guys did the heavy lifting."

Her excitement was contagious. He felt more upbeat just hearing her talk about her reunion with her daughter.

"By the way, Kyle was there." She hung up her dress and sat at her desk.

He sat across from her. "Where?"

"Church."

Whoa. Add that to the day's many revelations. "*Kyle* went to church?"

"Yeah, he should be in any minute now. You can ask him."

"Wonders never cease."

She cupped a hand to the side of her mouth to stage-whisper. "I think Grace has something to do with it."

"That right?" He thought his son was into Lily, but then, seeing Lily with Dylan at the warehouse and the hospital, he wasn't too optimistic about Kyle's chances. Or maybe the kid already knew and cut his losses.

"Hey, boss." Tanner and Hernandez walked in together, gym bags in hand. They probably came from a workout or were heading to one afterward. Minutes later, Kyle joined them, looking refreshed.

"Saw Deanna heading to the lab. Said she'd be right out." Hernandez dumped his bag against the wall.

After they all settled in and the forensic guru showed up, Ron started the briefing. "Sorry to call you in on a Sunday. We'll make it quick, but we better compare notes while everything is still fresh on our minds. And also to make sure we didn't miss anything. Deanna, you were eager to report something last night. Why don't you start?"

"Yeah, boss." She snagged the clicker. Email correspondence showed up on the screen. "Like I said, the vic's laptop had a hidden folder. I also found drafts of emails going back and forth with Silver Fox. Here's a few of those." She pointed to a couple of them with a laser beam. "You can read that he wanted to retire from this business, citing his legit business was doing well. But Silver Fox didn't like the idea."

"Didn't we decide Silver Fox was William Hunt?" Tanner was squeezing a stress ball—for fun, this time.

"Yes, but he went by Silver Fox in the emails." She glared at him. "Our vic also communicated with Nunez. Both basically told him the same thing—you can't quit in this line of work. After some back-and-forth"—her grin got bigger—"here's the good part. He kept his kill logs. Everything. The dates. The orders. He used that as leverage. So, Silver Fox caved on one condition. He needed to do one last job."

Ron nodded. Exactly what the detectives got from Nunez. Except according to Nunez, Rook ordered the hit. That would mean Rook and Silver Fox were one and the same.

"And that was to kill Kyle and Grace." Ana voiced what everyone was thinking. "I bet he knew he couldn't kill Sheila's son, so he refused. Correct?"

Deanna shrugged. "This part is not in any of the communications. Although I can show you the computer-generated, age-progressed images of Uncle Bill and Officer Bill." She clicked the remote and the images popped up on the screen. "And here is the photo of Hunt with the vic."

"So, Hunt was also Uncle Bill and Officer Bill!" Tanner fumbled, dropping the stress ball.

As Tanner scrambled to scoop up the ball, Ron had to agree. The images looked convincing. And it made sense from what Olivia told him about what she'd found out. "Coming back to what we were talking about, yes, that's correct. Doug couldn't kill Kyle." Ron then briefed them on his meeting with the detectives.

"Now, we're on the same page." Deanna beamed again, pressed a button, and brought up new emails. "Silver Fox and Rook are the same person. Here, you'll see Silver Fox telling our vic his new code name is Rook."

"Whoopee!" Ana squealed. "Silver Fox is Rook. And they're

William Hunt. Hunt is the fake O'Shea, the one who goes to see the Ghost. We have the connection!"

Everyone cheered.

Hernandez turned his computer screen around. "Just curious. What's the motive here?"

Deanna's response was evasive, her gaze flickering away. "Something about avenging Jade," she muttered, her voice barely above a whisper.

Tanner, still squeezing away, frowned. "Boss and Ana were present during the… incident." His gaze darted to Kyle, who sat stoically, his jaw set in a hard line. "Targeting Kyle makes sense. After all, he's the boss's son. But Grace?"

The implication hung in the air, an unspoken question, one everyone seemed hesitant to voice.

Ron looked at Ana, understanding passing between them. He then turned back to the group, his expression firm. "It doesn't matter. What matters is she's safe now."

A beat later, Hernandez ventured, "I'm looking at the notes here. According to Ana, the agent told her Silver Fox ordered the hit. And just now, according to the boss, Nunez said it was Rook. I know they're the same person. Just wondering why he would use the old code name."

Good question. Ron addressed Deanna. "Is Silver Fox his old code name from the CIA?"

She tapped her tablet furiously for a few moments. "Yes, boss."

"Wouldn't it be ironic if he wanted to get out from under the Ghost? You know, ditch the Rook code name and revert to Silver Fox," he mused. Then he shrugged. "Guess we'll never know."

# CHAPTER 75

## FEDERAL DETENTION CENTER

*OLIVIA*

Olivia strode through the sterile Federal Detention Center corridors, her gait purposeful, her heart pounding. Each breath brought in air thick with a palpable tension, a blend of despair and cold authority. As she entered the designated room, the Ghost was already seated at the table, with her ankles and hand shackled.

The Ghost leaned forward. "Is Dylan okay?"

The question took Olivia off guard. Surely, the notorious criminal mastermind didn't care about her nephew. "Yes, he's fine. But you're losing one of your attorneys. Adam O'Shea—or should we say, Rook—is dead."

Was that a glimmer of relief at the mention of Dylan? Whatever it had been her usual mask of indifference soon replaced it.

"People die, so?" The Ghost shrugged as if discussing something as mundane as the weather.

Olivia braced both palms on the table, pushing into the Ghost's space. "We know who he was. Silver Fox. Rook.

O'Shea. William Hunt. They're all one person. Now, you have no more insider information."

The Ghost's lips curved up. "Do you think he was my only source? By the way, I heard you'd been an FBI agent for decades doing a lot of classified assignments. I'm curious. Why did you leave your infant daughter? And fake your death? Don't tell me the Bureau wouldn't allow you to have a family."

Her heart pounded. This woman was sniffing, but she was getting too close for comfort. "I was young and didn't want the responsibility of raising a baby."

"Yet, here you are, about to marry the father of your child."

"Well, staring at death a few times made me realize what I really want in life—a family."

The two women stared at each other. Olivia kept her composure. She couldn't allow this woman to see through her lies.

"Oh well. So how did it go with Martinez?"

Olivia stifled a sigh of relief. "The Martinez operation was a success. He is dead. His underlings were all arrested."

"Good to be of service." The Ghost sat back. "How's my new dwelling? Progressing well?"

"It's going, as far as I know."

"Will you give my nephew my regards? Tell him he's welcome to visit any time."

"I doubt he'd want to see you again."

"Ah, but he came when the one he cares about was in trouble. Oh, didn't he tell you?"

Enough. Olivia wasn't taking her bait to get personal. "You'd better have a new name for us next time I come."

# CHAPTER 76

## RECEPTION HALL

***RON***

R on, clad in a dark suit that mirrored the somber mood, stood amid the muted buzz of conversations in the reception hall. He picked at the hors d'oeuvres on his plate, the array of delicacies a stark contrast to the heavy atmosphere following William Hunt's memorial service, the hushed tones only interrupted by the occasional clink of glassware as people paid their respects.

Vera, a picture of dignified mourning in her all-black attire, stood near the bay windows, her gaze lost in the distant horizon. He sidled up to her, his steps careful and measured. He cleared his throat before speaking. "What's next for you? Back to DC?"

She turned toward him, her expression composed, a tiredness in her eyes. She sipped her sparkling water. "Virginia, actually."

How well he understood the weight of her words. He leaned in, his voice lowering. "Is this why you came here?" Was that the flicker of recognition in her eyes? Ah, so she understood the underlying question, the unspoken inquiries about her motives, her presence.

She offered an almost imperceptible smile. "I had an order to do a job here. It's been completed, so now it's time to go."

As her steady voice revealed nothing more than what she chose to, his gaze lingered on her, searching for something more beneath the surface. "Is this your cover? Or your real job?"

She paused, her gaze meeting his for a moment of silence, a brief interlude in their conversation that spoke volumes. "I do what needs to be done, and of course, I serve at the pleasure of the commander in chief."

"Let's forget your position right now. Let me ask you as a friend. How are you doing? It couldn't have been easy for you." He wasn't in the need to know, but he could put two and two together. If he had to guess, Hunt was a sanctioned kill. He didn't have all the answers, but she had to have foreknowledge of the event.

Those amber eyes blinked at him. Then she smiled. "I swore an oath. You know, duty and country. But I should have seized what was good for me."

Memories of their time together flashed in his mind. "Well, we were both workaholics. Kyle just started reconnecting with me then. I couldn't—"

"I understand. A parent's love is powerful, a strong motivation. Look at Olivia and Agent Ruiz."

"You knew?"

She had that smile again. "What can I say? Part of the job, but it stays with me."

They looked at each other for another moment. He opened his mouth, but she put a finger on his lips. "Let's not bring up the past. If you ever come north, give me a holler."

He nodded. "You take care, Vera—Deputy Director."

She hugged him. "You too."

## *SHEILA*

Sheila stood in a quiet corner of her residence, the solemnity of the funeral still shrouding her. The room buzzed with hushed conversations and the clinking of glasses as attendees navigated the delicate balance between mourning and mundane pleasantries. Platters of half-eaten snacks and half-filled glasses littered the tables, a stark contrast to the emptiness she felt inside.

Ron's team was a great support. They all showed up, although Ron himself was a little late coming from another memorial service. Even Lily, her parents, and Dylan attended.

Kyle navigated the crowd and sidled up to her. In his hand, he held a flash drive. "Mom, our forensic guru found a letter in a hidden folder in Doug's laptop addressed to you. It's in here."

Her heart skipped a beat. A letter from Doug. She reached out to accept the flash drive. "What does it say?"

He shook his head. "As soon as we saw that it was personal, we didn't read it."

What did Doug have to say to her? More lies? "Thank you." A hint of resignation pressed down on her. "I must not know how to pick men. When I was married to your dad, he was married to his work. And Doug…" She sighed, the revelation still heavy on her. "He was an assassin."

"But he was trying to get out of the life. Remember that." Kyle leaned closer. "And if it makes you feel any better, I don't have much luck in picking girls either. First Eva, now Lily."

Her heart ached for her son. She put an arm around him, drawing him into a half-embrace. "Oh, honey. I'm sorry. I know you care about her. But I'm sure you'll find someone."

After a pause, she asked, "What's the name of that young woman who got stuck with you in protective custody?"

He blinked, apparently taken aback. "Grace. What about her?"

She shrugged nonchalantly, masking the keen interest behind her question while trying not to smile at his defensiveness. "Oh, nothing." She waved the hand not holding the flash drive. "Heard you attended church services with her. In my book, she's a good influence."

His phone must have vibrated since he took it out and frowned. "Peters," he answered. "Yes, this is Special Agent Kyle Peters.... Alex?... Slow down... What? When?... Where are you?... I'll be there in twenty. Yes, I'll let Ana know." He hung up and gave her a peck on the cheek. "Sorry, Mom. Gotta go."

She grabbed his arm. "What happened?"

"Grace got snatched."

*Hidden Secrets,* the next gripping installment in the Mirror Estate series, is available on Amazon and Kindle Unlimited. Grab it now!

In case you miss it, here's where you can download book 3, *Forgotten Secret*, or any previous books you've missed.

# THANK YOU!

Thank you for diving into *Tangled Secrets*! Writing this story has been such a wild ride and knowing that you've spent time with the cast means the world to me.

I hope you loved reading it as much as I loved writing it. If you'd be so kind as to leave a review on Amazon and/or Goodreads to share your impressions with others, I would greatly appreciate it. Your insights will help other readers find the book.

# BONUS SCENES

# BONUS SCENE 1

## THE MITCHELL RESIDENCE

*DOUG*

The airport's arrival lobby bustled with the usual cacophony of rolling suitcases, intercom announcements, and murmuring travelers. Doug Mitchell crossed the floor, his steps brisk, purposeful, each stride carrying the weight of a man accustomed to danger. But even he wasn't prepared for what awaited him just beyond the sliding doors.

Greek, a hulking figure with a scarred face that seldom smiled, stepped into his path, flanked by another muscleman whose presence spoke of menace. Without a word, Greek extended a hand and slipped him a piece of paper. Doug didn't need to unfold it to know what it was. His heart sank as Greek's gravelly voice broke the tension.

"This is your next job." His tone left no room for argument.

Doug met his gaze with a sense of finality. "Remember my deal with Silver Fox. This is the last one."

But as he unfolded the paper, his stoic facade crumbled. The targets' images sent a cold shiver down his spine. There, among the faces, was Kyle, his wife's son, his stepson. The revelation struck him like a physical blow.

"I can't do this." His voice barely breached a whisper, laden with an uncharacteristic tremor.

Greek's expression hardened, his eyes narrowing. "You have no choice."

But Doug was already shaking his head, desperation birthing a plan. "You don't understand. I won't do it."

The realization hit him then—they would find someone else to complete the job. Panic surged, along with a dangerous resolve. He'd been meticulous, keeping logs and details of his every job for the cartel. Turning to the FBI was a nuclear option. And the only way out now.

He hurried home, his mind racing faster than his sports car. He twisted his grip on the steering wheel, sweating now. He'd gather his evidence. He'd make this work. He'd save Shelia's son.

But fate, it seemed, was not on his side. As he stepped into the safety of his house, he was greeted not by the familiar quiet, but by Greek and his henchman.

"Sorry, pal." Greek grimaced, almost apologetic, and the gesture scrunched up the scar running from his ear to his chin. "Business is business. You know nobody quits this line of work."

Doug darted his gaze around for an escape, a way to warn Sheila and Kyle. His hand, trembling, still clutched the kill order. In a desperate move, he crumpled it and tried to swallow it. Perhaps the autopsy would find it and warn Kyle.

Then the garage door rumbled open, its whir piercing the tense air. Sheila was home. Panic and fear collided in his chest. "Please," he begged, his voice strained, "spare Sheila."

But a sharp pain exploded in his head, cutting off further pleas, and his vision blurred. As darkness engulfed him, his last thought vanished in a silent prayer for Sheila's and Kyle's safety.

# BONUS SCENE 2

## CHURCH

*KYLE*

Kyle's relationship with churches had always been distant, a sentiment rooted in childhood memories of obligatory Sunday services. His mother took him to church now and then, but as the years passed, he'd drifted further from the pews. So, when Grace, with her infectious enthusiasm, invited him to attend a service, he couldn't find a good excuse to decline. He braced for a tedious morning.

As he entered the church, nostalgia hit him. The familiar scent of polished wood and hymnal pages, the soft hum of a congregation in quiet conversation was both foreign and comforting.

Pastor Benson, Grace's father, stood at the pulpit with an air of approachable authority, shattering Kyle's preconceptions of a monotonous sermon. The pastor spoke with an engaging warmth and humor. His words wove through themes of faith and daily life, punctuated with anecdotes that had the congregation chuckling.

With a twinkle in her eye, Grace leaned over, whispering, "Told you my dad could be funny."

After the service, a sense of community enlivened the atmosphere. Grace and her newly reunited birth mother, Ana, planned to have brunch with the Bensons, and Mrs. Benson extended the invitation to him with a graciousness he couldn't decline.

But that made finding a moment alone with Grace amid the post-service bustle a challenge. When he did, under the pretext of admiring a stained-glass window, he broached the subject weighing on his mind. "So, how are you taking it all in? Finding out about your birth mother like this?"

She waved, giving a light, almost carefree laugh. "It's all good. She's cool, you know? A federal agent and everything. She carries a gun, and did you see how those SWAT guys listened to her the other day? It's kind of awesome."

Her words trailed off, her expression reflective. "Not that my mom is boring or anything. She does important admin work here at the church. It's just... well, it's not as exciting as what Ana does."

He nodded, understanding the mixed emotions she must be enduring. It was a lot to process—discovering a birth mother who lived a life straight out of a crime drama, compared to the stable, quiet life Grace knew with the Bensons.

"You have an interesting family dynamic, to say the least." He nudged her elbow with his, trying to offer lighthearted support.

Grace laughed, the sound echoing in the near-empty church. "That's one way to put it. Life's full of surprises, isn't it?"

# HIDDEN SECRETS

A Thriller

BOOK 5
SNEAK PEEK

# CHAPTER 1

## LORRAINE'S KITCHEN, MIRROR ESTATE

*CONNOR*

As usual, Connor Murray went downstairs to the restaurant to help his wife, Lorraine, set up for the day bright and early. Lorraine's Kitchen didn't open until 10 a.m., but they needed to do a lot of prep work first. He'd made sure Sean, their ten-year-old son, was up and ready for school before heading downstairs. His family, along with his in-laws, Max and Kate Warner, all lived in the quarters above the restaurant, a perk of being part of the Marino household. Of course, they weren't related to the Marinos, but Max had been with the family for decades as the majordomo. Max's father had also been the Marinos' head butler.

"Morning, Connor." Kate joined them in the kitchen. Max had likely gone over to the main house to start his day. Kate always helped out, either in the kitchen or out front.

"Morning, Kate." Connor flashed her a smile as he began chopping vegetables while Lorraine bustled around, organizing the ingredients and ensuring everything was in its place.

"Here, Sean, your lunch." Lorraine held out his lunch pack.

The boy grabbed it and dashed off with a quick "Thanks, Mom!"

His chest swelling, Connor watched his son walk out the door. Turning back to his task, he focused on the steady rhythm of chopping, the sound oddly soothing.

While prepping her kitchen, Lorraine asked, "What do you think of the new priest?"

"Fr. Jeremy? He's young, but he seems nice." Kate handed Connor a bowl of freshly washed tomatoes.

Fr. Jeremy seemed about Connor's age, late thirties or early forties, but then Kate still called them kids. "Does that mean Fr. Phil is finally retiring? He's talked about it for a while."

"Seems like it." Lorraine arranged the tomatoes on a platter. "Fr. Jeremy's homily was good, though. Fresh perspective."

Connor nodded, thinking about last Sunday Mass. "Yeah, he is good. Brings a different energy."

He headed out to the dining room to set the tables. The morning light streamed through the windows, casting a warm glow over the neatly arranged room. This quiet time before the rush, the calm before the storm, was always a blessing.

"Hey, you guys open yet?" A voice hollered from outside the side door.

This happened once in a while. People didn't want to go out front to check the opening hours. Connor headed to the side door and peered out. The person he saw brought him back to that fateful day.

*Dad looked him in the eye through the mirror and mouthed, "Run!"*

*The man turned and looked into his eyes.*

In an instant, his heart raced, his hands clammy. He managed to mutter, "We're open at ten."

# CHAPTER 2

## MARINO HOTEL BAR

*SIMON*

In the dimly lit hotel bar, shadows seemed to dance along with the low hum of conversation and the clinking of glasses. Simon Roth spotted Javier Jimenez on a barstool.

Javier's presence was unmistakable, even from a distance. His frame, usually poised and commanding, slumped slightly over the counter, a clear sign of the weight he carried on his shoulders. The haphazard state of his hair and the absence of his customary tie painted a picture of a man unmoored, adrift in thoughts that offered little solace.

"Hey, Javier. How's it going?" Simon's voice broke through the ambient noise, a beacon of familiarity in the semidarkness.

"Simon! Good to see you, man." His smile didn't quite reach his eyes, which flickered with relief and something else—was it apprehension?

"How's the fam?" Simon nodded his thanks to the bartender who placed his drink in front of him. Scotch, neat, just the way he liked it.

Javier raised his glass. "Here's hoping Tyler stays clean this time." He took a sip of his bourbon. "I told Liz I won't bail him out again."

Simon's chest tightened. Javier had spoken of his stepson's drug addiction. Now that Simon had a daughter, a grown daughter, he could relate to Javier's concern about his kid. No matter the age, parents always worry.

"Enough about me. Now, tell me about your new fiancée and your newfound daughter." Javier raised his glass to Simon. He displayed photos on his phone. "Olivia is doing some consulting with the FBI, and Lily actually works here. She's in charge of the Private Select Program."

Javier leaned in to look at the photos. "Oh, I met your daughter. She checked me in and escorted me to my suite. I was so tired that I didn't even connect her to you." He swallowed and lowered his voice. "I've heard rumors about Olivia. Is she really with the Bureau? Or is she still a spook?"

Simon swirled his Scotch to consider his answer. "I can neither confirm—"

"Or deny it." Javier finished the sentence. "The standard answer. Pretty much tells me she's still attached to Langley."

"Why the sudden interest? What rumors have you heard?"

Olivia recently uncovered the mole. Everyone believed that was the end of it. Or did someone finally find out she was Phoenix?

Javier shrugged. "Just curious is all. The task force 629 you guys are consulting with is mysterious."

Simon wiped away a ring someone's glass must've left on the bar. He didn't even know they assigned a number to Ron's task force. He always thought of it as the Ghost task force. "Classified stuff is always mysterious. If it's an open book, it wouldn't be classified. So, tell me about Liz. Still trying to get you to lose weight?"

Javier laughed. "Always." They chitchatted in this vein until Javier clattered his glass back onto the counter. His scowl returned before whispered words rushed out. "I don't know what to do."

"About?" Simon's concern deepened at the shift in Javier's tone.

"The story about me growing up in a foster home was a lie." Javier kept his scowl fixed on the bar's worn surface.

Simon blinked. "Okay, why? You and your folks don't get along?"

Javier hung his head, a gesture heavy with more than just denial. "It's worse. The business, uh, I can't get involved in the business."

Simon puzzled over this. Sure, it wasn't uncommon for children to shy away from a family business, but to fabricate a story of foster care? That was a drastic step. Most didn't lie about it.

"My mother agreed not to spill the beans. But now..." Javier rubbed his eyes. "I don't know what to do."

Not knowing the whole situation, Simon didn't comment.

Javier sighed again, a sound heavy with unsaid words. "I may follow your footsteps."

Simon's resignation from his senatorial position months earlier had been a decision born of necessity, a path chosen amid a thicket of complexities. While Javier wasn't a senator, he was a US congressman. Was he facing a similar crossroads?

"You're thinking about resigning?" Simon kept his voice steady but his heart not quite so.

"I can't see another way out."

"What's the problem? Anything I can do?"

Javier turned, and an inner conflict twisted his features before they slacked into resignation. He opened his mouth, perhaps ready to unveil the storm within, but then he paused. A sudden movement, a glance that darted toward the lobby, and the moment shattered.

His friend stood, throwing some cash onto the bar with a haste that spoke volumes. "I'll see you Friday. Need to go."

Simon followed Javier's gaze to a man lounging in the lobby. The Hispanic man, engrossed in his phone, seemed harmless, but the tension in Javier's posture suggested otherwise. Who was he? A threat? A reminder of whatever storm Javier was navigating?

But before Simon could piece together the puzzle, Javier was gone, slipping away into the night as if trying to outrun his own shadow. Left at the bar, a witness to a friend's turmoil, Simon stiffened under the weight of unanswered questions. What was Javier involved in? Was it political, personal, or something sinister? The man in the lobby, now looking up from his phone, seemed to hold a piece of the puzzle, yet his role in this enigmatic evening remained a mystery.

# ABOUT THE AUTHOR

S.F. Baumgartner writes fast-paced Christian suspense thrillers. Book 1 of her Mirror Estate series, Living Secrets, was selected as one of the Top Picks in the thriller category at Killer Nashville, 2024. Her love for writing comes second only to her love of reading.

When she's not busy writing about complex characters, secretive operatives, and relentless agents, she spends her time binge-watching crime TV shows, such as NCIS, or playing with her cats. If you enjoy James Patterson's style—specifically short chapters—you'll love her Mirror Estate series.

To be the first to know about any sales, promotions, and new releases, sign up for our monthly newsletter. By subscribing, you'll stay informed about all the latest happenings and never miss an opportunity to explore this captivating world.

# ALSO BY
# S.F. BAUMGARTNER

**Mirror Estates series**

Buried Secrets, book 1

Living Secrets, book 2

Forgotten Secret, book 3

Tangled Secrets, book 4

Hidden Secrets, book 5

Shadowed Secret, book 6

Stolen Secrets, book 7

Box Set (Books 1-4)

**KC & Orlando Prime series**

Christmas Murders, a prequel

Fatal Invitation, book 1

# ACKNOWLEDGMENTS

Publishing a novel is not a solo endeavor, and I'm deeply grateful to those who made this book possible.

A heartfelt thanks to Deirdre Lockhart at Brilliant Cut Editing, Kelsey Darling and Chelsea Lauren from Represent Publishing for their invaluable guidance and support. To the team at 100Covers.com, your stunning cover design perfectly captured the heart of this story.

I also want to thank the amazing beta and ARC readers—your feedback and enthusiasm were crucial in refining this novel.

To my family, your unwavering support has been my greatest strength. And finally, to you, dear readers—this book is for you. Enjoy the journey!